EXPLOSIVE TERROR PLUMMETS FROM THE SKIES—AND ONLY ONE MAN WILL RISE TO STOP IT . . .

Alec Martin's trouble was that he was living thirty years in the past and had no grasp of the enormous technical odds he was facing. In his obstinancy, he would believe that sheer cunning and flying skill were enough to defeat the most sophisticated defensive system of the 1970s.

He was surrounded by a dazzling display of scientific expertise, all geared to pinpointing the ancient Spitfire and surrounding it with a blocking screen of aircraft as soon as it appeared.

Martin didn't stand a chance. But why didn't Martin himself realize that?

EARLY WARNING

CHRISTOPHER FITZSIMONS

AVON
PUBLISHERS OF BARD, CAMELOT AND DISCUS BOOKS

AVON BOOKS
A division of
The Hearst Corporation
959 Eighth Avenue
New York, New York 10019

Copyright © 1978 by Christopher Fitzsimons
Published by arrangement with The Viking Press
Library of Congress Catalog Card Number: 78-24151
ISBN: 0-380-50179-1

First Avon Printing, March, 1981

AVON TRADEMARK REG. U.S. PAT. OFF. AND IN
OTHER COUNTRIES, MARCA REGISTRADA, HECHO EN
U.S.A.

Printed in the U.S.A.

For Mary

MEMORANDUM TO: THE SECRETARY OF STATE FOR
DEFENSE

FROM: DIRECTOR, INTERNAL SECURITY
COORDINATION OFFICE

SUBJECT: EDINBURGH CONFERENCE, MAY 15-16

You instructed me to provide you with
regular, personal reports on the progress
of the arrangements for the security
program in relation to the above
conference.

The purpose of establishing this office,
it will be recalled, was to insure there
would be no overlap between the functions
of the various security organizations
operating in this country; in addition,
and more importantly, that there would be
no gaps within the total security screen.

The arrangements for this conference
provide the opportunity for the first
full-scale testing of the new system.
Already it has proved its effectiveness
by pinpointing several areas where two or
even more agencies were covering the
same ground. Their roles have now been

adjusted accordingly—although not without some recriminations, it should be added. However, the fact that this office has overriding authority to define security responsibilities has proved invaluable.

I can report that the security program for the conference is now complete and no major problems remain to be solved. Priority is, of course, being given to the personal protection of the conference delegates, representing as they do the major oil-producing nations of the world. As, by definition, these include several politically volatile Middle Eastern states, the dangers are self-evident.

There has been some speculation as to the possibility of a "strike" operation of one kind or another being aimed at the delegates indiscriminately, as opposed to individual assassination attempts. This seems an unlikely prospect for one simple reason: the presence at the conference (as an "observer") of the leader of the Palestine Freedom Front. Even though, in the past, this organization has earned the condemnation of every government for its terrorist activities, it has recently been seeking a more respectable status as the unofficial custodian of the Arab conscience relating to Palestine. There have been reports that the Arab delegates to the conference accepted the PFF as part of their bloc with some reluctance ("blackmail" is a word which was used) but

the fact remains that the PFF will be there.
It follows that concerted terrorist action
agains the conference can to all intents
and purposes be ruled out.

I consider that the arrangements which
have been made for the personal protection
of the delegates are as watertight as they
can possibly be. The only difficulties I
face are on the administrative side, in
insuring the (sometimes reluctant)
cooperation of the various security
agencies.

To sum up, I can assure the Minister that
there is little risk of the Government
being embarrassed as a result of this
decision by the oil-producing nations to
hold their conference in the capital of the
newest oil-producer of all.

                         H. BLAIR
                         Director

1

Just over an hour after the British Airways Trident penetrated the low cloud to land at Heathrow, Alec Martin stepped from a taxi in Whitehall, at the corner with King Charles Street. He had spent the flight attempting to sort out the turmoil in his mind. Now his head was aching and what he really wanted was a drink, a bath, and some sleep.

The uniformed guardian of the Foreign Office held him at bay for five minutes. During this time Martin admitted he had no pass, no appointment, and no idea of the name or position of the person he wished to see.

"I'm a businessman and I've just arrived back from East Germany," he explained with diminishing patience. "I've some information I want to pass on to someone in authority."

"By rights you should send us a letter," the doorman told him. "That will be sorted out and passed on to the appropriate office. Then they will write a letter if they wish to see you and make a proper appointment."

There wasn't a machine gun or a coil of barbed wire in sight. Yet the civil service appeared to have erected a defensive screen around itself as impregnable as anything he had seen behind the Curtain. Moreover it was all done with a maddening surface politeness that must have been polished on hundreds of obvious cranks like himself.

"Look," said Martin finally, "is there, anywhere in your department, a man whose job it is to deal with the awkward customers? You know, the ones who threaten to chain themselves to the railings unless you buy their death-ray from them?"

The doorman looked dubiously for a moment at this late-fortyish, square-faced man with tired gray eyes, a crumpled suit, and a well-worn overnight bag. He went to the telephone behind the desk and dialled a number, keeping an eye on Martin as he did so.

Martin put down the bag and leaned wearily against the pillar of the doorway. The odds were that he was making a first-class fool of himself. The sheer scale of the information made it unbelievable, for a start. Yet he had believed it at the time. It was only when reviewed in the cold light of an April morning in the middle of London that it took on the appearance of fantasy. Really it needed Greta to tell it all over again in that voice of hers, tight and urgent with fear.

It wasn't a pin-striped bouncer who came down the stairs in response to the doorman's call. This was a serious-featured young man with long fair hair and a brisk, skip-trotting gait.

Martin thrust a business card into his hand.

"I don't want to waste anybody's time, including my own. That's who I am. Is anyone interested in some information I've just brought back with me from East Germany?"

The young man said cautiously, "We might be. Do you have it with you?"

Martin tapped his forehead. "It's all there. Now don't ask me to go away and write it down. It's too urgent for that."

The young man took only a moment to make up his mind. "I'll arrange for someone to see you," he said. "Before I take you inside, you'll have to go through the procedure."

While the doorman searched the overnight bag, the young man entered Martin's name in a book at the reception desk. When the blue-serge centurion was satisfied the bag held no bombs or firearms, the young man led the way up two flights of stairs.

Martin followed him along a narrow corridor and into a small bare room with cream walls, brown linoleum, and a deal table with two chairs.

"Do sit down," the young man said. "We shan't keep you waiting."

He was as good as his word. Three minutes later he was

replaced by a thin, middle-aged man with flat gray hair and a lined forehead. His spectacles were basic National Health issue and the shoulders of his baggy gray suit were speckled with dandruff.

The man placed a briefcase on the table, arranged a pad of foolscap paper before him, and held a pencil poised above it as he looked questioningly at Martin.

"My name is Cole. I understand you have some information you wish to convey?" he said in a flat, uninterested tone. As Martin was about to answer, he went on, "I think we should start with your identification."

"Martin. Alec Martin."

Cole said patiently, "Written identification, if you please."

Martin took the passport from his inside pocket and passed it across. Cole first wrote down the passport number on his pad. Opening it, he compared Martin with his own photograph for a few moments. Apparently satisfied, he copied out all the written details. Next he turned to the stamped pages and studied them for several minutes, making notes all the time.

Finally, he handed the passport back and said, "Now, what have you to tell us?"

Watching the calculated pendantry had served to intensify Martin's headache. He said bluntly, "During the next five weeks, Britain is going to come under attack from hostile forces."

Cole held his pencil above the paper as he stared at Martin without any change of expression. After a pause he said, "So that is your information: there is going to be a war?"

It appeared they kept a file of War Warnings into which Martin could fit pretty neatly.

"Not a war as such," Martin said irritably. "There are going to be various attacks on British interests of one kind or another, with the object of ruining our credibility as a nation able to protect itself or others. It's all tied up with this oil business—"

"Just one moment." Cole held up his hand, then straightened the pad of paper once more and brought his pencil two inches nearer its surface. "Let us start with where and how you obtained your information, and then detail the information itself. What were you doing in East

6

Germany? Were you acting in any official capacity on behalf of our government, either overtly or covertly?"

"You've seen my passport," Martin snapped. "I'm a businessman, not a diplomat or a spy."

"I appreciate that, but some businessmen abroad do undertake additional tasks at the request of certain government departments. This was not the case with you?"

"It certainly was not. And I can tell you that if the government did ask me, I'd tell them to go and stuff themselves. The thought of getting regularly involved in"—he waved his hand at the pad—"all this red tape would kill the patriotism of Nelson himself."

Cole displayed no reaction to the outburst. "You were in Germany simply on business?"

"How many times do I have to make it clear to you? I own a medium-sized engineering company. We make—"

"The name of the company?" Cole was actually writing now.

"Martin Engineering, of Kenley. Our specialty is one-offs—that is, individual tailor-made parts for any type of machine you care to mention. Obsolete plant is our bread and butter. Some countries will buy a whole factory or power plant second-hand—say from the UK or another European country. They get it cheap, but their problems arise when it goes wrong. The original firm that made the plant has either gone out of business or doesn't keep very old spares in stock. So then they come to us and we machine the part for them."

"So this is overseas trade?"

"Very largely. The developing nations use us a lot."

Cole wrote for a few moments, then said, "Does East Germany have a lot of obsolete Western machinery?"

"Obsolete parts isn't all our business. We'll tackle any specialized small-scale engineering job, and as we've got the experience and the expertise, we're very competitive indeed. There's a man in Paris who acts as a freelance agent and he got us the contact in East Germany. I've been going over there for a couple of years now, and they're very satisfied with our work." Martin paused until Cole finished writing. Then he said, "Is that enough of the company prospectus for you? If so, I'll get down to what I really came about."

"It's all relevant," Cole said. "Carry on, please."

"This last trip was to meet the usual people, headed by a man called Bruno Lukas who's in charge of purchasing for one of the biggest VVBs in East Germany." Cole glanced up and Martin explained, "One of the nationalized industrial trusts. Bruno and I are quite good friends by now. I spend a week going round various plants and he fixes my appointments and guides me through the red tape. In fact his secretary does the donkey work—a girl named Greta Beckmann. An efficient and very intelligent girl.

"On this occasion I got the feeling things weren't quite normal. Nothing specific—just an undercurrent of strain and unease that had not been evident before. It was particularly so with Greta—Miss Beckmann."

He felt the need to describe Greta, but what sort of picture could he paint that would bring her alive to this man? The blonde, shoulder-length hair, the natural grace, the warmth—no, the radiance—how could anyone really describe that? You had to feel it to know it. You had to feel that physical ache that he felt right now when he thought of her.

Cole was impatiently tapping his pencil, and Martin went on: "On the day before I was due to leave Germany, she took me to meet a man called Frisch. This visit wasn't on my official schedule, and I was a bit unhappy about that. But I had come to rely on Greta and she had always kept me out of any sort of trouble.

"The strange thing about Frisch was that he seemed to have no particular connection with the engineering business, and in fact, he knew almost nothing about it. It was late at night when I met him in his office—but I couldn't tell you what the building was, as we went in at the rear. The office itself was impressive enough, large and well furnished. Frisch was impressive too. Bulky, wearing a well-cut black suit, bald, and with a pair of the most penetrating eyes I've ever seen. One hears that expression about eyes that see right through you, but I never thought of it in the literal sense until I met Frisch. They weren't hypnotic—just the opposite, in fact, because they made you feel thoroughly uncomfortable. It was as though he was reading the hidden depths of your character that you'd never want anyone to know about.

"He was easy enough to talk to. Good English, and he

knew a lot about this country. My conversation was geared toward business, naturally enough, but he seemed more interested in me personally. He extracted from me complete details about my background, my opinions on various matters, and my political convictions—which, if you're interested, are rather right of center. It was all done so skillfully that I didn't realize until later that I'd done most of the talking. Then the meeting ended abruptly."

There was the sudden sound of several vehicles coming to a halt in the street outside. For the first time a trace of emotion appeared on Frisch's face. His eyes clouded over so that their piercing quality appeared to diminish and his forehead creased into a frown. Then Martin saw the thin film of sweat appear and he realized that Frisch was afraid.

He stood up and moved quickly from behind his desk, ushering the two of them toward the office door. He muttered something in German to Greta, who went pale as she nodded. The phrase stayed in Martin's mind, and he later translated it as "They have come sooner than I expected."

Frisch opened the door for them, then put his hand on Martin's shoulder and said quickly and with restrained emotion, "We need your help, Mr. Martin. The reason you were brought here tonight was so that I could assure myself that you could be trusted. Now I see that Greta was right in her belief that we can rely on you."

There was the sound of footsteps in the street and Frisch glanced nervously over his shoulder. He turned back to Martin and dropped his voice.

"Later on, Greta will be giving you some information. Accept whatever she tells you as being completely authentic. Then please, I beg you, do all you can to ensure that that information reaches the appropriate authorities in your own country."

Martin started to say, "I don't want to get mixed up with anything like that—" but Frisch was pushing the two of them through the door.

"Quickly, you must go now," he said urgently. "And—best if you walk back to your hotel."

Greta was already hurrying along the corridor that led

to the rear of the building. Martin found himself following her in a state of bewilderment, caught up despite himself in the atmosphere of urgency and danger. Most of the building seemed to be in darkness, and he had to rely for guidance on the sound of her shoes clattering down the stone stairs. She obviously knew the route well.

She led him into the yard, where she cautiously opened the gate. After looking in either direction she beckoned him to follow her outside. As he was about to speak she placed a finger to her lips.

They walked rapidly along the street, keeping in the shadow of the high wall and so avoiding the moonlight which spilled over the roadway. As they neared the end of the block, a sharp crack echoed from somewhere at the front of the building. It was followed by three more in rapid succession.

"Poor Frisch." Greta bit her lip. "We must hurry."

Taking his arm she led him running to the end of the street. As they reached the Alexanderplatz, traffic was at a halt. People stood in groups, looking toward the front of the building. A van maneuvered its way through, siren blaring.

"Do not stop," Greta said in a low voice. "Go straight to your hotel now. Stay in your room and I will contact you later tonight."

"Now just one moment, Greta," Martin protested. "Isn't it time I had some explanation as to what's happening?"

But she had disappeared among the crowd.

As Martin made his way along the street he glanced back. Police were clearing people out of the way of a convoy of cars that was pulling away from the front of the building. The cars sped past him and he tried in vain to see through their darkened windows.

His anger grew. In all his dealings in East Germany he had kept scrupulously to the very clear rules that governed his sort of activity. No discussion of politics, no casual conversation with strangers, no travel anywhere not on his approved schedule. He was fully aware that the slightest transgression could mean the end of all his trade with the country. Now, thanks to Greta, he had only just avoided being embroiled in some very messy police business. Just who was this Frisch? His bearing and his surroundings indicated some senior official position. It followed that any trouble he found himself in had to be serious. The cracks he had heard, if they were gunfire, seemed to confirm that.

But by eleven that night, Martin's anger was replaced by concern. He stood at the window of his hotel room and looked down at the empty street. There was literally no one in sight. Any approach she made now would have all the impact of a spotlit entertainer coming onto a bare stage. But she had promised to contact him and she had never yet failed to keep an appointment, missed an item on his schedule, or overlooked any aspect of the complex paperwork he generated.

He glanced at the telephone, but he knew that whatever she had to tell him would not bear transmission by that means. What the hell was he waiting here for, anyway? Not only his business but his life could be in jeopardy. It was Greta, of course. He didn't give a damn about Frisch or whether the information he valued so highly was smuggled out of Germany or ended up in the wastepaper basket. But he did care about Greta, to an extent that surprised him. He had to know that she was all right after what had happened.

Twenty minutes later there was a faint knock at the door. He opened it and she stepped in quickly, pushing the door shut behind her. She was pale and lines of tension were deeply engraved around her mouth.

Before he could speak, she shook her head abruptly, then went over to the washbasin and turned on both taps.

"To prevent anyone hearing us," she explained. She spoke quietly, and he had to strain to hear her words above the sound of running water.

He led her over to the chair and she collapsed into it. He sat on the edge of the bed facing her and watched in silence as she huddled there, her face in her hands. Then she took out a handkerchief and began to dab at her eyes.

Finally she looked at him and said, "I am sorry, Mr. Martin. Please believe that I would not have involved you in this matter if I could have avoided it. But we are desperate, you see. Everything is falling to pieces and you are the only hope now."

Martin shook his head. "Whatever role you've cast me in, you can forget it. I can guess the sort of thing you're trying to involve me in, and I want nothing to do with it.

All right," he went on, holding up his hand as she was about to speak, "you've got problems and so has Frisch. But that's no reason why I should start creating problems for myself. I'm here in the GDR on my own business, and when I go home tomorrow I want to forget all about your country and its politics. That's selfish, yes, but I have my own worries."

"But you won't give me a chance to explain. The reason we are approaching you is because it is your own country that is involved."

"That still doesn't concern me."

She shook her head wearily. "It is not easy to explain. It is a long story—"

"Which I don't wish to hear. Look, you'll feel better if you have a drink."

He washed out the glass under the running tap, then poured an inch of whisky from a bottle he took from the bedside cabinet.

As she sipped the whisky, she said, "Please let me tell you a little. I have gone to so much trouble to come here." She watched him for a moment as, in silence, he poured himself a drink into the toothglass. With a trace of hesitation she went on: "We have been operating for a number of years. We are all people with a loyalty to Israel and it is to there that we send information which will help the country in its fight for survival. Frisch is our most important source of information. He is an official of the SSD—the secret police." She paused. "Something has gone badly wrong. We had no advance warning. Clearly that is because they have at last connected Frisch with our activities."

Despite himself, Martin wanted to know more. "Surely Israel's problems are with the Arab states? What information could you provide from here?"

"The Arab terrorist movements are mostly left-wing. The very extreme ones have their sympathizers in Communist countries. On occasions they can be given help from here. That is what will happen in the attack on your country."

Martin put his glass down on the dressing table. "You did say an attack on Britain? By the *Arabs*?"

"Let me explain a little more. Your country is to have a special conference on energy starting on May fifteenth, in the city of Edinburgh. The oil-producing nations are all taking part."

Martin nodded. "Since oil was discovered in the North Sea, off the Scottish coast, Britain has become a major energy producer. So the other countries decided to hold their meeting in the capital city of Scotland as a 'welcome to the club' gesture."

"Most of the nations represented will be Arab," Greta went on. "The conference will start on the morning of May fifteenth, at ten a.m., when a special ceremony will be held at the castle within the city. Is that not so?"

"In Edinburgh Castle? Well, I suppose it's an appropriate spot."

"There is an open area in front of the castle upon which there will be much pageantry. You do not know about this?"

"Not really," Martin admitted, "but it's not a subject which interests me particularly. I assume the Scots would push out the boat for such an occasion with that sort of thing."

"There is something else you may not know, because it has not been publicized widely. The Palestine Freedom Front is being allowed to send an observer to the conference."

Martin was surprised. "With their reputation for bombing and shooting I didn't think they were welcome anywhere these days. Who's the chap who leads them? Name like Zaddi—"

"Zaidi. He is attending personally."

"Strange. What's his interest in the world's energy problems? Apart, maybe, from creating some more by blowing up pipelines."

"It is all part of the new image that the PFF is trying to create for itself. It has been working hard recently to show it is something more than a terrorist group like all the others. It would have the world believe it has discarded its terrorist tactics and is now interested more in the long-term economic development of the Middle East."

"Why should it want to do that?"

She shrugged. "Maybe Zaidi has political ambitions. No one really knows, and such is Zaidi's character that no one wants to probe too deeply. As far as the Arab nations are concerned, it is something of a relief to them that Zaidi is now more prepared to talk than to kill. This

13

is why they have agreed to include him in their bloc delegation." She paused. "The fools."

"Why?"

"Because common sense should tell them that he must have some other, more sinister, motive. As indeed he has. Let me tell you what is really going to happen. Zaidi will arrive at Edinburgh later than the other delegates, as they are not asking him to participate in the official opening. They are worried that the event might be spoiled by demonstrations if he is there. In fact, his special aircraft is scheduled to land at Edinburgh Airport at the time the opening ceremony is being held. That way, any demonstrators will be drawn to the airport rather than to the opening ceremony. But all this is acceptable to Zaidi, because such timing is the key to the whole operation."

Martin was staring at her, openmouthed. "How the hell did you get all this information—"

"Let me finish. Zaidi's aircraft, on its way from the Middle East, will land in Germany to refuel. It is a small charter aircraft, you see. There, secretly, Zaidi will leave the aircraft. It will then take off for Scotland with a crew of only two people aboard. They are volunteers—fanatics, like the Japanese pilots in the last war. For when they reach Edinburgh, they will crash their aircraft onto the many people assembled on the forecourt of the castle. There will be an explosion, for the aircraft will be loaded with bombs, and many people will be killed."

Greta sipped her whisky while Martin tried to absorb what she had told him. Finally he said, "If that was so, it just wouldn't make sense. Many of the people killed would be Arabs themselves. What would Zaidi gain from that?"

"That many martyrs. Immediately afterwards, Zaidi himself would appear in public. He would claim that Israeli agents hijacked his aircraft in Germany and that they carried out the attack. He would back this up with carefully arranged evidence. You can see what he would gain then."

"My God, I can." Martin stood up and walked restlessly around the room. "It would unite the Arab nations in retaliating against Israel. Another Middle East war—and the Palestine problem solved once and for all." He turned and faced her. "You really can vouch for the authenticity of this—oh, no. It's bloody ridiculous. How could you possibly get all this information—and guarantee that it's genuine? I mean—just where did it come from, Greta?"

"From within the State Security Department, which is where we get much of our information from. I cannot tell you who the person is. It was only this evening that I was able to get the final details from him. This is a system Frisch arranged—so now that he is taken, our contact will soon be taken too."

"Normally, what would you do with this information?"

"I have another contact, who gives it to Israeli intelligence. But he has gone as well. We are only a small group you see, without any official links with the world outside. Now the whole network is broken and I think I am the only one left." Her hands were tightly clenched around the glass. There was a tremor in her voice as she went on. "Perhaps I will be picked up soon. But they will not touch you. They have no reason to think you know anything, and you will be safely back in Britain tomorrow."

The water gurgled ceaselessly into the washbasin. Martin stood at the window looking down into the road.

"You can't stay here, Greta. You see that, don't you?"

"Where would I go?" she asked. "I belong here in the GDR. This is the only place I know."

"You can come with me. You'll like it in Britain—"

She laughed bitterly. "It is as easy as that? I simply get on your airplane with you and fly away? No, we must be serious. I have given you the information, and what is important is that you should get it safely to Britain. Do not worry about me."

He grasped her arms and eased her from the chair.

"You know very well what I feel about you, Greta. I would have asked you before, but I suppose I lacked the nerve. Now I can offer you something at least that's better than this."

He could feel her trembling as he held her arms. She refused to meet his eyes and said, as she looked at the floor, "Do not talk of things that cannot be done. You make me even more unhappy. You cannot take me with you, no matter what means you were thinking of trying. Our security forces are too experienced and too efficient.

15

We would both be caught and the information would never get through."

She looked up at him and they stared at each other in silence for a few moments. He said, "I find it hard to believe I am the only person who can get the information out. There must be someone in contact with Israel—"

She broke away and said wearily, "I have explained that it is not so. And even if I could find someone else, would they believe me?" She turned back to him. "But you know me, and you know I would only tell you the truth." She came close again and stared into his eyes. "You know it is the truth? Believe me—please?"

As he nodded she stared at him a moment longer. Then she kissed him lightly, turned, and hurried to the door.

He followed her. "Which way did you come? I was watching the street."

"Through the kitchens," she explained. "I will go out that way. Please do not come any further. Goodbye."

Two minutes later there was a light tap on the wood. As he opened the door she whispered, "They have locked the door at the back of the hotel. What am I to do?"

He stood aside. "There's nothing else you can do. Come in." Then he went and turned off the taps.

The next morning she had dressed before he was properly awake. He stretched an arm over to the other side of the bed, which was still warm from her body, then looked up sleepily as she moved quietly across to the door. "Why are you rushing away?"

"It is best. I did not want you to wake. Goodbye, Alec."

As she left the room she turned, gave a slight smile, and said, "It is only fair for me to tell you that the kitchen door was not locked last night."

By the time he had struggled out of bed she was gone. He looked at his watch. Seven-thirty. He could dress and race after her, but he had no idea of the direction she had taken. Where did she live? In all the time he had known her, she had never given any clue as to where she lived or, indeed, any detail of her personal background.

She should be at the office by eight-thirty. After breakfasting on a single cup of coffee he went to the telephone in the lobby and, at eight thirty-two, dialed the number of Lukas's office.

The operator cut in and said, "The number you are calling is unobtainable."

It took him a moment to translate the German. He said, "That can't be so. There's more than one line."

"All the lines are out of order," she said and cut him off.

He replaced the phone thoughtfully. Lukas's was a busy office, so they should repair the line quickly . . . if indeed it was out of order.

He stepped out of the kiosk and looked around the lobby. There was no one in sight except the receptionist. He nevertheless felt the sudden chill of exposure, as though he had gone outside without a coat.

If what Greta had told him was true, the security police could already be seeking her. Could, in fact, have found her . . . and followed her the previous night to see who would be the recipient of her information.

His British citizenship would be no protection against a charge of espionage. If he had any sense at all, his aim would be to get out of Germany as fast as possible. But still—he really should say goodbye to Lukas before he left. That meant calling on him at his office.

When he reached the glass and concrete building at the corner of Unter den Linden and Schadowstrasse, two uniformed Vopos stepped forward to block his entrance. It was something that had not happened before.

"I wish to see Herr Lukas." He tried to sound as matter-of-fact as he could.

He expected to be asked for his papers, but one of the policemen simply said, "Herr Lukas's office is not open today."

"But I have business with him. I am from Britain and we have arrangements—"

"You have an appointment?" the Vopo asked politely.

"Not exactly."

"Herr Lukas is not here today," the Vopo said with finality, staring over Martin's shoulder at the street beyond.

Either they had caught up with Greta and now the whole office was under investigation, or perhaps they were waiting for her to arrive . . . in which case he might be able to warn her.

He walked across to a small coffeehouse that stood at the junction. From the main window he had a clear view

17

for a hundred yards of anyone approaching the building.

As he sipped the coffee he watched the Vopos talking to a man in a raincoat and a dark hat of Bogart style. After a few minutes the man came across the road and entered the café. He made his way straight to Martin's table and sat down.

"Papers," he said quietly, studying Martin's features as though to memorize them.

Martin handed over his passport and visa and the man flicked through them.

"When do you return to UK?"

"Today."

"Then there is no purpose in your being here?"

"I wanted to have a word with Herr Lukas—"

"He is away," the man cut in, handing back the papers. "So you do not need to stay here any longer."

He rose and waited pointedly for Martin to stand, then followed him into the street.

The man stood watching as Martin walked away without a word. It was hard to gauge the extent of their suspicion of him, but it would be lunacy to tempt them any further. With conscious and deliberate effort he pushed Greta from his mind and headed for the hotel.

He went straight to his room and was packing when there was a call from reception to say someone wished to see him.

He went down to the lobby to find standing there the manager of a tractor-engine plant he visited regularly.

"Why, Erich," Martin said in surprise, "I thought we had completed our business."

"Something urgent has arisen, Herr Martin," Erich replied in a loud voice. "We need your help and we would like you to come back to the factory before you leave." He was breathing heavily as though he had been hurrying.

"I was just packing—"

"Please, Herr Martin. I have a car outside."

They drove straight to the factory and Martin was kept there for the rest of the day, while complex drawings of machine parts were produced and hair-splitting haggling took place over the contract, which Martin thought had been settled two days previously. It wasn't their usual style, as Erich was one of the best-organized and most incisive industrial managers Martin had met in Germany. It was after six by the time they had finished.

Then Erich insisted on taking him to his home for dinner, which made it nine by the time he got back to the hotel. Utterly weary by now, he decided he might as well stay the extra night.

He was just starting to undress when there was a knock on his door.

His surprise at seeing Greta there left him speechless for several moments. She was wearing her black coat and her hands were thrust into the deep pockets. She stared at him unsmilingly and he saw dark rings under her eyes.

As she stepped in he grasped her by the shoulders.

"I've been sick with worry," he said disbelievingly. "I thought I was never going to see you again."

She pulled herself away from his hands and walked to the center of the room. Hurriedly, he closed the door and went to take her coat.

"No," she said dully, holding it closely around her. "I cannot stay. I came with more information for you."

"Sit down," he said, leading her to the chair. "What on earth happened to you? Lukas's office was crawling with police." He studied her more closely. "You look as though you've been crying, Greta. Did they—?"

She shook her head. "I managed to avoid them. I did not go near the office today. But I have more information which you must memorize."

As he poured her a whisky, Martin said gently, "Keep it to yourself. If it's so important that it should get to the West, then you must take it there yourself."

"You know I cannot—"

"I know that people escape to the West practically every day of the week by one means or another. If we apply our minds to it, we can get you over that border somehow. You're tired now and you need a good night's sleep—"

Abruptly she got to her feet and thrust the glass into his hand.

Her voice was harsh in a way he had never heard before as she said, "Listen to me now. There is a NATO naval exercise in the Mediterranean this month. On April eighth a British warship will be sunk—either by a mine or a torpedo, I do not know which. On April tenth something will happen to one of your oil-rigs in the North Sea. Again I do not know the details, but there will be an explosion followed by a fire. Then on April twelfth a British airliner flying to Berlin along the corridor will be forced down by fighters over the GDR. Can you keep all that in your mind?" She was breathless and there was a vivid pink spot in each of her cheeks as she faced him but failed to look directly at him.

He shook his head slowly. "Greta, you can't expect me to accept all these remarkable items of information seriously. I don't know where they're supposed to come from—"

"From the same source as the information I gave you last night."

"But it's all a bit overwhelming, to say the least. If it all were true, this would be so secret that a professional intelligence agent would be doing well to get just a fraction of it. But I, who have no interest in espionage at all, am handed it on a plate. Why?"

"I've explained it already—"

"I know—the Israeli spy network. But these incidents you're talking of now don't concern Israel."

"Our contact has access to intelligence of all kinds. This information only came into his hands today, and I am passing it to you for the benefit of your country. The intention of the Warsaw Pact is to humiliate Britain so much that she will not be seen any more as a nation of power and influence, despite her new wealth from oil. And that will make a serious weakness in NATO."

"Can't you tell me who your contact is?" Martin said. "That could help give some weight to the information."

She shook her head. "I have told you all you need to know. When your government sees what happens on those dates, that will be proof enough."

She turned and walked to the door. He hurried after her.

"Where are you going now?"

"That does not concern you, and it is safer if you do not know. Don't worry about me, Alec. Please take care for yourself."

She faced him, then leaned forward and kissed him on the mouth with a sudden and unexpected passion. She said, almost in a whisper, "I want to help. Please understand and believe that."

He tried to hold her as she opened the door, but she angrily shook free of him.

"Leave me alone. I am going, and you must not attempt to follow me. You understand that?"

His bewilderment was complete. "I don't understand anything. How are we going to meet again?"

She shook her head. "Goodbye, Alec."

"And that is all?" Cole asked.

"That was yesterday. I spent a sleepless night wondering first of all if she was all right, and second, when the police would get round to me. But this morning I booked out of the hotel, crossed the border without any trouble, and caught the flight home."

"The East German police did not question you?"

"Showed no interest in me at all. For that reason I'm hoping that Greta is still free. That's where your people come into it."

Cole put down his pencil. "In what way do you mean?"

"Bringing her over here. You must have ways and means." Martin watched him expectantly.

"You want the Foreign Office somehow to extract this lady from the German Democratic Republic?"

"You can't tell me you don't operate some kind of system for smuggling people out when it's important to you. In Miss Beckmann's case I should think it's the very least you can do. She went to a hell of a lot of trouble and risk to get this information for Britain." There was silence for a few moments as they stared at each other. Martin said impatiently, "Well, don't look at me like a bloody zombie. What can be done?"

"It isn't up to me," Cole replied. "My job is simply to make a report on what you've told me. If you wish, I will put in an addendum containing your request."

"Then do it," Martin snapped. "I've a feeling there isn't very much time. Who makes decisions on these things?"

"I really couldn't say," Cole replied, pointedly gathering his sheets of paper together and putting his pencil away.

"Well, what will happen next?"

"My report goes to my superiors. If they want to speak to you further, then doubtless they will get in touch with you." He stood up and opened the door with a poor imitation of a smile on his face. "Thank you for coming in, Mr. Martin."

As he walked along Whitehall watching for a taxi, Martin's anger came into full flower. He'd been treated like a child. Mother listened patiently to his fantasies, then patted him on the head while she concerned herself with important matters.

So his information was from an unproved and unauthenticated source. But surely an efficient intelligence system followed up every lead, no matter how insubstantial it might be. All he could hope was that Cole's superiors would show more interest than Cole himself had displayed —assuming that the report ever moved further than Cole's desk.

2

Martin was the only passenger to alight when the train reached Kenley at fourteen minutes past noon. The main rush would come with the flood of returning commuters in six hours' time.

He found Fred Williams's hire car on the station forecourt. The driver was just as pleased to see him: a fare at this time of the day was a bonus.

"Home or office?" Fred asked, taking the bag from him.

"Home first, Fred. The works have survived a week in my absence, and another hour or so should make little difference."

More than anything he wanted a shower and a change of clothes.

"Where was it this time, Mr. Martin?" Fred asked as he steered the car along the narrow lane, the hedges shining with the previous night's rain. "La belle France or der Fatherland?"

"East Germany again," Martin told him. "That means not a lot in the way of fun and plenty of hard work."

"No joke dealing with those square-headed bastards," Fred said sympathetically. "Even after thirty years I still hate their guts. When I think what we went through because of them . . ."

What Fred had gone through was an untroubled three years with an ack-ack unit in the Shetlands. Martin had long given up listening to the same monologue each time he came back from Germany.

Then his attention was caught as Fred went on, "Two of them, there were. Can't think why they wanted to come here. Got me to drop them at the Greyhound, but Michael tells me they never stayed the night with him."

"Who was this?"

"These two Jerries. Yesterday. Got off the train and asked to go to the village. Don't know why, because they seemed to disappear once they got there."

"How do you know they were Germans?"

Fred said patiently, "Square heads. That's not just a nickname, it's a physical fact. I can tell them a mile off. And their voices—guttural is the word."

He halted the car in the lane outside Martin's house.

"Miserable buggers they were, too. Never a word from them. Reckon they're still sore from the hiding we gave them."

Martin got out of the car and watched Fred drive the remaining two hundred yards into the village, no doubt anxious to get in his lunchtime pint at the Greyhound.

As he made his way up the path, he noted the height of the grass in the front garden. Ellen had always argued that the front lawn should have a razor-cut neatness, whereas he maintained that, in the country, a certain degree of dishevelment was permissible. When she first moved out he had taken a childish satisfaction in letting it go. Now he just found it irritating—another indication that advancing years brought a greater appreciation of the joys of conformity.

He entered the house and found the usual mail on the floor of the hall. As he stooped to pick up the letters, he paused. Ellen had nagged him for years to fit a basket behind the letter box. He never did, and the mail continued to fall on the mat, which meant that the door, when opened, pushed all the letters back. If there was a quantity of mail, the door sometimes jammed.

But the door had opened now to meet no resistance at all, and the letters were piled neatly to the left.

Cautiously he put the mail unopened on the hall table and looked into the lounge, then the dining room, and finally the kitchen. Nothing appeared to be disturbed downstairs and he made his way up to the bedrooms without knowing just what he was expecting to find. Everything upstairs seemed normal and he reentered the lounge wondering if he was becoming neurotic.

He opened the bureau. Impossible to tell if that jumble of letters and bills had been turned upside down and inside out. Then his eye was caught by the bookshelf above the bureau—the *Concise Oxford Dictionary* was the right way up. When he took it down and opened it, the pages were upside down. Some years ago he had backed it with self-adhesive plastic and only when he finished did he realize he had the dust jacket the wrong way up. He referred to the book rarely, but never, when replacing it, did he deliberately turn it the other way round. It always appeared on the shelf with the cover upside down.

No one had a key to the house save himself. There was Ellen, of course, who might have kept one, but she had never even spoken to him since the divorce, least of all come to the house.

The place had been entered skillfully, and everything had been thoroughly searched, including his books. The obvious candidates were the two Germans Fred had delivered to the village. But he himself had been in Germany at the time the break-in presumably took place. If they suspected him of having received information, why did they let him leave the country? He could understand it if the Germans arrived now, hot on his trail, just having discovered how much he knew. But all this seemed to have happened twenty-four hours too soon . . .

As soon as he had taken his shower and changed, he walked into the village. Fred's car was still outside the Greyhound and he found the driver in the bar, finishing what appeared to be the last of several pints.

"Didn't take you long to find your way here, Mr. Martin," he chuckled. "Want to taste some decent beer after that Jerry rubbish, I suppose. What'll you have?"

"Nothing just now, Fred," Martin said. "I want to know about those two Germans you picked up yesterday. Have you any idea where they went after you dropped them?"

Fred reflectively took a pull from his glass. "I never saw them again. And Michael told me they never stayed here overnight. Hey—Michael!"

The rotund manager shuffled across from the alcove leading into the residential part of the inn. His perpetually worried face creased into a grin when he saw Martin.

"Nice to see you, Mr. Martin," he said in a soft Irish voice. "You'll have one on the house."

"I haven't time just now, Michael—"

Fred cut in, "You saw those Jerry bastards I brought in yesterday, Michael. Did you ever find what happened to them?"

The manager pondered for a moment. "It was only for a few minutes they were here. They didn't have a drink— just said they were looking for Glovers Lane. I told them where it was and then they left. I've not seen them since."

Fred turned to him. "Why are you concerned about these Germans, Mr. Martin? Friends of yours, would they be?"

"Certainly not friends," Martin said. "But they sound like business acquaintances. Thanks for your help, anyway."

Fred swallowed the rest of his beer and followed him out.

"Give you a lift back to your house, Mr. Martin," he said expansively, opening the passenger door of the car. "I have to go that way."

It was only a short walk but Martin couldn't be bothered arguing. Fred regarded anyone who used his legs for locomotion as deficient either in money or intelligence, and he himself almost lived in his Cortina.

As the car turned into Glovers Lane, Fred leaned across and said in a voice of beery confidentiality, "Having trouble with those Jerries, Mr. Martin? Couple of crooks, are they?"

"I don't know yet who they are," Martin said truthfully. "I'm just trying to establish their identity."

"Never trust a Jerry in war or in business," Fred droned on as they came to Bridle Way. "They'll slip a knife between your ribs without you feeling a thing—"

"Hold it, Fred! We're here." Martin put his hand against the dashboard as Fred stood on his brakes outside the house. "Thanks for the lift."

As a responsible citizen, he should have gently suggested to Fred that perhaps he was not in an ideal condition for driving. But such a suggestion would, he knew, meet with disbelief and anger. He justified his silence with the thought that there was little traffic on the road down to the station, except where it crossed the main Bainton road.

As Martin got out of the car, he was dismayed to see Fred climbing out as well, still discoursing on the iniquity of the Hun.

"You only have to read the books to see what type they are. And you're not trying to tell me they've changed their character in thirty years." He followed Martin to the gate. "It's all there in the history books for anyone to read. They've never changed in the past and they won't change now."

"I have to go, Fred," Martin cut in gently. "I've got to drive down to Kenley and make sure the works is still there."

"I'll drive you there if you like, Mr. Martin. You'll still be tired after your trip—"

"Thanks all the same," Martin said quickly. "But I'll need my car today anyway."

He picked up his briefcase from the hall, then went to the side of the house and swung up the garage door. To his dismay Fred followed, apparently determined to complete his dissertation.

"We should have bottled them up in nineteen forty-five, instead of letting them run riot again, flogging us their cars and cameras. . . ."

Martin opened the door of the Rover, noticing as he did so some new oil stains on the garage floor. He'd had that oil seal fixed at the last service, but it looked like another botched job by Samuels. He'd have it out with them later in the week.

Fred's flow ceased only when Martin sat in the car and firmly closed the door. His watery eyes blinked and he stepped to the rear of the car.

"Sensible, that," he said. "I see you back your car into the garage so you can drive straight out." He chuckled and added, "I daren't do that. Takes me all my time to steer the car forward when I've had a skinful at the end of the day!"

Martin smiled wearily and started the engine. It required a calculated degree of rudeness to get away from someone like Fred.

The driver jumped to one side as the car edged forward.

"Okay, Mr. Martin," he called. "Don't worry—I'll shut the garage for you."

With a sigh of relief Martin drove out onto the road and headed for Kenley. The sun was directly in his eyes and he lowered the visor as he built up speed to a steady fifty. As he neared the Bainton crossroad he started to brake. There was no response from the car and the pedal felt spongy. He pumped it several times but there was no build-up of pressure. The crossroads was a hundred yards ahead. He pulled on the hand brake and the car slowed slightly.

Martin felt a cold band of perspiration across his forehead as he held up the brake lever with all the force he could muster. The car was vibrating, but it was not going to halt before the crossroads.

It was so damn stupid, the way life could have such a feeble and arbitrary ending. A man devoted his life trying to create something worthwhile, only to see it all finish in something as mundane as a car crash. The main road ahead was solid with traffic. He had five seconds before he hit it. Five seconds of life left to him. What could he do with them? Treasure each moment of the day, my boy, came the voice of Chippy Taylor, his fifth-form master, chiding him for his daydreaming. A fleeting thing such a moment may be, but your life is made up of them and nothing more. Weigh them, my boy, value them and use them. The sweat was running from his hands, making the steering wheel slippery. You must treasure every one of those fleeting moments, watch them jealously, because one will slip past you and that is the final one that takes your life with it. Strange. He'd never recalled Chippy's words until now. Even in 1944, when he faced death three times a day as a front-line operational pilot, life had never seemed such a desperately precious possession. Of course that was due to Colin, with his gift for leadership that made you really believe that success in battle transcended all personal considerations.

Two seconds left and every articulated lorry and furniture van in southeast England is queuing to enter Bainton, population ten thousand five hundred, market day Saturday, early closing Wednesday.

The gear box! Down into third. The engine screaming but too late. Slicing into the middle of the cross traffic. Horns and tire squeals above the sound of the engine. A thud of a lorry bumper hitting the rear wing, lorry driver red in the face as he stands up pushing the brake pedal with his whole weight. Hold the rocking car on course.

Disbelieving, Martin found himself on the other side of the junction still doing a steady forty and still on the road. No time to wonder how he had survived; he had to stop this damn-blasted car. Go down to second—what about the ignition? Marveling at his thoughtlessness, he turned the key to off. Then he marveled further at his stupidity: that key also locked the steering column.

Unwaveringly the car took a course along the rough grass lining the ditch. The engine, starved of power, dragged the speed down.

The suspension could absorb the bumping no more and Martin was thrown up and down in his seat as the wheels began their inexorable progress further into the ditch. That was the most effective brake of all. Water spraying its side, the car slid into the ditch and shuddered to a final halt.

The first driver to stop had to be Fred, of course.

"Fancy bit of driving, that," he observed with heavy humor as Martin climbed out of the ditched car.

"Brakes failed," Martin said shortly. "Where's the nearest phone?"

Fred obligingly took him half a mile to a kiosk, from where he telephoned Samuels's garage and arranged for them to tow the car in for an inspection and estimate.

Fred waited for him. "You'll want a lift to the works I suppose?" The grin had an element of smugness now.

He drove with a surprising degree of care considering his condition, and twenty minutes later he halted outside the long brick building which bore the words "Martin Engineering." The factory was bounded by fields with a small airstrip across the road hidden by trees. Based here was the Molyneux Aircraft Museum, of which Martin was a trustee. He constantly marveled at the good fortune that had allowed him to establish his business next door to such a haven of escapism and nostalgia.

"You'll be without your car for a few days, I'd say," Fred observed before he pulled away. "I can do you an exclusive hire at a special rate. I'll be available any time you like."

"I don't think so, thanks," Martin said. "There's a company car I can use."

It was a four-year-old Viva used as a runabout by anyone at the works who needed transport, and its condition reflected its haphazard life-style. But it would be worth putting up with to avoid Fred's continuous droning.

When he walked into the office Sheila was typing a complex tender document. She looked up with a smile.

"Good trip, Mr. Martin?" Then she looked more closely and a note of concern came into her voice. "You're very pale. Are you feeling all right?"

"Bit of trouble with the car," he told her. "All I need is a cup of that witch's brew of yours, and I'll be fine."

He sat in his chair as Sheila scuttled round with the electric kettle. His hands were shaking slightly and he kept them below the level of the desk. The desk itself was clear except for the opened correspondence standing in a neat pile on the blotting pad.

Sheila did an excellent job. Those letters would represent only a quarter of what had come in, she having disposed of the rest with as much efficiency and dispatch as he could himself. His dependence on her was absolute as far as the business was concerned. While she ran the office like clockwork, her principal virtue was that she knew how to handle Martin himself. His short temper would long since have driven any other secretary in tears to an industrial tribunal. He no longer tried to analyze the reasons for his low boiling point. Years of stress in building up the business, maybe: that was where Ellen put the blame for their marital breakup, the reason why no woman could be expected to live with him. He had never been too sure whether or not cause and effect were being confused here. Wouldn't a more stable atmosphere at home have eased the stress of his work? He didn't know, and he'd given up trying to work out an answer. The simple facts were that he could be a bastard to live or work with, he knew he was a bastard, he sincerely tried to do something about it when the realization crossed his mind, and he always failed.

Sheila's method of survival was to absorb his shouting and sarcasm like a sponge and carry on cheerfully doing things her own way. This was fine as far as Martin was concerned. What did wear him down, however, was her tendency to be overprotective.

She poured out his tea and stood to one side of the desk as though to supervise him while he drank it. She was plump, about thirty, but her rosy face was that of a girl some years younger. She had a husband whom she worshiped but no children. This must have represented a major gap in her life, a gap Martin sometimes suspected he was being used to fill.

"Is that better?" she asked as he finished the tea. When he nodded, she went on, "Now listen, Mr. Martin, there's nothing too urgent here, so I think you should go back home and spend the rest of the day in bed. You're tired out and I think that's your trouble."

"I'm fine," Martin told her. "That tea of yours would get a dying elephant on its feet again. Let's hear about all the problems of this past week."

Still watching him doubtfully, she outlined the half-dozen matters requiring his attention. Only one brought an uplift to his spirits.

"I didn't know Algeria was operating Derry-Stevens equipment," he said as he studied one of the letters she placed before him.

"They bought it second-hand two years ago," Sheila told him. "Maybe they didn't know it was obsolete."

"They know now, when they're trying to get spares. And this is going to be an expanding market for us as the machines get older."

"Can we supply those parts within a month?" Sheila asked. "They want a reply quickly."

"We can do it. Draft a letter to that effect and get it off today." He leaned back. "Strange, isn't it, the way we prosper because other firms go out of business. I suppose we're carrion crows in a way, living off the scraps other people leave behind." He got up from his desk to look out of the window. A stacker truck was passing, loaded with pallets. "I sometimes feel it would be nice to be making something that was really our own—a Martin original."

"And what would you make?" Sheila asked bluntly. "Some fancy machine that would probably make *you* bankrupt—and then someone else would come along and make money selling spares for your machine. You should be grateful for the nice steady business you have."

"I am, Sheila. I really am." He turned from the window. "Ask Arthur to call in and see me, will you."

A dull pain was developing in his right shoulder, which he remembered bumping against the door pillar when the car hit the ditch. It could be a sprain or just a severe bruise. He'd take a look after he'd sorted out the works problems with his chief production engineer, Arthur Parry.

31

In fact those problems occupied the rest of the afternoon. Then, as the engineer left, Sheila put through a call from Samuels.

"We've finished looking over your car, Mr. Martin, and we're a bit puzzled. Did you bleed your braking system at any time?"

"That's a daft question," Martin said. "No one lifts up that bonnet except you."

Samuels said carefully, "I hope you're not going to blame my lads for this. According to our records it's four months since we gave it a service. But all the fluid has been drained out of the brake hydraulic system. There's no sign of a fracture in the lines, so it can't have leaked away."

Martin thought for a moment. Then he said, "No one is blaming you, Mr. Samuels. It must have been vandals. I'd like you to go ahead with the repairs now."

"It could take about a week." Samuels said. "Depending on how easily we can get the parts. There's a fair bit of body damage there. But we'll do our best."

Martin replaced the phone thoughtfully. Somehow the news had come as no surprise. It explained the stains on the garage floor. He should have guessed those two Germans were not simply investigating his reading habits. But why had they left it this late? They must realize that, by now, he would have passed on all his information. And even then, surely they could have found a more direct and effective means of killing him. If he was as dangerous to them as all that, they should be stopping at nothing to remove him. If they succeeded, he thought with wry satisfaction, it would make those Foreign Office cynics sit up and take him seriously.

Martin got up and walked restlessly round the office. The Germans would see it that way, too . . . which was why his death had to appear accidental. Through the window he could see the works car parked by the main engineering shop. The Viva would be their next target once he started to use it.

He opened the office door. "Sheila, get hold of Fred Williams, will you, and tell him I'll take him up on that exclusive hire he was talking about. He can start by picking me up in an hour's time and driving me home."

Martin found it difficult to sleep that night because of the pain in his shoulder.

At two o'clock he got up, put on his dressing gown, and went down to the lounge. Sitting at the bureau he wrote a brief summary of everything that had happened over the past three days, including his visit to the Foreign Office and the details of the accident.

His final paragraph read: "My death will not be as accidental as it appears. All the circumstances should be investigated, particularly with regard to the activities of the two Germans who were reported in this area on April 4."

He signed the last sheet and sealed the pages in an envelope. This he put into a further envelope together with a note addressed to his solicitor:

> Dear Brian,
>   The enclosed envelope is to be opened in case of my death. With luck this should not be for many years yet, but there is the possibility something may happen in the more immediate future. I'm not being deliberately morbid: after all, that's the premise insurance policies are sold on.

Having sealed the outer envelope, he went to the kitchen, swallowed three aspirins, and went back to bed. Within the next hour he finally drifted off to sleep.

In an office off Whitehall, three men sat round a table listening to the playback of a tape recorder. When the cassette finished its run, Cole stood up and switched off the machine.

Hector Blair leaned back in his chair, putting a match to his pipe while his eyes studied the ornate ceiling. "When," he said, "are you Foreign Office people going to invest in a decent tape recorder? Parts are unintelligible."

"The machine was concealed in a briefcase which I placed on the table while he spoke," Cole explained. He passed over a sheaf of papers. "I've had a complete transcript made, based on the recording and my own notes. My chief feels two of the items mentioned concern your office to some extent—the oil-rig and the Edinburgh business. Technically speaking, both are internal."

Blair grunted as he glanced through the papers. "How much credence do your people place in this man?"

Cole took off his glasses and polished them slowly. "I'm the only one who's actually met him. He's a strong-minded man and he seems genuinely to believe in the information himself. He doesn't appear the type who would have the ability or the need to invent it."

Blair picked up a buff-colored file from the table. "I've been looking him up. Regular visitor to the GDR, sound steady export trade in noncontroversial areas, never overstepped the line." He flicked through the pages. "No question of his loyalty up to now. Served in the RAF, commissioned nineteen forty-four, came out in forty-six. Closely connected with the Molyneux Aircraft Museum, which might indicate a tendency to live in the past—still wallowing in the remembered glory of his wartime flying days, maybe." He stopped and checked back on some of the pages. "Nothing here about his marital status—which could be significant in this case. You'd better check on that, Jenkins."

The third man in the room gave a nod. He was in his early thirties, tall, with his dark hair cut short and with a small moustache. His face was alert but uninvolved as he absorbed everything that was said with routine efficiency.

"What about the background details to his story?" Blair asked Cole. "Are those names genuine—Frisch, Lukas?"

"We know that Lukas does hold the position referred to. We're trying to find out about Frisch at the moment. That's no easy thing to do, if he's with the secret police."

"How about the Israelis? Have they recently lost an agent?"

"It's not as straightforward as that. They do have a source of information, but it's strictly a one-way system. They have to wait for what he gets out to them, and they have no way of contacting him directly. He's not a regular agent, you see. The Israelis regard what they get from him as just a bonus to their normal means of intelligence gathering. It's not unusual for weeks to pass without hearing a word from him."

Blair sat in thought for a few moments, smoke billowing from his pipe. Finally he said, "This is a real dog's breakfast, when you think how many departments it involves: Defense, Foreign Office, Home Office—Energy, too, with an oil-rig in the picture." He gave a self-satisfied smile. "Proof, if it were needed, of the indispensability of ISCO. Imagine all those departments tripping each other up, trying to sort things out."

Cole nodded and put the tape recorder back into his briefcase. "You'll be reporting through your own channels, of course, but we would like to be kept in touch with developments."

"I doubt if there will be many of those," Blair said, standing up and weighting the transcript in his hand. "The whole thing has that phony smell to me."

When Cole had gone, Jenkins said, "Where do we start?"

"With Martin himself. If it's been set up by the opposition, they'll be watching him themselves to make sure he does what he's supposed to—namely, lead us up the garden path."

"Could be. There's the report that came in yesterday, if you recall. Keller is believed to have entered the country recently."

Blair shook his head. "I don't believe it's a setup—not by the opposition, anyway. My view is that it's a half-baked stunt by Martin himself to get that girl from behind the Curtain and over here." He sighed. "Bloody nuisance. We have to work our balls off just because the sap runs strong in his."

3

Over the next two weeks Martin watched the papers and listened to radio news bulletins in a mood of anxious anticipation.

The start of the NATO exercise in the Mediterranean, with the usual reports of Soviet "trawlers" and aircraft shadowing everything that moved, heightened his feeling of tension. On Thursday, April 8, he took a transistor radio into the office, where it provided a continuous background to his day's work. It meant trying to close his mind to the solid slabs of pop music and reopening it for the news bulletins. The whole thing left Sheila utterly bemused and he did nothing to enlighten her.

By the end of the day, nothing had come through: no report of a mystery sinking, or, conversely, of a Soviet submarine being rammed. The following morning's *Telegraph* simply reported that the exercise was completed and NATO had flexed its muscles very convincingly.

Had anything happened? Had an attempt been made by the Soviets—and frustrated by pre-emptive action on the part of the NATO forces?

It suddenly occurred to him that, if so, the odds were the whole affair would be hushed up anyway. If NATO had successfully dealt with the matter, they wouldn't be banging the drum about it at this stage. It was the sort of incident that could be played up by either side for its own benefit from a propaganda point of view, so both versions would cancel out.

Whereas a strike against an oil-rig would be a much more clear-cut affair. . . .

Three days later Martin had to start questioning his own

gullibility. Should he have taken Greta's warnings at their face value? The deadlines for three of the four "incidents" had passed without any evidence that they had taken place. Wasn't the man besotted with a beautiful woman the easiest mark of all for the confidence trickster? Had he simply been used as a ready-made and convenient pawn in some complex game of espionage?

The presence of Greta in the center of it all was something he couldn't accept. He could offer no rational justification for his faith in her and what she had told him. But the faith was there and it was enough to sustain him.

"It's the bloody 'D' Notice system," he muttered to himself, throwing the newspaper into the basket on his desk. "The government just tells the press that publication will jeopardize national security and the news media have to obey the censor."

But surely he, at least, was entitled to be told what was happening? Or did those dummies in Whitehall classify him simply as a delivery boy—drop off the parcel, lad, but don't ask what's in it because it's none of your business.

Sheila came in and started tidying up the drawings cupboard. Chattering in her usual way she said, "As a trustee, you should know. There's nothing special about the Molyneux airfield, is there? I mean it's not RAF or Ministry of Defense—just a collection of old planes?"

"That's probably an accurate layman's description," he said, "but don't let any of the other trustees hear you call it that. Why do you ask?"

"The past couple of days I've noticed two men in a car driving up and down the road between here and Molyneux. They go very slowly as though they're keeping an eye on something."

Ten minutes later he told Sheila he was going to the machine shop. He headed that way, but once clear of the offices he changed direction for the main gate.

There was no traffic on the road outside.

Willy Crow, who doubled as timekeeper and gateman, had his office just inside the grounds and Martin asked him if he'd seen anything.

"I don't have time to watch traffic driving past, Mr.

37

Martin," Willy said heavily, pushing his pencil behind his ear. "I'm fully occupied with my two jobs."

Willy had been demanding a raise for some time, on the argument that in his dual role he had to work twice as much as anyone else. The fact that each of them was barely half a job made no difference from his point of view. Martin intended to give him a raise but also planned to make him wait a little longer for it. Willy might think it too easy otherwise.

Martin said to him, "A couple of men in a car have been hanging around recently. They may be casing the place for a break-in. If you spot them, give me a ring."

"I'll be watching, Mr. Martin," said Willy, his interest aroused. Now he had a reason for spending the day at the time-office window, which meant his work wouldn't get done, would it? And that would prove something.

It was three o'clock in the afternoon when he called Martin across.

From the time office Martin looked out onto the road at the Marina cruising slowly past the gate. Sheila had been halfway right. The men were keeping observation, but on the Martin works and not on the airfield. They both seemed in their mid-thirties, wore suits and ties and expressionless faces. Two clean-cut, innocent, respectable—what? They could have been anything.

"That's the third time they've been past in half an hour," Willy said conspiratorially. "They're looking the place over very carefully."

"There doesn't seem anything sinister about them," Martin said after a while. "They're probably looking for a development site. Forget about them now, Willy."

Leaving Willy looking disappointed, Martin walked around the engineering shop to the other perimeter fence, where he had a quick inspection. It seemed sound enough, as it should considering the money it had cost. In a place like Martin Engineering a certain degree of security was a basic requirement. The sort of stock the works carried could be very tempting to certain people, metals like titanium, brass, and copper being both valuable and easily negotiable. But there was no way to stop a really determined man from getting into any factory, short of surrounding it with armed guards.

38

As he went back to the office, once again he had that feeling of angry impotence he had first experienced when leaving the Foreign Office. Someone was planning something unpleasant for him. All because of a matter he had been involved in entirely against his will.

Then, as Fred was driving him home at six o'clock, he spotted the Marina parked across the road from the works entrance. The occupants made no effort even to hide their faces behind a newspaper. They watched without expression as Fred's car turned onto the road; then the Marina edged forward to follow.

Martin glanced back as Fred drove towards the Monkswell Road and saw they had positioned themselves a steady fifty yards behind. Although there was a fair amount of traffic heading for Monkswell, with cars constantly overtaking each other, the Marina stayed glued on their tail, thanks to what Martin could see was pretty smart driving. He kept looking back until even Fred noticed.

The driver glanced in his mirror and said, "Know the people in the Marina, Mr. Martin?"

"No, but you might. Are they the two Germans you picked up the other day?"

The driver screwed his eyes up as he looked in the mirror. "Can't tell from this distance. Have they got square heads?"

"I never really noticed. But they're a bit of an embarrassment to me."

Fred nodded. "Leave it to me."

He put his foot down and started a leapfrog overtaking routine around the cars ahead. It was a hairy experience on a two-lane road. Fred seemed able to calculate matters to within a yard, although his style provoked a lot of flashing headlights and blaring horns. But he managed it well considering that, as far as Martin knew, he had not had less than his normal daily intake of beer.

The Marina was several cars behind now but working hard to catch up.

"When we reach Monkswell, I'm going to leave you, Fred," Martin said. "You know the side road on the left by the post office? Turn into there, stop just long enough for me to bail out, than carry on to your own place. I'll see you at the usual time tomorrow."

That was the way it worked. As the car pulled into the side road Martin had his door already open. Out he rolled and Fred was off within two seconds. Martin stepped into a phone box and watched as the Marina appeared round the corner. The two men saw Fred's car and continued the chase.

Waiting until both cars were out of sight, Martin then looked up a Monkswell taxi firm in the phone book and arranged for a cab to come and collect him.

He reached home half an hour later, not leaving the taxi until he could see there was no sign of any other car parked in the vicinity. He entered the house feeling rather pleased with himself in a childish sort of way.

As he went up to bed he savored the thought of the men's reactions when they realized they'd been fooled. Then he thought wryly that things had come to a sorry state if his only pleasure lay in such small satisfactions.

Just over an hour after he'd gone to bed the doorbell rang. He went down to find a police sergeant and constable at the door.

Fred's car had crashed, he was dead, and the police wanted to know if Martin could help with relevant information. Fred was on exclusive hire to him at the time and they wondered when Martin had seen him last.

His mind misty with sleep, Martin took some time to absorb the news. Finally it got through and he felt sick.

"Yes, he was on hire to me," he told them, "but I left him at Monkswell and he was supposed to be going home from there. What happened?"

"He took a bend too wide," the police sergeant said. "Met a car coming the other way and hit a stone wall trying to avoid it."

Martin thought for a moment and said quietly, "Are you sure that's what happened?" Then, suddenly conscious of the flimsy evidence his own suspicions were founded on, he added, "He was a professional driver. He knew the road well and he wasn't the type to make silly mistakes."

"He was a regular drinker, too, from all accounts," the sergeant said. "I've little doubt we'll find his alcohol content was above the permitted level. Why did you leave

40

him at Monkswell, Mr. Martin? Had his driving been dangerous in any way?"

"Not at all. He'd been driving particularly well. I wanted to make some urgent telephone calls so I sent him on his way while I used the call box."

It must have sounded thin and the sergeant looked searchingly at Martin while the constable wrote it all down.

"And that's all you know, Mr. Martin?"

"It is. I'm terribly shocked by this. Are you sure that was how the accident happened?"

"The people in the car behind him have confirmed it. Thanks for your help. We'll be in touch if we need anything more."

After the police had gone Martin gave some thought to the characters in the Marina. Had they forced Fred off the road and then reported it as an accident? If so, the driver had died as proxy for him.

Why the hell did he ever keep that appointment with Frisch? He'd put his own head in a noose and now a harmless old soak like Fred had been crushed to death just because he got in the way.

Bitterness and anger burned inside him as he went back to bed.

In the morning he phoned Sheila at home and she agreed to give him a lift into the office. At eight-fifteen her white Mini pulled into the drive and she gave a toot on the horn.

Martin was reading the morning paper at the time. Reports of planes getting into trouble while crossing East Germany were what he was looking for now. Waiting for news of an oil-rig attack was something he'd given up, along with his belief in the independence and integrity of the news media.

"Did you get to bed at a reasonable hour?" Sheila demanded as he climbed into the car.

"Eleven-thirty," he told her. "I chased the girls home by telling them a dragon in a white Mini would come and scorch them with her breath in the morning otherwise."

"It really isn't funny."

He didn't think so either. Making feeble jokes was a reflex against the depression that Fred's death had cast over him. He had barely slept at all after receiving the news, and he was still trying to fight off a feeling of guilt, which threatened to envelop him. The guilt related not only to the fact that Fred had died in his place, but also to the mental abuse he had so often poured on the old chap's head.

Sheila steered the car toward the works and, as usual, her habit of staying in gear until she'd reached forty served as an abrasive to his nerves.

"You might think it's clever and you're making a lot of money by staying up all night. Well, there are no pockets in a shroud, Mr. Martin."

From the way she said it he knew she was repeating a comment she'd made to her husband over breakfast. Martin had gathered that Tom was a long-suffering and silent audience to her views on the world in general and the running of Martin Engineering in particular.

Taking a right-angle bend in top gear, she went on, "I wish you'd find some way to relax out of work—"

"Just a moment, Sheila." An item of news on the car radio caught his ear.

"The aircraft made an emergency landing at an East German airfield. None of the fifty-six passengers on board was injured. It is understood that the plane's captain decided on the forced landing after a loss of power in one of the engines. Now for some home news. Three men will appear in court this morning. . . ."

He felt a small and quite inappropriate glow of triumph. Whatever had or hadn't happened in the North Sea and the Mediterranean, Cole's crowd would find it difficult to disguise this one. Fifty-six people knew what had happened and would make sure some blunt and loud questions were asked.

He found it hard to concentrate on his work that morning as he kept an ear tuned to the transistor radio.

Finally, at one o'clock, there was more news about the incident. A flame-out was apparently the cause of the forced landing, and the East German air-traffic control had cooperated in helping the aircraft safely down. The passengers had been transferred to buses, which had taken them on to their destination.

Martin switched off the radio in a state of utter confusion. Not only were they going to brazen it out, but they were giving the East Germans a pat on the back. What sort of international diplomacy was that?

By any standards he reckoned that he was now entitled to be brought fully into the picture. He telephoned the Foreign Office and asked for Cole. To his surprise he got straight through.

"Yes, Mr. Martin. What can I do for you?"

"I just want to be brought up to date. How have things worked out? I know all about the Offical Secrets Act, but I feel I'm in a special position, having started things off so to speak."

There was a pause; then Cole said in his flat voice, "The matters you communicated to us proved to be unreliable. I assumed you had realized that by now."

"Unreliable?" Martin thought for a moment, and then grasped the euphemism. "You're trying to say I was lying?"

"Now, I did not say that, Mr. Martin—"

"It sounded very like it, as translated into your Civil Service weasel language." Martin was striding angrily round the office as he grasped the phone. "What about that incident reported this morning? How unreliable was I on that? Don't tell me that didn't have you all running round in circles!"

Cole sounded genuinely puzzled. "What incident are you referring to?"

"The forced landing in East Germany! Isn't it just as I warned you?"

"Just one moment, Mr. Martin." To Martin's pleasure a note of irritation had crept into his voice now. "The facts in the case of that particular incident were exactly as they have been reported by the news media. There was a mechanical failure in one of the engines. The captain was worried about a possible fire risk, which was why he decided to make the emergency landing."

"Have you had a report from your man on the spot?" Martin demanded. "I think you'll find there's more—"

"We have received all the information," Cole said firmly. "One of my colleagues has in fact been liaising with the East German authorities. We've enjoyed the utmost cooperation from them."

Martin felt utterly lost now. After a moment he said

43

feebly, "You must realize I find that hard to believe, in the light of the information I brought back—"

"I'm sorry I cannot help you, Mr. Martin." Cole's voice was its neutral self now. "We appreciate your coming in to see us, but that particular file is now closed."

Martin put down the phone and slumped into his chair. His head ached, as though he had been banging it against a wall.

Sheila came in with her diary and said, "This meeting with the shop stewards this afternoon—"

"Cancel it," he told her. "I'm going up to London this afternoon."

The doorman phoned Cole and he was down in two minutes flat.

"We didn't make any appointment," he said reprovingly.

"True," Martin agreed. "But as I couldn't get any sense from you over the phone this morning, I thought I'd try what the politicians call an eyeball-to-eyeball confrontation."

They looked at each other in silence for a few moments, unblinking. Then Cole went and signed the book and said, "You'd better come upstairs."

He took him to the same interview room; Martin sat down, while Cole remained standing by the door.

"I don't think there's anything left for us to discuss," Cole began, but Martin held up his hand.

"If you're talking about yourself and me, then I agree. Clearly you don't know what's going on, as you're probably at too low a level to be kept informed. So now I want you to arrange for me to see your superior."

For the first time he saw the man react—a faint pinkness came over his face. That, for Cole, probably represented fury.

But his voice was only slightly more tight than usual as he said, "That isn't possible—"

"A man died yesterday," Martin interrupted. "To my knowledge he never harmed a soul in his life. He wasn't important to anyone. But that poor bloke died in place of me—in what was the second attempt on my life." He paused, Cole remained silent, and he went on, "I've just about had enough, and now I intend to do something about it—and I don't just mean writing to the *Daily Telegraph*. As far as I can see the British security network—of which I assume you are a vital segment, possibly one of the holes in the net—is either incompetent, inhuman, or both. Now, I'm quite prepared to make that fact known to everyone I can think of and produce the evidence for anyone who wants to see it." As Cole sniffed, he added, "Oh, yes, you'll have plenty of means of discrediting me. I'm well aware of that. But you can't deny it's going to cause you a lot of work and embarrassment while it lasts."

There was silence as their eyes locked in on each other again.

Finally Cole said, "Just wait here," and he went out. No "please" this time or "would you mind." Mr. Cole had clearly had a bellyful of Mad Martin, the amateur secret agent. Well, it was mutual.

It was ten minutes before Cole returned. He had his coat on and he said, "Come with me."

Martin followed him in silence out of the building and along Whitehall. They went down a smaller street to what seemed a side entrance to one of the larger buildings. There was the usual fuss with security at the door; then Cole led him up three flights of stairs.

He opened an oak-panelled door, stepped inside, and announced Martin as though it were the Lord Mayor's banquet. He also managed that suggestion of contempt in pronouncing the name that butlers take years to develop.

Martin walked in and Cole went out, closing the door behind him. It was a large office with a good carpet, which, however, was short by a foot all round of being wall-to-wall. The size of the carpet was, Martin had heard, an accurate indication of rank in the Civil Service. This chap was well on his way but not yet right at the top.

He was in his fifties, with thick gray hair and the build of a weight-lifter—a short weight-lifter, as Martin realized when the other man stood up behind his desk. He had a reasonably pleasant smile on his face as he came across with hand outstretched.

"Good afternoon, Mr. Martin." There was a trace of Newcastle in his voice. "Hector Blair. I think you want a chat with me."

As they shook hands, Martin said, "If you're in a position to tell me what's been done about the information I gave to Mr. Cole, then you're the man."

Blair indicated a chair in front of his desk and busied himself pouring tea from a metal pot into two blue cups.

"No sugar," Martin said in answer to his questioning glance.

As Martin sipped the tea, Blair sat down again and placed a buff-colored folder on his desk.

He said, "Everything is here that you told Mr. Cole. And, contrary to your belief, we took it seriously—as we do all information that reaches us from people such as yourself." He tapped the file with his finger. "None of the incidents of which you warned us have in fact taken place. The NATO exercise—no interference at all. There's been no trouble with our North Sea oil-rigs, and the air corridor over East Germany remains open—"

"What about that incident yesterday? You're not trying to tell me that aircraft genuinely suffered a flame-out?"

Blair shrugged. "If you're not prepared to take our word for that, then I can't do anything to convince you— except suggest you interview any of the passengers you wish. I can arrange for you to have a copy of the passenger list."

Martin thought that one over for a moment. A rigged passenger list? Possible, but so complicated as to be unlikely. Which seemed to leave him with no ground under his feet at all.

It must have shown in his face, for Blair said sympathetically, "No one's questioning the fact that you came here in good faith. But we need more than faith to work on."

Martin said, "Don't patronize me, Mr. Blair. You claim my information was false. But I've never been taken seriously since I first came here. Cole's attitude was one of disbelief from the start."

Blair put his elbows on the desk and rested his chin on his hands. He said with easy informality, "You had a personal relationship with this girl, Greta Beckmann? A close relationship?"

"Yes. So what?"

"And as a result you want us to try and get her into this country?"

"That was my idea. I've since realized what a vain hope

it is, expecting you people to give a helping hand to any-one—least of all someone who's gone to a great deal of risk to help this country."

"Be that as it may," Blair said, "you must see that your personal involvement casts a certain amount of—" He paused. "Let me put it this way. A person might present such a story simply to persuade us to bring the lady out." He held up his hand as Martin went to speak. "I know. I've impugned your integrity. But, Mr. Martin, we would be very naïve if such a thought didn't cross our minds."

"You can think what the hell you like," Martin said with anger, "but I'm no liar. Before we go any further, do you believe that or not?"

Blair stirred his tea, tasted it, then started lighting his pipe. Through a blue haze he said, "I can't guarantee the honesty of any man, but fair enough: let me accept what you say as being the truth—as it was told to you. Has it occurred to you that Miss Beckmann herself might have invented this for the same reason—using you as her mid-dleman?"

Working hard to keep his temper, Martin said, "Of course it occurred to me. But I offered to help the girl es-cape. I begged her to come with me. And she refused. All she wanted was that this information should reach Lon-don."

"Let me cast another fly then: the information was de-liberately planted by the East Germans, using her and yourself as pawns."

He watched for a reaction, but Martin simply shrugged. "What would be the point?"

"Let's think of a few. Maybe they wanted to test our reflexes—see how smartly we reacted to a threat. More likely they would simply want to embarrass us. If we'd taken the warnings too seriously, we could have messed up the NATO exercise, disrupted our North Sea oil pro-gram, and cancelled a lot of our European flights. And, most important of all, stirred up the whole Palestine situa-tion before the Edinburgh Conference even started. Quite a haul of credits for them, at the cost of bluffing one Brit-ish businessman."

"All this proves what I suspected," Martin said with disgust. "Nothing I told you has been taken seriously. You've never believed a word of it."

47

"I never said I disbelieved your story, Mr. Martin—only your sources. A man comes from the east with a package of goodies like yours—well." He smiled through the smoke. "If you were in our position, wouldn't you feel that this is one gift horse that needs its teeth examined very carefully?"

He stood up, presumably to indicate the interview was at an end. "In the light of events—or nonevents—I suggest you forget the whole affair, Mr. Martin, and concentrate on running your business."

Martin remained seated and said, "There's nothing I'd like more. But that's difficult to do when people are trying to kill you."

That sent Blair's eyebrows up. "Kill you?" His mind was changing gear, Martin could see.

"There was a man I knew called Fred Williams," Martin said. "He was a pretty nondescript sort of bloke who had some irritating ways, but there was no harm in him at all. Last night he was mangled to death in his car by two people who thought they were mangling me." Blair's forehead was now creased in puzzlement. "This was the second time someone tried to kill me. I can't help worrying in case those responsible take consolation in the theory of third time lucky."

Blair pressed the button on his desk intercom and said, "I want Jenkins." He released the button and turned to Martin. "We've had people watching you since the day after you first came here. They've not reported anything untoward."

Interesting, Martin reflected. He wouldn't have mentioned that if he hadn't been pushed into a corner.

Martin said, "Then they're doing a poor job. The first attempt was the day I came here, when the brakes on my car were sabotaged. I only survived because of a gap in the traffic and a lorry driver with lightning reflexes. The second occasion—"

There was a knock and in walked the man who had been driving the Marina.

"Jenkins, have you any evidence of one or more attempts on Mr. Martin's life?"

"But this is one of them," Martin protested. "He was driving the car." He looked at Blair. "You mean those men were sent by you?"

48

"It was considered appropriate to keep an eye on you for the time being. If, by any chance, your information was genuine, then conceivably you could have been a target for—the other side."

"We saw no sign of an attempt on your life, Mr. Martin," Jenkins said politely. "In fact, there was no evidence of anyone out of the ordinary taking an interest in you."

"But the car I was in crashed just after I'd left it—"

"Quite true," Jenkins put in, "and for a while we thought you were still in it. My colleague and I witnessed the whole thing. The driver took that bend far too wide."

There was a pause; then Blair said quietly, "So that is one of the so-called attempts on your life dealt with. What was the other?"

Martin struggled to adjust his mind to the changed situation.

"All right, I was wrong about that one. But there's no doubt my car was interfered with so that the brakes would fail."

"You have clear evidence of this?"

"The fluid had gone from the hydraulic system. Someone drained it off."

Blair looked at Jenkins with a "what can we do with him?" expression.

In that moment Martin realized he'd had enough. He stood up and said, "You've made up your minds, and I'm not going to change them for you, I can see that. I've explained how I got involved in this business and how it was entirely against my will. Having done all I can to get other people to face up to their responsibilities, I now intend to take your original advice and forget the whole bloody affair."

"I think it's best," Blair said, gently holding his arm and steering him to the door. "We appreciate it was your public-spirited attitude that brought you here in the first place, but you must leave us to be the final judges in matters like this. I'm sure you'll see everything in a more balanced light in the morning after you've slept on it."

The door was opened for him by Jenkins. Before going out he turned and said, "You think you've persuaded me of something. And you have: God help this country if you're the sort of people running its security system."

The bitterness in his voice had no effect on them at all. The door was shut quietly and firmly behind him.

The doorman even gave him a salute as he left the building. Christ, he thought, I must be beginning to look like one of them.

4

Martin tried pushing the whole matter to the back of his mind. This proved not too difficult as he became immersed in the problems of meeting the increasingly urgent demands of the Algerians.

"We'll have practically built them a new power station when we've finished this," he said, studying the telex list that Sheila had already placed on his desk when he came in the next morning.

"You're not complaining, are you?" she asked. "Because here's another one just in from Paris."

He snorted as he read it. "That's ridiculous. We can't bring delivery forward two weeks. I'm not sure we can meet the original contract date as it is. What's got into these people?"

"Boulin?" Sheila said. "He probably gets a bigger commission if he can manage early delivery. It's a great pity we can't deal with the Algerians direct."

Martin shrugged. "It's through Boulin we got the business in the first place, so we can't very well bypass him. And he's pushed a fair amount of stuff our way over the years." He reflected that it was Boulin who had first put him in contact with Lukas: how much should he thank him for that? "I'd better see Arthur, then."

The chief production engineer gave a defensive laugh when Martin showed him the two telex messages. "Not a hope, Mr. Martin. You know the amount of machining that's required on those turbine fittings. And it's not hack work either. We could have to scrap them and start again three or four times."

"I agree with you, Arthur. It's completely unrealistic. Forget this and carry on doing the best you can."

When the engineer had gone, Martin said to Sheila, "Get Boulin on the phone. I want to acquaint him with the facts of economic life."

The agent was his usual friendly self. "It is a delight to hear from you, Mr. Martin. You received my messages? I get you plenty of good business."

Martin said, "This isn't business you're offering me. It's an invitation to run my works and my staff into the ground. These delivery dates just aren't on, Boulin, and you know it."

"But I do not know it, Mr. Martin," said Boulin, sounding hurt. "I am under pressure from my client. In the first place I gave you this work because I understood you could offer a fast and efficient service. Now you say you cannot adapt to a slight variation in the agreement."

"Slight variation! You want the delivery time halved. No one can work within those sorts of limits."

"I know someone who can."

"Then why don't you go to them?"

"Because I have an agreement with you, Mr. Martin. But if you wish to break our agreement, please say so, as I must make my alternative arrangements as quickly as possible."

"Who is this alternative supplier?"

Boulin chuckled. "You know I cannot tell you his name. He is very reliable. Not as cheap as you, I agree, but fast—much earlier with his delivery dates than you can be."

Martin thought for a moment. Then he said, "I'm coming over to see you, Boulin. Tomorrow."

"As ever, I shall be delighted to see you," the agent said placidly.

As Martin put down the phone, Sheila was looking at him questioningly. "It's all right," he told her. "Boulin is playing one of his games. He's a greedy beggar, as you know, and he's trying to squeeze me for a bigger commission."

"Will you give it to him?"

"I'll give him something eventually. The stuff he's pushing our way makes him worth it. But I've got to go through the bargaining routine. Try and book me on a flight tomorrow morning."

He spent the rest of the day rearranging the production program to try to fit in the extra items. It was a tricky process, involving new bonus arrangements, which had to be agreed upon by the men. Finally it was done and at six-thirty he set off for home.

Samuels had done a good job on the car and it seemed to be running better than ever. When he opened the garage doors, prior to driving the car in, he took another look at the stains on the floor. There was no leak in the hydraulic system, according to Samuels. So who drained it off? The two disappearing Germans? Then they must have realized by now that their plan had failed. So why had they not tried something else?

With the sudden suspicion that they might have done, Martin opened the front door with more than usual care and stood in the hall for several moments looking around and listening. Nothing seemed to be abnormal.

He went through the house rapidly, putting on the lights in each room. No hooded figures stood behind doors, no booby traps were wired up to switches.

Relaxing slightly, he made himself a cheese sandwich, opened a can of beer, then settled down to eat in front of the gas fire and the television. He watched a double agent outwitting the KGB by means of sheer intellectual capability based on a straight left and a handgun that fired an unlimited number of bullets.

Martin tried to apply his mind to the meeting with Boulin and the negotiating tactics he should use. Instead, the picture of Greta kept appearing. It wasn't Greta looking her best. It was as he had last seen her, strain and tension combined with anger in her eyes as she battled against his skepticism.

"I want to help," she had said. "Please understand and believe that."

Could she have been using him? Had their brief affair been carefully arranged and controlled in order to make him more amenable to the role of message-carrier . . . and then, in his gullibility, to apply to the message the gloss of authenticity? He had no illusions about his appeal to women. His own wife had not been able to live with him, with his short-fused temper, his blindness to other people's feelings. Even his recognition of his own short-comings and his fruitless attempts to erase or at least soften them had failed to strike any responsive chord in Ellen. So why had Greta tolerated him?

Then he began to realize that it never had been like that with Greta. His nerves were never rasped, his hackles never rose at the wrong word or lack of understanding. Leaving aside the actual consummation of their affair, he reflected on the hours they had spent working together: each moment with her had been relaxed, harmonious. They really had belonged to each other from the start, although, typically, he had been blind to the fact until it was too late. She had never seen the irascibility, the impatience, because, quite simply, they ceased to exist when the two of them were together.

It couldn't be a setup. Let Blair believe what the hell he liked, but he hadn't met Greta, listened to her desperate pleading, or been touched by her burning sincerity. The problem was, you couldn't describe sincerity, not in words that would convince someone like Blair.

So had Greta herself been used? That made no sense at all, not in the light of what had happened since. The only reason the Germans could have for trying to kill him was that the information he had obtained was genuine and he therefore represented a real security threat to them.

Later, as he struggled for sleep between the cold sheets, a black curtain of depression began to cover his mind. Rationally, he should now forget everything that had happened in Germany. Having done all he could to pass on the information, he should be left alone both by his conscience and by the people involved. But did he really want that? It would mean accepting that he would never see Greta again, and that, in the bleakness of the small hours, was too unbearable even to contemplate.

5

Traffic from Charles de Gaulle Airport into Paris was heavy. Martin sat in his taxi and took from his briefcase the wad of papers that would form the basis for negotiation with Boulin.

He knew exactly what he intended to offer, but he had to decide on a lower starting point from which he could be edged upwards. Boulin would be doing the same in reverse, and with any luck, they should meet at a mutually acceptable figure. It was a game, of course, but Boulin would feel he wasn't earning his money if the charade was not acted through. Even in his twilight world people had their standards.

It was a day that showed off Paris at her best, sunlit and sparkling, as the taxi halted outside Boulin's office in the Rue de l'Orme. Chestnut trees framed the entrance to the elegant white stucco building, which was the headquarters of a merchant bank. Even the lift had a subdued dignity that reflected a feeling of wealth and substance. The drawback was that it only went as far as the third floor. Here the marble staircase gave way to linoleum-covered wooden stairs that seemed to get narrower as they neared the fifth floor.

Boulin's office was at the end of a dark corridor that was lined with mops, pails, and all the resources necessary to maintain the elegance down below.

Martin knocked at the door and entered. Boulin's plump figure was standing looking out of the window and he whirled round, a welcoming smile on his face. His chubby hands grasped Martin's free one and pumped it up and down.

"Delighted to see you, my dear Mr. Martin," he said, his bright eyes dancing with what seemed genuine pleasure. "You had a pleasant journey, I trust? Everything all right at home?"

"The answer is yes in both cases. And you seem as prosperous as ever, Boulin," Martin said, disengaging his hand.

The Frenchman shrugged with his hands upturned. "It is a very uncertain business we are in. But with people such as yourself to deal with, business becomes a pleasure."

Careful, Martin thought, he's turned on the big guns. It's going to be a long battle getting him to accept my figure.

"Please do sit down," Boulin said, lifting a bundle of papers from the leather armchair beside his desk. "I have some coffee ready and we shall relax a little before we discuss important matters."

As he poured the coffee from the glass pot, Boulin said casually, "You have had a lot of matters on your mind recently? White, isn't it?"

He added the cream and handed the cup to Martin. As usual it tasted better than any coffee he could find anywhere at home. Yet Boulin was able to produce it from the old, unimpressive drip machine that had stood in the corner of the office for years.

"We are very busy at the moment," Martin said. "Your latest orders are stretching us to the limit."

Boulin nodded. "But do you find you can devote all your time to the work? You do not suffer from distracting affairs of other kinds?"

Martin looked at him. "What affairs do you mean? There aren't any female entanglements, if that's what you're referring to. Just what are you referring to, Boulin?"

Boulin was not smiling now. He sipped his coffee absently and said, "I was thinking of other kinds of business. Never mind—"

"Just a moment." Martin thought he could see what Boulin was getting at. "Does this relate to the new delivery date you've asked for? Are you suggesting I've got other orders on hand and they get priority over your business? Because that's not true. I've always dealt straight with you, Boulin."

56

"My dear friend, I do know that. I was not implying anything. It was just that I heard you were under a great deal of pressure and my only concern is with your health."

Now where on earth has he heard that? Martin wondered. And why the lingering emphasis on the word "health"?

Suddenly Boulin rediscovered his smile and said, "But you came to discuss how early you can supply my needs, did you not? Let us do that."

The discussion went on for an hour. Boulin was his usual shrewd self and it soon became clear that Martin's instinct had been right: commission, rather than delivery dates, was the point at issue.

The dealing moved gently to and fro, neither man showing his hand, and both bringing out new arguments at carefully timed intervals.

Then, at fifteen minutes before one o'clock, Boulin suddenly said, "I accept. An extra commission of three-quarters of one per cent if I can persuade my clients to accept the original delivery dates."

"Surely there's no 'if' about it, Boulin. You claim you're the only man who can negotiate with the Algerians. But if you can't get the results, I'd be prepared to have a go at them myself—and save the commission."

"Consider it definite, then," Boulin said with a quick smile. "I will explain to them that they must be patient if they want the best." He stood up and took his hat and cane from the corner. "And now we will go to lunch. I have discovered a new bistro, by the way. I am sure you will be impressed."

Martin followed him out of the office, somewhat surprised that the dealing had finished so abruptly. He had been prepared to make it the full one per cent, and Boulin must have realized it needed only a little more argument and pressure to achieve that figure. Perhaps it was a sign of age, but there were no signs of it elsewhere. Disdaining the lift, Boulin was almost bouncing down the stairs ahead of him.

"We shall walk," Boulin announced when they reached the street. "Paris cannot be seen at her best from a taxi or a bus—and certainly not from the métro."

"How far is it?" Martin asked, striding out alongside him.

"It will take us about fifteen minutes."

Martin found it a pleasure walking along the busy streets. Perhaps it was because his place of work was in the country, but he never lost the feeling of exhilaration that any city, and Paris in particular, could provide.

In the Rue du Rossignol they stopped to wait on the curb edge for a gap in the traffic.

As Martin stepped off the pavement with Boulin on his left, without warning the Frenchman grabbed his arm and Martin found the walking stick thrust between his ankles. He lost his balance and fell back, assisted by a strong thrust from Boulin's arm.

He hit the pavement with a crash and lay on his back, stunned and breathless. Boulin was crouching beside him.

"My dear friend," he said with concern. "You had such a narrow escape."

Several passers-by had stopped and were gathering round. Martin struggled to get up but found his upper arm pinned down by Boulin's knee.

"Are you not able to get up?" Boulin asked sympathetically. "You must have been hit by the car."

"I would be able to get up if you moved your blasted knee!" Martin snapped. "What the devil were you up to, anyway? It wasn't a car—"

A gendarme pushed his way through the group of people. Boulin said something to him about his friend being struck a passing blow by a car that did not stop.

Again Martin tried to struggle up and this time Boulin allowed him to get to a sitting position.

"It seems there are no broken bones," Boulin said to him, "but I have told the gendarme I will take you into the hospital for a check. Fortunately we are right outside the Hospital of the Sacred Heart."

"There's nothing wrong with me!" Martin was angry now and trying to get to his feet. Boulin seemed determined to make it as difficult as possible.

Finally Martin made it. But Boulin's arm was around his shoulder and he tried in vain to shake it off.

The gendarme moved away and Boulin started to help Martin toward the white building behind them.

Trying to control his temper, Martin said, "Boulin, I

don't know what the hell you're doing, but would you take your arm off me?"

Boulin ignored him and pushed open the glass door into the hospital. Only when they were seated on a bench in the casualty room did Boulin relinquish his hold.

He gave Martin a sad smile and said softly, "Please accept what is happening, Mr. Martin."

"What the hell *is* happening? First you trip me up, then you blame a car——"

Boulin put a finger to his lips and nodded toward a white-coated houseman who was approaching.

Boulin told him his friend had been in a road accident. There appeared to be no injuries, but it would be best to make sure. Despairing now of being able to make any sense of what was happening, Martin allowed himself to be led to a bed. He stripped to his underclothes as the doctor directed and lay down to be probed for broken bones.

The doctor asked him to raise his right arm. He did so and felt the pain in his shoulder. Noticing the grimace, the doctor started feeling his collarbone. In halting French Martin explained that this was an existing condition and was simply a muscular sprain.

At last he allowed Martin to dress. Then the door opened and Boulin hurried in.

"He is all right?" he asked the doctor. Without waiting for an answer he turned to Martin. "While we are here, my friend, I want you to see somebody."

Pulling on his shirt, Martin said carefully, "I don't know what experience you have planned for me next, Boulin, but as far as I'm concerned you can stuff it."

Boulin nodded. "I know just how you feel——"

"Do you, indeed? You know how it feels to be tripped up, knocked to the pavement, and frogmarched into hospital? I don't believe you do, Boulin; otherwise you'd realize that's a most ineffective way of influencing people to your way of thinking. I don't want to see any of your damned friends."

Boulin was pleading now. "You will understand all this in a short time, I promise you. Please come with me now."

Despite his anger, Martin's curiosity led him after Boulin into the corridor and then to the lift. Not a word was said as they travelled up to the sixth floor. Once there

59

Boulin led the way along a corridor that was lined with individual wards.

He stopped at one near the end that had a card on it reading "A. Braun". He glanced in, then beckoned to Martin and led the way into the room.

It contained a single patient with an intravenous drip connected to an arm. His face was thin, almost emaciated, and he had short gray hair. His eyes were closed.

Boulin went up to the bed and spoke quietly, and the eyes opened. They looked at Boulin for a while until the Frenchman said something else. Then they focused on Martin.

Only then did Martin recognize Bruno Lukas.

"Mr. Martin, it is good of you to come." Lukas's voice was soft and it was clearly an effort for him to speak.

Martin clasped the German's right hand and said, "I'm very sorry to see you like this, Lukas. What has happened to you?"

Boulin said, "It is an unpleasant business. Certain people administered to him a substance which has made him very ill. But he has kept up his spirits, nonetheless. Isn't that so, Lukas, you old dog?" he added cheerfully.

As though to justify Boulin's optimism, Lukas forced a faint smile. It made his sunken features appear even more skeletal. Martin was appalled at the condition of the man now, compared with only a few weeks ago.

"Is there anything I can do for you?" he asked foolishly, as though the man were not surrounded by the best resources of French medicine.

Lukas's voice, although weak, was matter-of-fact. "I do not have very long. That is something of which I am well aware. I asked Boulin if he could arrange for me to see you, as I have something to say to you. It concerns Greta."

He paused, and Martin said, "How is she?"

Lukas looked at him with some puzzlement for a moment. Then he said, "I am sorry—I thought you knew. Or that at least you would have guessed. They took her. The SSD. Now she is dead."

The faint noise of Paris traffic reached even to this height although the window was closed. The sun filtered through the venetian blinds and formed a pattern on the counterpane. Martin recalled a similar pattern being shaped by the moonlight on the bed he shared with Greta. The one night they had been together.

"You are sure of this?" His voice was a whisper.

The man in the bed managed a slight nod. "She was taken the day after you met Frisch. I was picked up at the same time."

Martin walked over to the window and stood looking out. Lukas was gasping slightly now and his eyes were closed as Boulin watched him closely. When Boulin looked toward him, Martin beckoned him over with a slight movement of the head.

He spoke very quietly. "Is he delirious or confused in any way?"

Boulin shook his head. "He has been quite rational in everything he has said to me. Why do you ask?"

Martin pondered for a moment, then said, "Is it safe for me to ask him any questions? He doesn't look too good and I don't want to make things worse."

Boulin shrugged. "Things could not be any worse for poor Lukas. It was a corrosive poison. He has no stomach left. It was he who asked for you to come, so you ask him whatever questions you wish."

Martin went back to the bed, pulled up a chair, and sat close to the head of the bed.

"What you just said to me—about Greta—does not make sense," he said.

Lukas opened his eyes. "It is true. She is dead."

"Lukas, I saw her on the evening of the day you say she was arrested. She came to my room and talked to me for some time. You must be mistaken."

Lukas shook his head. "I have it on the best authority." His brow wrinkled in thought as he absorbed what Martin had said. "She came to you? But how . . ." Then his head began to nod slowly. "This second time you saw her. Did she tell you anything? Did she give you more information?"

"Yes. A lot of information."

"But did you notice anything different—or strange—about her? Was she like Greta always was?"

Martin said firmly, "You're not going to tell me that it wasn't really Greta—because that's nonsense, Lukas."

Lukas waited for his breathing to settle. Then he went

on, "It was a different girl in a way. Because she had been in their hands. They only released her for a short while so she could go to see you—and give you that additional information."

Martin stared at Lukas. He told himself that this was a sick man. A dying man. You couldn't expect rationality from a man whose stomach had been eaten away by a corrosive poison and whose remaining span could be measured in days, if not hours.

Lukas was nodding his head slowly. There was shrewdness and cunning in his eyes still. "You must see what was happening, Mr. Martin. When they picked her up, they realized that she had given you some information. For all they knew, you could have passed on that information by then—to another contact, perhaps in your own embassy. So they had to neutralize that information. And the way to do that was to discredit you."

It made sense. Martin was forced to admit that. To have taken action against him—arrested or even killed him—would have added authenticity to any information he might have passed on. Instead, they simply fed him with more information that, in a short time, would prove to be false. All the information he brought out of East Germany would then be classified as "unreliable" in Cole's language. And so it had proved.

"I cannot accept it," he said finally. "Greta just would not betray what she believed in so deeply."

Lukas sighed and said, "My friend, anyone will betray what they believe in, if the right pressure is applied to them."

"But what pressure could that be in Greta's case?"

Lukas said, "I was also in their hands, remember. I can understand it now, whereas I was puzzled at the time. They released me, you see. That was the only way they could persuade Greta to cooperate: they offered my life as their side of the bargain."

Martin looked across at Boulin. "They released you? Then what—"

Boulin said, "He then managed to get across the border —but their people followed him, of course." His voice grew bitter. "You do not think they would allow such a bargain to bind them, once they had got what they wanted? I do not know how the poison was administered, but it was a miracle that he survived for so long, was able to shake them off and get into France. It is the only part of their scheme to go wrong."

The strain that Greta showed, the anger when he tried to pick up the emotional threads of the previous evening . . . he understood now. Beneath it all, for her, as well as the feeling of self-disgust at having to lie to him, was the knowledge that everything they said was being monitored. She had not turned on the taps on that occasion, clearly under instructions not to do so. Yet even then she had conveyed, as best she could, her feelings for him. It was just that there was someone else who had to come first. . . .

Lukas was looking at him intently. "She was my daughter, you understand. Not in the legal sense, but she had been with us since three months after her birth. We were very close." He paused. "You can see how great were the pressures."

Martin nodded. There was coldness in his voice as he said, "What I cannot understand is a man who would allow his daughter to sacrifice her life for him."

Lukas looked puzzled. "I do not understand *you*, Mr. Martin. Her life was beyond saving. Nothing I could do would alter that."

There was a knock and a nurse entered. Boulin hurried over to have a brief conversation with her. Finally she went out, closing the door.

Boulin explained, "It is nearly time for his medication and we should go. I persuaded her to allow us a little longer—that is, if you wish to go on, Bruno."

Lukas nodded. "I asked for you to come, Mr. Martin, for a particular reason. Greta was allowed to see me before I left—I think it was part of the agreement. There was little we could say to each other. But she was allowed to kiss me—and that was when she passed this to me."

He raised himself up and attempted to reach the drawer of the bedside cabinet. Boulin gently pushed him back onto the pillows and opened the drawer for him. He found a small envelope, which he passed to Lukas. The German tore it open and took out a small piece of gray paper, about one and a half inches square. It had been folded several times and had the texture of blotting paper.

Lukas passed it to Martin. "This was her last message."

The paper was covered with blurred pencil marks. They were tiny shorthand symbols, except for the signature, which read "Greta."

"I have had it transcribed and translated," Lukas said, taking a larger sheet of paper from the envelope and passing it to Martin.

This was typed and read: "Dearest Alec, forgive what I had to do. Only on that first night was it the truth. I love you. Please remember me."

The long silence while Martin stared unseeingly at the paper was finally broken as Lukas said, "I need to rest, please. I can do so now that you have received the message, Mr. Martin."

Martin made an effort to stabilize the thoughts tumbling in his mind. "You are sure—certain—Greta is dead?"

"Without question," Lukas said softly. "It was inevitable."

"And the information she gave to me—about the conference in Edinburgh—that is true? It came from Frisch himself?"

"He arranged for the information to come, although he did not have all the details himself at the time he was arrested. Greta had to pick that up later that night."

Despite himself, Martin had to check. "Usually your information was passed to Israel. Why was this not given to them?"

"Because our contact disappeared and the link was broken. I have no standing with them. At that time we turned to you." Lukas raised his hands helplessly. "We did not know what else to do. Everything was falling apart. I am sorry we had to involve you, Mr. Martin, but there was no alternative. Even now I have no status with the Israelis. They will not accept anything I tell them." He looked questioningly at Martin. "Have you passed on the information to your security authorities?"

"Yes. Including what Greta told me at our last meeting."

"That will cause problems." Lukas's eyes were closing now. He was clearly exhausted.

Martin nodded to Boulin, who was hovering near the door, then stood up and took Lukas's hands.

"Thank you for what you have done, Bruno."

The man's eyes opened slowly. "It was Greta's wish. I only hope it is a help to you. Goodbye, Mr. Martin."

The eyes had closed again as Martin followed Boulin out into the corridor. The Frenchman was looking anxiously at his watch.

"We must not be seen to be spending too long in the hospital. It could seem suspicious."

"Do they know Lukas is here?" Martin asked as they entered the lift.

"No. But I have no doubt they have been watching you since you arrived in Paris." He looked at Martin as they headed for the ground floor. "Do you understand now why you had your little accident? There had to be a convincing reason for you coming in here."

Martin stared back at him. "What's your connection with all this, Boulin? I knew you were friendly with Lukas —you put me on to him and the East German trade in the first place." The lift doors opened and they stepped out. "Did you contrive to smuggle him into France?"

"Why do you want to know?"

Martin shrugged. "I'm intrigued to see you in the role of Scarlet Pimpernel. No disrespect, Boulin, but I always thought your interests were confined to business and nothing more."

As they reached the hospital entrance, Boulin stopped and said vehemently, "Then your supposition was exactly right. Business *is* my only interest—although I *will* occasionally help a friend who is in trouble, on a personal basis only. I hope it is quite clear to you that I have no political sympathies one way or the other—none at all." He paused, then went on more quietly, "You do not realize how important that is to my business. If it was thought for a moment that I favored one side as against another —Israeli or Arab, East or West—then overnight I would have no business at all. Up there, for example"—he nodded toward Lukas's room—"I grasped what the problem was. Communication. Passing information to the Israelis. You wonder why I never volunteered to help?" He threw up his hands. "Because that would mean breaking my cardinal rule—getting involved in politics. You understand?"

Martin nodded. "Very well. You've convinced me—if that's worth anything."

They went out into the street and Martin stared for a moment at the frantic traffic swirling around them. If Boulin was right, someone out here was watching him.

Boulin gave a slight smile and took his arm. "I think we should get a taxi. We cannot risk any more accidents, can we?"

6

Dusk was falling as Martin's flight landed at Heathrow. In the terminal building his name was being paged.

"Your secretary telephoned," the girl at the information desk told him. "She has arranged for a car to collect you from outside the terminal building. A yellow Triumph."

Sheila knew he would be weary and was sparing him the fuss of finding a taxi. He never stopped to wonder how she knew which flight he would be on.

There was a yellow Triumph 2000 immediately outside the door. A young man in a short leather jacket was smoking as he leaned against the wing. He threw his cigarette away as Martin approached.

"Evening, Mr. Martin," he said. "Car as arranged."

Taking Martin's bag he opened the rear passenger door and Martin climbed in. The door was slammed shut behind him and it was only then that he realized the car already contained two men. One beside him, and the other in the driver's seat.

"I didn't realize I was sharing a car—" he began when the leather-jacketed man jumped into the front passenger seat and the car took off with a jerk. Martin was thrown against the man alongside, who showed no reaction, but continued staring straight ahead.

The car whipped in and out of the traffic as though in a hurry to get clear of the airport.

Martin said, "Hold on a minute! What the hell is happening?"

The man alongside him said, "A free ride to your home. Why should you complain? I am providing this car as I want the opportunity to talk to you." He was not

English but his accent was so slight as to be barely noticeable. In the faint light Martin could only make out a middle-aged profile, a sharp nose, and thinning dark hair. Without turning toward him, the man said, "Do you know who I am?"

"I can guess," Martin said, suddenly consumed with weariness. "Of course, you could be our own security people, because they act in peculiar ways too. But from your accent I'd say not."

"Let us say my name is Koster. The particular country I represent does not matter. Our concern is peace throughout the world. Better minds than yours have applied themselves to achieving this and it seems that you, in your ignorance, are seeking to jeopardize their efforts."

The car stopped behind a line of others held up by temporary traffic lights. Martin edged his hand toward the door handle.

"Childproof locks," Koster said without even looking at him. "A very useful safety feature: the door cannot be opened from the inside."

The line started moving forward again. Koster did not resume his conversation but leaned back in his seat and stared at the traffic ahead.

Martin's weariness was now being replaced by a growing anxiety. What was more disturbing than the immediate situation was the man himself. There was an air of cold professionalism to him, an impression that death could be one of the everyday tools of his trade.

Finally Martin said, "You wanted to talk to me. I'm listening."

"We have plenty of time," the man replied. "It is an eighty-five-minute drive to your home."

He relapsed into silence. The car was on the M4 now, heading into London. Its yellow headlights sliced through the night and showed only moderate traffic on the motorway.

Martin recognized the technique. His nerves were being stretched by the silence, suspense being used to cultivate fear. As a technique, it was undeniably effective. He decided to resist the temptation to speak, so as to force a reaction from the man. Whether he could gain anything by concealing his nervousness he didn't know. At least he could try to retain some self-respect.

They reached London and the time of night meant they had practically a clear run through the city. The driver picked up the A2 and stayed on it until the A249 to Maidstone. There he turned off the main road and headed south-east, following the same country lanes that Martin would have used. And with the same apparent familiarity.

Twenty minutes later, when they were about ten miles from his home, Martin's nerves were ready to snap. It was then that Koster spoke.

"We know you have been in Paris today, talking to certain people. The discussions were not concerned solely with your own business."

He paused and Martin said, as evenly as possible, "Are you asking me or telling me?"

"What I am telling you is that you have somehow become involved in a mischievous way with matters that should not involve you. Let me make something clear: whatever you do or have done will in no way affect the ultimate action to be taken. But, by your interference, you could create certain problems—of embarrassment and inconvenience, nothing more."

Martin said, "You're going to extreme lengths just to avoid a bit of inconvenience."

For the first time Koster showed some reaction. It was in the form of a faint smile. "You call this extreme? I must say, Mr. Martin, you're more of an amateur in these matters than I realized." He leaned across to the driver. "Stop here."

The car halted by the side of the empty road. The man alongside the driver climbed out, opened the passenger door, and nodded briefly for Martin to join him.

Koster, who was still staring straight ahead, said, "Out. Now."

Martin obeyed and stood by the open door. The driver's mate looked him straight in the eye and, without altering his expression, lunged forward with his right fist.

The punch exploded into Martin's lower stomach with a force he found unbelievable. Then, welling up inside him, came pain and sickness that was only too easy to believe. He found himself rolling on the ground, his arms wrapped tightly around his body. At that moment he cared for nothing but the searing ache in his lungs as he desperately tried to draw breath. If the man had produced a gun and finished him off then, it would have been nothing but a blessed relief.

His eyes focused on a pair of shoes. The man stood motionless in exactly the same position. What came next? The kick to the face?

Incredibly the road became bright. A pair of headlights. Another car coming to a stop. Voices.

"Can we help?"

"Nothing serious. Charlie has had too much to drink. We'll be all right."

The car driving away. Silence.

Now he could breathe. Two hands dragged him to his feet but he could not straighten up because of the pain that seared through his gut. He was lifted bodily into the car, the door was slammed, and they were moving again.

Now Koster was smoking a small cigar and the smell compounded Martin's nausea. He sprawled against the door desperately trying to contain the bile that forced its way up.

"On the films one often sees a man receive a punch like that," said Koster conversationally. "He bounds up again and continues the fight. But you, Martin, know that such a thing is not possible. Few blows are so simple yet so disabling."

"I suppose," Martin breathed hoarsely, "it's the only language you know."

Koster nodded as he appeared to give this serious consideration. "Let us say it is the most effective language we know. By that very brief demonstration we have proved to you that we are unpleasant and dangerous people. It might have taken hours to convince you of that simply by talking." He flicked the ash from his cigar. "The message I have for you is quite a simple one. Forget the nonsense you heard when you were in the GDR. Just carry on quietly with your own life, and you will not see or hear from me and my colleagues again."

The pain was diminishing to some extent, but there was still a great emptiness in the lower part of his body.

"You're too late. I've already passed on all I know."

"We are aware of that," Koster said. "Fortunately, your own security authorities did not believe you—which is understandable, in view of the bizarre nature of the information you chose to impart."

Koster wound down the window, threw out his cigar butt, then settled back. Martin waited, but the conversation seemed to be over for the moment. The car raced smoothly through the night, the driver seemingly in no doubt about the route.

When they were two miles from Martin's home, Koster spoke again. "Simply remember one thing, Martin. At any time during this journey we could have killed you. As you lay on the road, the car could have driven over you. But I don't think death is necessarily the answer to every problem of this kind. My views are tempered by a humanitarian outlook. If I think the person concerned is intelligent enough to understand and abide by a serious warning, then I am inclined to let him live."

Christ, Martin thought, he sounds like a Mafia patriarch: beating you up one minute, conferring favors the next.

The car finally halted outside Martin's house. The leather-jacketed man came from the front seat and opened the rear door. Before Martin climbed out, Koster touched him lightly on the arm.

"I think you understand the situation now. It comes down to a very simple proposition: mind your own business and you will be permitted to live."

Martin made no answer. As he climbed out, Koster called, "Don't waste your time noting the car's alleged registration number."

The door was slammed shut behind Martin and he turned to enter the gate of his house. Leather-jacket tapped him on the shoulder. Martin turned and in that fraction of a second knew what was going to happen but it was too late to move. The fist seemed to connect with exactly the same point in his body, only this time it plumbed undiscovered depths of pain. As he pitched to the ground a wave of blackness tinged with red swept through his mind. For a few moments he thought with gratitude that he was losing consciousness.

But there was no escape from the pain. From its central position in his lower gut it sent jarring signals throughout his whole body. Somewhere a car was starting up. In the jumble of his mind was a recollection of a threat to drive over him. But the sound of the car faded into the distance.

He became aware of small, very unimportant things. The gravel of the path directly under his face. He did not want to get up or move his limbs in any way, not while there was a chance the pain would dribble away. The dull everyday gravel that he took for granted was there now when he needed it, supporting him. He hugged the gravel, then found that by moving his head slightly he could see the gatepost nearby. There were the old screw-holes left after he rehung the gate. That had followed months of nagging from Ellen. He should have filled in those screw-holes. He meant to, but the time wasn't there, the weather wasn't right, he had no putty.

Raining very slightly. Just the start of a drizzle. The kind you could absorb for hours and not feel wet, just be conscious of a dampness pervading every part of you. Tentatively he moved his legs. Next he grabbed the gatepost and got onto his knees. After a minute he was on his feet. He saw his bag on the ground and picked it up.

His path up to the house was slow and erratic. When he reached the front door, he slumped against the support post of the porch while he felt in his pocket for the key. At last he got the door open. Inside he carefully made his way to the downstairs lavatory, where he spent five minutes vomiting.

Back in the lounge. Climb slowly onto the settee. Drift off into a half-world where the misery of pain is balanced by the realization that it is gradually diminishing.

It was twenty minutes before pain ceased to be the dominant matter in his mind, to be replaced by angry rationality. He picked up the telephone and dialled 999.

While waiting for the police to come he poured himself a large whisky. He sipped it carefully at first. When his stomach did not rebel, he finished it off quickly and poured another. This was in his hand when the patrol car arrived.

He told the two constables exactly what had happened since he arrived at Heathrow.

The younger of the constables said, "Have you any idea why they picked you up like this?"

"Yes. They told me quite clearly what it was all about." Martin sipped his whisky. "They were East German

72

agents. I was over there some weeks ago and given some secret information affecting Britain's security. These men were trying to persuade me that I should keep this information to myself."

The constables looked uncertainly at each other. The older one said, looking at the glass in Martin's hand, "I think Special Branch may be interested, in that case—"

"I should damn well think so," Martin said. "But the most immediate thing to do is to try and pick up that car. It's a yellow Triumph Two Thousand."

The constables radioed in the information, and half an hour later they were replaced by a plainclothesman.

"I'm Detective Sergeant Langley," he said.

"Special Branch?"

"That's right."

"You got here quickly from Scotland Yard," Martin said suspiciously.

The detective said patiently, "They aren't the only people with a Special Branch, sir. I'm attached to the local force. Now would you give me the whole story from the beginning?"

The long-faced detective showed no reaction as Martin went through it all, but simply made notes.

When Martin had finished, the detective said, "Who were the people you spoke to at the Foreign Office?"

"Cole and Blair—although I don't think Blair actually belongs to the Foreign Office as such. But you won't get much encouragement from them," Martin added wearily. "I know I haven't. They've never taken me seriously from the start."

Langley looked at him sharply, then wrote down the names and closed his notebook.

"We shan't bother you again tonight, sir," he said as he went out. "You look as though you need a rest. We'll be in touch."

The next morning Martin found to his surprise that he had enjoyed a good night's sleep. His stomach was sore but it was a muscular pain that did not prevent him from keeping down a light breakfast. He went into the lounge and stopped as his eye caught the bookshelf. The dictionary was there with its cover the right way up.

He opened the bureau and the first thing he saw was the letter from his solicitor acknowledging the "in case of death" package. He distinctly recalled pushing that letter to the bottom of the pile in the bureau, feeling vaguely embarrassed at the time by the melodrama of it all.

He read the letter again.

Dear Alec,

This is to acknowledge your recent communication. I will of course comply with your request and only open the enclosed envelope in case of your demise. To say I'm intrigued is putting it mildly, but knowing you as a level-headed, down-to-earth sort of person, I take your instructions seriously— hoping, of course, that the thing will gather dust in my safe for many years to come.

He sat down in the chair and stared at the letter. They must have come into the house while he was in Paris, looking for evidence as to how far he had taken the matter. This letter was the only reason the car had not been driven over him last night. While Koster had claimed that nothing he said or wrote was going to affect the ultimate plan, his solicitor would have stirred up so many problems that, on balance, it was worth leaving him alive.

For the moment.

7

Several times Martin caught himself glancing over his shoulder as he drove to Molyneux. Christ, was he turning paranoid?

Maybe, but at least it was clear he wasn't being followed.

He'd phoned Sheila to say he would go straight to the trustees' meeting instead of stopping in at the office. He added, with conscious irony, that "a bit of tummy trouble" had made him decide to take things easy for an hour or so before the meeting.

He swung the car off the road, through the wrought-iron gates, and along the gravel driveway that curved toward the graceful Georgian house. Behind the trees to the left was the airfield, and as he switched off the car's engine he could hear the phut-phut of one of the aircraft being put through a ground test. In the tranquil Molyneux atmosphere, the shadow of Koster seemed to diminish. As always when he came to Molyneux, he felt a pang of regret for ever losing touch with the world of practical flying. He could have kept in his hand somehow if he had made the time. Now, of course, it was far too late.

This had been a family home until Sir Philip Molyneux had moved to London some years previously. The museum had been established in memory of his father, who had been one of the Bleriot-age pioneers and had left the nucleus of the collection in various sheds scattered around the grounds. To these primitive aircraft had been added more substantial models picked out by Sir Philip from the mass of war matériel that was going for a song in the late 1940s. In the process he had built up another fortune for the family, simply by buying up most of the Royal Engineers' inventory and reselling it to construction companies around the world. Molyneux wasn't on the same scale as some of the better-known museums, such as the Shuttleworth Collection at Old Warden, but it could put on a good show when the occasion demanded and it had a loyal following among the enthusiasts.

There were eight trustees present at the meeting. It was held in the Octagon Room on the first floor, which was one of the most relaxing rooms Martin had ever been in. Its Wedgwood-blue walls and large windows not only made the room bright but somehow gave the impression that it was suspended in space. The sills were high, which meant that all one could see when sitting down was the sky. The occasional vintage aircraft lumbering by added to the sense of timelessness. It was a room where Martin often felt himself being taken back thirty years to his own golden days when, as a flyer, he had discovered and reveled in a freedom of spirit that transcended anything he had experienced since.

Arthur Henshaw was in the chair. Sir Philip rarely appeared now, although he was nominally chairman, preferring to leave matters to his cousin. Being retired, Arthur was able to devote a large proportion of his time to museum affairs.

The other members had also been on the board for years, except for Wing-Commander Beacham, who was the non-voting representative nominated by the Ministry of Defense. This link was important as there was a good deal of cooperation between the museum and the RAF. Vintage aircraft were often provided by the museum for flying displays, and the RAF supplied information to help maintain the aircraft and keep them airworthy. Their aid was confined to providing this expertise: the cost of parts and labor had to be met by the trustees.

The agenda was a routine one. Requests for aircraft to appear at exhibitions and demonstrations were considered individually. The surprising thing to Martin was that interest now centered more and more on World War Two aircraft and the early jets. Already the Meteor and Vampire had achieved vintage status.

Mike Lowe, the only paid employee of the trustees, gave them a rundown on the condition of each of the aircraft. If ever there was a misnomer, in Martin's view, it was Mike's title of "curator." Mike was an engineer, a practical mechanic, whose blackened fingernails were witness to a life spent immersed in engine oil.

"We've had a bit of a problem with the Spitfire," he told them. "One of the air-compressor cylinders that powers the brakes and flaps is U/S. We've tried patching things up, but it's got to be reliable. As we can't get hold of a new one, it looks as though we'll have to have one made."

All eyes automatically turned to Martin, who knew full well why he had been invited to join the trustees in the first place.

He said, "Let me have the old one and I'll see what we can do. It's pretty high pressure, isn't it?"

"Three hundred pounds."

Martin nodded. "It might be as well if we replaced the other one for you while we're at it."

Arthur said, "Once again we're indebted to Mr. Martin. I speak for all of us, I'm sure, in expressing our gratitude for his assistance."

When the meeting ended, Wing-Commander Beacham said to Martin, "I often wish we in the service had a setup like yours to fall back on: someone who could supply one-offs on the strength of a phone call, with no paperwork."

"If I was supplying parts to the RAF," Martin countered, "you wouldn't be getting them for nothing. It's when money is involved that the paperwork starts to breed."

"But it must cost your company money," Beacham observed.

"It's my own company, so I don't have to account to anyone. What I get from it is personal satisfaction. That Spitfire, now: it's a real pleasure to be able to do something to keep a lovely plane like that flying."

"You were in the service?"

"Only a temporary commission. I was on Spits from nineteen forty-four. It was the tail end of the war, of course—once I qualified, Hitler saw the game was up." He paused. "Occasionally I wonder why I ever left the RAF. I suppose we all think back to the war with unjustified nostalgia, but there just seemed to be a different type of person around in those days." Martin looked at the wings on Beacham's chest and the DFC ribbon. "In

77

the service did you come across a chap named Colin Raymond, by any chance? My old squadron commander. He stayed in, and he reached air commodore the last I heard."

"No. I was with Coastal Command before going to the Ministry," Beacham replied. "It's not practical, but I'd love to see a Sunderland flying boat among your collection here."

Martin grinned. "You give us one, and I'll personally supervise the digging of a bloody great pond that we can moor it on."

During the afternoon he put in a couple of hours' work at the office. Once Sheila had gone home he telephoned Detective Sergeant Langley.

"Afternoon, Mr. Martin," the detective said. "Are you feeling any better?"

"A little. I was expecting to hear from you."

"There's nothing to report so far, sir. We've not been able to trace the car."

Martin said, "Have you passed the word on to Blair?"

Langley said cautiously, "We are in touch with his office."

There was a pause, and Martin said impatiently, "Well —what was their reaction?"

"None at all, so far."

Martin drew a deep breath. "Listen, I've something to report now—something new. I've realized they must have broken into my house."

"They?"

"The people behind the kidnapping—Koster's people. They were looking for information."

"How do you know they broke in?"

"My dictionary was the right way up—I mean the cover was. You see it's upside down and I always keep it that way. But someone else putting it back wouldn't realize that." Oh, Christ, he thought. "I'm not making much sense, am I?"

"Not to worry, sir," Langley said soothingly. "You've had a rough time—"

"Look, there was another thing—a letter in the bureau. It had been looked at. I know that because I buried it under a pile of papers and there it was on the top."

There was a barely concealed sigh at the other end.

"Thank you for letting me know, Mr. Martin. I've made a note of all that. As I told you, I'll be in touch when there's something to report."

He rang off, leaving Martin looking foolishly at the receiver in his hand.

Wearily Martin got up and put on his coat, turned off the office lights, and went out to his car. He had to face the reality of the situation: so far as both the security people and the police were concerned, he was at best a crank and at worst a nuisance. Why the hell did the British have to be so bloody phlegmatic when they weren't being downright cynical? A girl was dead and a man was dying in a French hospital because of the information they had given to Martin. At least three men in this country were vitally concerned that the information should not be taken seriously by those who could do anything about it.

Martin almost laughed out loud at the thought of the effort they had put into frightening him last night. If they but knew it, they had nothing at all to worry about. Their security would remain intact as long as the British security service had anything to do with it.

That night he deliberately avoided the whisky bottle until ten o'clock, when the image of Greta became too strong. He poured himself a double and drank it quickly.

By midnight the bottle was empty and he could sleep.

Brian Woods was a partner in the firm of Threep, Ransom and Coddle. Despite his vast experience he had not yet reached the degree of decrepitude that would qualify him to have his name included in the title. Martin telephoned him from his office and arranged to see him at eleven o'clock.

As Sheila assured him the works could run without him for another day, he took the train into town and was at Brian's office at three minutes to eleven.

As they shook hands Brian said, "Bit under the weather, Alec? That's not your usual rubicund expression."

"It's a long story," Martin said, "and I won't bore you by reciting it. Principally because it's all written in here." He produced an envelope. "It's to supplement the material you already have, and I'd like to leave it with you on the same condition."

Brian took the package and held it gingerly. "What do you think could happen to you, Alec?"

Martin shrugged. "Nothing, I hope. But if it does, I'll leave you to do what you think is best with it."

Brian looked at him curiously. "Is it something to do with the business?"

"Goodness no. That's going fine. We're thinking of going public shortly, and that's my other reason for coming to see you."

Brian was surprised. He leaned back in his chair. "You do realize how such a move would complicate your personal situation?"

"It's bound to, and that's why I want you in at the start. But as I see it, I can't lose. It would give me more security, as I'd be gambling with other people's money more than my own."

The solicitor shook his head. "I'm referring to your position in relation to Ellen. She hasn't remarried, you know."

"Of course I know," Martin said. "I'm still maintaining her, aren't I? Even though she's all but married to that Harrington character—and look at the money he has!"

Brian pressed the button on the office intercom. "Jean, bring me in the file relating to the Martin divorce—Alec Braithwaite and Ellen."

When the girl brought in the file, Brian flicked through the papers quickly. Finally he said, "Yes, it's as I thought. Under the settlement, you undertook to pay her maintenance. But you also agreed that, if you ever realized the value of your capital assets—house, business, that sort of thing—she would be eligible for half the proceeds."

Martin stared at him. "You mean she picks up fifty per cent of whatever I get? But she doesn't own any of the company."

"Only because it wasn't possible at that time to realize the financial worth of the company without selling out. She was being very considerate about the whole thing, according to her solicitors."

"Oh, no." Martin stared at the file on Brian's desk.

The solicitor said, "I'm sure I explained all this to you at the time, Alec. It was certainly in the documentation supplied to you—"

"I'm sure you did. It couldn't have registered properly in the general air of euphoria which, I recall, was very evident then. Now look, Brian, this is ridiculous. If she gets half my equity in the company, I won't have control over it any more." A thought struck him. "And I wouldn't put it past her to persuade Harrington to buy a block of shares when they come on the market. Between them they'll be able to run the company."

"I can't see that she would want to do that—"

"Wouldn't she just! Having me as her employee would really appeal to her. God, how she'd delight in rubbing my nose in it."

Brian said, "You're taking this far too seriously, Alec. There are ways of floating a company so as to secure your own position."

"No. Not in this case. Ellen always did try to run my life for me—that was one of the things which finally led to the breakup. This would put her in the same position all over again." He paused for a moment. "You know, Brian, until now I never really thought it through—going public. It just seemed a sensible thing to do. But now I begin to see what it really means—not just Ellen, but the fact that other people will be able to tell me how to run my own company."

"It's a sobering thought," Brian agreed, "but I should have expected you to have considered that right from the start. The difference is, as you said yourself, that it will be other people's money at stake. They must have some sort of say."

"I just had an impression of a group of shadowy figures hovering in the background and coughing up the cash as required," said Martin. "It's when they materialize in one's mind as a board of directors that it hits home."

There was a pause. Then the solicitor said, "Does that mean you're having second thoughts?"

"I don't know." Martin looked at the file Brian was holding. "My financial wizard tells me I have to do it. We can't survive without new capital. But if it means giving in to people like her—well, I wonder if it isn't preferable to let the whole bloody thing go to pot in its own way."

"I'm sorry if what I've said has upset your plans," Brian said. "But it was my duty to make the situation clear to you."

"Nothing for you to worry about, Brian," said Martin, getting up from his chair and going to look out of the

81

window at the traffic below. "It's my problem, not yours. I've had some difficult matters to handle recently and it's left me somewhat frayed around the edges." He turned from the window. "Anyway, how about some lunch so you can tell me how Shirley is and that fine young son of yours—Gavin, isn't it?"

"Gareth. He's fine. They both are. I'd love to have lunch with you, Alec, but today's just not on, I'm afraid. Tuesdays we eat with the senior partners. Another time?"

Martin went to the door and waved a hand. "If there is another time—certainly. Take care of those papers of mine, won't you?"

The lunchtime crowd in the pub thinned out as two o'clock approached, leaving tables littered with the remains of cheese sandwiches and limp ham salads.

Martin had ordered a roast-beef sandwich, but one bite had been enough. His stomach wasn't as right as he had thought. Strangely, it could accommodate liquor with no trouble at all.

He started on his fourth double Scotch. From his corner seat the plastic-and-chrome decor was now less obtrusive than it had been when he first entered the pub. He had selected it only because, of all the ones in this area of the Strand, it didn't have music. And the alcohol was doing a grand job in battening down that damn conscience that said he should get back to the works. Why the hell should he? It wasn't going to be his works for much longer.

Those premidnight or early morning hours when he had pushed his flagging mind and body came back to him in a flood of nostalgia and self-pity. What had driven him on had been the simple, selfish knowledge that it was all for his own ultimate benefit. The work had only one objective and that was to build up Martin Engineering so that—so that what? So that a flock of vultures led by Queen-bitch Ellen could swoop in and take over.

"If I'd made a failure of it, no one would have been interested," he muttered into his glass. "Least of all Ellen."

In the *Evening News* that somebody had left on the seat alongside him there was a two-column picture of a young girl in traditional Scottish dress under the heading

"Margo (11) will sell the schottische to the sheiks." Young Margo, it appeared, was one of ninety children who would be taking part in the opening ceremony for the Edinburgh Conference four weeks hence. The Scots were taking this opportunity to display to the assembled delegates a sample of their cultural heritage. They were planning to do almost everything in thirty minutes flat, short of tossing the caber.

Martin stared at the story and almost laughed out loud. Those sheiks were going to get a damn sight more than they bargained for. Talk about bringing the house down! He started to sip from his drink, then put it back on the table. He felt sick.

Things were clouded now and he found he couldn't really focus his eyes at all. Something was spinning round his mind concerning the Edinburgh Conference. The PFF was going to attack it. Fly a plane into it. But he knew that already: that was what had amused him about all those people expecting to be entertained. . . .

His stomach was rebelling. He managed to focus his eyes for long enough to find the "Gents" sign, and there he locked himself in and gave way to the muscular reflex of his stomach.

After a few minutes things seemed to have settled and he could see more clearly. He made his way out to the bar and ordered a tomato juice.

It must be true: Lukas had assured him of it, and a dying man had no need to lie. But why was he the only one who would believe it?

"They'll only believe the damn thing after it happens," he muttered thickly.

"Yes, sir," the barman said, looking at him curiously.

The tomato juice helped. But even if no one was prepared to believe it was going to happen, why take the chance? Cancel the thing, move it . . . or at least warn everyone that they were sitting it out at their own risk. Ninety children. The delegates. Ministers. The staff of the place, doorkeepers, caterers, electricians to keep the microphones working. But ninety children . . . !

I know it's going to happen. It's up to me to convince someone to do something. Cole and Blair. Waste of time. Civil servants who won't rock the boat. Has that detective really passed on to them everything I told him? What happened in Paris. Koster. What Koster's man did. God in heaven, isn't that proof enough?

A public phone in the corner. Don't need the book. Know that Whitehall number by now. Dial it straight off. Ask for Blair. Hold on, please. Long, long wait. Who's calling, says operator. You're back, are you? Thought you'd gone to sleep. Tell him it's me—Alec Martin, that's who. Urgent. Put me through, will you. Only then does she say Blair is not in.

"Lying bitch!" he shouted before slamming down the receiver.

Coming out of the box he found himself facing the stairs leading to the street. He climbed them slowly until the daylight blinded him. He leaned against the pub wall as the Strand traffic thundered past, and waited for his head to settle.

He was going to do something. Right now. He would do . . . what? It had come into his mind while he was dialing. Tell someone . . . of course. The press. How did he go about that? He wanted a serious newspaper that was reasonably unblinkered.

He beckoned a passing taxi.

"Sunday *Times*," he said. Where was it? Not to worry, the driver seemed to know. What's that yellow car behind? There are thousands of yellow cars around, and Koster can't be in all of them.

When the taxi halted in Gray's Inn Road he still had no idea what he intended to do. He took a deep breath and told the doorman he wanted to see a reporter about an important news story. There was apparently nothing unusual about his request, for he was shown without fuss into a small interview room. A few minutes later there appeared a young man with long hair and an air of general confidence.

"My name is Johnson. You've something to tell us, Mr.—"

"Martin. Alec Martin. I own an engineering company. I have to go to East Germany sometimes and the last time—"

"Just a moment." The young man produced a notebook and sat down on the other side of the table. "I'll need to take a few notes."

The similarity to the interview with Cole gave Martin a

feeling of depression. He found himself gabbling his story, as though afraid of losing the reporter's interest. As he went on he noticed Johnson took fewer and fewer notes and was looking at him curiously.

Then Johnson said, "Let me get this clear, Mr. Martin. You say you went to the Foreign Office and told them all you'd heard in the GDR?"

"That's right."

"And what was their reaction?"

"Well—what you'd expect, I suppose. Typical civil service. They're floored by anything that isn't covered in their manuals."

"But they did listen to you. Then what did they do?"

"Nothing—except put a couple of security men on to tail me."

Johnson nodded thoughtfully. "Did they say what value they placed on your information?"

"That's the whole point. The first three incidents never took place—because they were set up to mislead us. Fakes. On the strength of that, our security people did exactly what they were supposed to do—lost interest. But the really big strike—the one in Edinburgh—is going to take place. That's definite and I know it for a fact."

"You know it for a fact?" There was skepticism in Johnson's voice.

Martin took a deep breath. His stomach was tightening and there was sweat on his forehead.

"Could I have a drink of water, please?"

Johnson slipped out and brought back a paper cup. Martin sipped the water, but he felt no better for it.

He went on hoarsely, "In Paris I met the man who had put me on to the story in the first place. Bruno Lukas. In the Hospital of the Sacred Heart. He was dying—because they got to him."

He had stopped gabbling now because he wasn't sure whom he was talking to. Everything was out of focus again. He'd been talking about Lukas and it was Lukas who had told him Greta was dead. Her face was there before him now, and he was overwhelmed suddenly with the harrowing feeling of loss that he had up to now managed to fight off. A bleak despair began to grip him and tears poured freely down his cheeks.

Johnson sat looking embarrassed, but it didn't matter any more. Martin stood up, swaying slightly.

"Are you all right?" Johnson asked awkwardly.

Martin wiped his face with the back of his hand, but the tears wouldn't stop.

"I'm just a bit—off-color. I'll go now. If you want to know anything more, get in touch."

"I'll do that," the reporter said quietly and led him to the door.

As Martin stumbled out into the street, Johnson stood looking after him for a few moments, then went back to his office, and telephoned the Foreign Office.

"Martin? Our people know him well," the press office spokesman said. "We wondered when he'd get around to you. Has a fascinating supply of fairy stories. Was he sober?"

"Let's say he was tired and emotional."

"You follow it up as you wish. But he's slightly unballanced, if you want our opinion. Got mixed up with some bird in the GDR and he's not been the same man since. He's cost us a lot of time and energy, and if you take my tip you won't waste yours on him. There's not a vestige of truth in anything he's told us."

Johnson made one further call, to the Hospital of the Sacred Heart in Paris. They had no record of a patient by the name of Bruno Lukas. Johnson drew a line through his notes and hoped a decent story was going to turn up that would give him a by-line in this week's paper.

8

Martin slept badly that night. He had dozed on the train and gone three stations past his own. By the time he finally crawled into bed it was ten o'clock.

There was a man standing by the bed, looking down at him. Koster's face was half hidden by shadow, as it had been in the car. Martin rolled away to avoid those pale, chilling eyes.

He found it hard to move and more difficult to breathe. If he could throw off the choking weight of the bedclothes it would be easier, but then he would be exposed to the figure standing by the bed. Sweat poured from his body and his head was banging.

The feverish heat of his body turned to a chill and he started to shiver. He reached up and pulled the light cord, then sat up. The room was empty. His shattered nerves were overstimulating his imagination. As he turned out the light the feverish feeling returned.

Soon the figure of Koster was there again. He burrowed under the sheet in desperation to hide. Whichever way he turned he could see the same face, studying him silently. He was in the car with them again on a journey that was going on for hours and the pain in his stomach was growing more intense all the time.

A cold breeze across his skin finally brought him back to reality. The bedroom window was open and the curtains were flapping. He shivered and tried to recall if it had been open when he came to bed.

He got out of bed and went over to the window. He saw a movement in the garden below. Then he realized that small clouds scuttling across the moon were turning the ground into a mass of shifting shadows.

He slammed the window shut and drew the curtains completely across. The thought of returning to his nightmare-tossed bed gave him a feeling of nausea, but his head was aching so much he had to lie down.

He somehow endured the rest of the night, his mind saturated by a vivid montage of Koster, newspapers, explosions, and over all the face of Greta, at once beseeching and reproachful.

There was a jangling sound which eventually materialized into the telephone beside his bed. Sheila's voice penetrated the weary edges of his mind and dragged him into wakefulness.

"It's ten o'clock, Mr. Martin. I understood you were planning to come in today, and I wondered if anything was wrong."

"I'm fine," he mumbled automatically. Then as a pain seared the back of his eyes he said, "No, I'm not. I feel rotten, Sheila, and I'm not coming in. Tell everyone to try and keep things going, will you?"

He put down the phone and lay back in the wreckage of his bed. This was no mere hangover. He'd not felt so bad since an attack of dysentery in the Canal Zone many years ago.

He was drifting into a doze when the front-door bell rang. He tried covering his ears with the pillow but the ringing went on. Finally he tottered out of bed, opened the bedroom window, and saw Sheila looking up at him with an elderly, impatient-looking man alongside her.

"I've brought Doctor Patterson," she called up. "Throw down your keys."

While the doctor slipped him a thermometer and took his pulse, Sheila tut-tutted over the state of the bed and started straightening things up.

"Virus infection," the doctor finally pronounced, scribbling on his prescription pad. "Our old standby when we're not quite sure what it is. Could be 'flu. Anyway it means bed, hot drinks, and an antibiotic. And time, of course. Don't get up for at least three days—not that I imagine you'll want to."

Within half an hour Sheila had his bed comfortable, the windows open, and a hot-water bottle at his feet. Next she collected his prescription from the chemist and also brought back bottles of fruit drink and cans of soup.

Martin finally persuaded her that she had done all that could possibly need doing, and that he would spend the rest of the day trying to sleep. As soon as she had gone he slipped back into a doze.

Now he saw the children screaming as the explosion tore them apart. He was somehow detached from the chaos, a horrified observer, yet standing at the very center of the carnage. Then the flames surrounded him and his skin was burning.

He forced himself awake and found he was drenched with perspiration once more. The rest of the day passed wearily in this way, alternating between unbearable dreams and consciousness.

Sheila called in the evening on her way home. She tidied him up and made sure everything was to hand for the night.

"Any problems at the office?" he asked.

"Forget about work," she instructed him. "Everything is under control there. You just concentrate on getting yourself better." She tightened the cap on a newly filled hot-water bottle. "By the way, I arranged with the post office this morning to have your service temporarily disconnected. Otherwise, believe me, you'd have no peace at all. People have got to learn that not even Alec Martin is indispensable."

He picked up the phone. "It's dead. So I can't make calls either."

"That's right. I asked if they could just stop incoming calls, but apparently it's all or nothing." She smiled at him maternally. "Really, it's a good thing, too. Otherwise you'd be calling us at the office all day, trying to keep your finger on everything."

He said, as patiently as he could, "I have no intention of doing that. But you realize that now I have no contact with the outside world in case of emergency."

"That's nonsense. Anyone would think you were at death's door. You've only got a touch of 'flu, for heaven's sake."

He had no energy to argue further. He said, "Sheila, before you go will you make sure all the doors and windows are locked? Upstairs as well as down."

She looked at him curiously. "Listen, Mr. Martin, do you want me to stay overnight? Tom would understand—"

"No, of course not. I just like to know the house is secure."

She made a great show of testing every window after she had closed it, like a mother assuring her child there were no bogeymen hiding anywhere. It was a relief when she finally left.

Sleep, when it came, was no better than the previous night. The same images dominated his mind as his temperature soared up and down. Koster was there again. He was entering the bedroom with young Leather-jacket, the man who had punched him. They stood in the doorway looking across at him for a moment. Martin tried to escape the faces by rolling away. He opened his eyes and saw with relief that the trick had worked.

But it hadn't. A hand was on his shoulder and the voice was Koster's.

"Such a stupid man, Martin. You had your warning from me, but you ignored it. Did you really think the people at the newspaper office would believe you? And did you think we would not know about it?" The voice was soft but penetrating and he could feel the man's breath on his ear. "You regarded my warning as no more than a form of words, because I allowed you to live on that last occasion that we met. Well, there was only one reason for that: your sudden death might have given some note of authenticity to the statement you had given your security authorities."

The hand on his shoulder turned into a vise and twisted him round. Koster was there, smiling at him. But it was different: for the first time Martin could see his whole face.

There was a long silence while the two men studied him.

Then Koster went on, "I think you can hear me, Martin. I want you to know that we are no longer inhibited by that consideration. Our information, from an unimpeachable source, is that your stories are now completely discredited in those dusty offices of Whitehall. Your character has been assessed—rightly, I feel—as 'unstable.' Indeed your accidental death, caused through your own carelessness, now would fit very neatly into the personality profile they have drawn up for you." He

90

paused, his eyes searching Martin's perspiring face. "George, are you ready? Now Mr. Martin, as your dentist says, this will only hurt for a moment." He turned to the other man.

George took Martin's shoulders and pulled him to a sitting position. Then he moved back, out of the range of Martin's vision. Martin felt a piercing pain as the heel of the man's hand struck the base of his spine. His whole body went rigid as George let him fall back into the pillows.

Martin lay with his mouth open, breathing hoarsely, his limbs paralyzed as the two men busied themselves at the bedside table.

"He won't move for a few minutes," George said.

"Open the pack of cigarettes," Koster instructed. "Where's the bottle?"

Something was sprinkled over the sheet and blankets. Next Koster lit a cigarette, puffed it a few times, then stood holding it in his hand.

"Filthy habit," he said, and dropped the cigarette onto the bed.

Three seconds later there was a "whoof" and a flash as the bedding started to burn.

Martin never heard Koster leave. He closed his mouth to try to avoid the smoke and fumes drifting upwards toward him. The heat was penetrating the blankets around his body. As the smoke crawled into his nostrils he started to cough. His head was spinning and he was back among the children dying in the explosion. He would have joined in their screams if only his vocal cords had worked.

The whole ground was lifting and he was rolling over. Voices with alarm in them, one sounding like Sheila. Suddenly the heat was gone and it was blessedly cool.

He was lying on the bedroom floor with Sheila looking down anxiously at him. Over her shoulder a man had the bedroom window open and for some reason was bundling blankets through it.

"Are you all right, Mr. Martin?"

Life was creeping back into his muscles. He was still coughing the smoke from his lungs although the room was now clear.

The man finished pushing out the blankets and came

across, dusting his hands. He had square, cheerful features and was wearing a polo-neck sweater and slacks.

"You were right to be worried about him, Sheila love," he said. "Never could understand people smoking in bed."

"We've got to get him back there." Sheila was stripping the bed. "Find the linen cupboard, Tom, and see if there are any sheets and blankets."

By the time the bed was remade, Martin was able to crawl back in with their assistance.

"Thanks," he croaked with real and profound gratitude. "How did you come to be here?"

Sheila tucked in the bedclothes so tightly that he could barely move. "When I got home I kept telling Tom I was worried about you being on your own. Now Tom's a man who prefers to do things rather than talk about them. In the end he said why don't we both go and stay overnight? There's no one at home who needs us, so we might as well be in your house. And what did we find when we arrived?'

"The smell of burning," Tom said. "We rushed up here and found your bedding on fire. Another minute and you would have been nicely barbecued."

Sheila ostentatiously took the cigarette pack from the bedside table and handed it to her husband. "Take care of that, Tom. We don't want a repeat performance in the middle of the night."

"I wasn't smoking," Martin protested. "I can't stand the taste of cigarettes at the moment."

"Then how did your bed catch fire?"

Martin said slowly, "You'll find it difficult to believe, but I think there were two men in here. They poured some stuff on the bed and dropped a lighted cigarette on it."

Sheila looked pointedly at her husband. "I see. And how did they get into the house? Through the keyhole? This place is more secure than the Tower of London."

"These men are capable of getting through any door." Martin felt a terrible weariness. All he wanted now was sleep. "Very well, I probably dreamt it all. Thank you for what you did."

Sheila was bursting with self-satisfaction. "Think nothing of it, Mr. Martin. Every good secretary should be on hand to put out her boss when he catches fire."

He tried to smile, and Tom said, "I think we'll let Mr. Martin sleep, Sheila."

"Call us if you need anything, Mr. Martin," she said. "You've nothing to worry about now."

He listened to them making up the bed in the next room, then finally drifted into sleep.

Martin was in bed for the next three days. Sheila and Tom spent each night in the house and she made his meals morning and evening. His fever diminished and he started to eat solid food.

It was Tom who noted that these signs of physical recovery were not matched by an uplift in his spirits.

"Is he always as morose as this?" he asked Sheila, as they prepared for bed.

"He's not himself," she said, "but there's always depression after 'flu. He must be on the mend, because he just told me he'll be all right now on his own."

"Do you think he will be?"

"I'll call in mornings and evenings to make sure he's eating, but I don't think we need sleep here any more." She shivered slightly as she looked round the room. "I've had enough of this place, Tom. It always seems cold, somehow."

Martin got out of bed the next day after Sheila and Tom had left. Despite some initial dizziness he was able to make his way downstairs, where he brewed some tea.

Then he picked up the telephone. Sheila had promised to have the line reconnected that day and the dialing tone showed she had been as good as her word.

Detective Sergeant Langley was in his office. It seemed to take a few seconds for Martin's name to register with him.

"Nothing to report, Mr. Martin," he said, adopting a tone of weary patience. "No trace of those characters or their car."

Martin said, "They've been back."

There was a pause. "You've seen them?"

"They broke into my house the other night and set fire to my bed."

The pause was longer this time. "When, precisely?"

"It must have been Wednesday. I've been in bed for three days. Yes, Wednesday."

"I see," Langley said brusquely. "It's not much good

93

telling us about it after this time. How did they get in?"

"I don't know. The house was securely locked up, so they must have got a key from somewhere." Martin went on, "I know what you're thinking, Sergeant. I don't expect you to take any of this seriously, but would you just do one thing? Make a note of what I've told you and file it away somewhere. You may need to refer to it at some time in the future."

Martin spent the rest of the day in an armchair, looking out into the back garden. He was still there when Sheila let herself in at five-thirty.

"How's the patient today?" She looked at him doubtfully. His eyes were unseeing as he stared out into the garden.

He shivered slightly, then he turned to her with a smile. "Much better, thanks to you and Tom. I really feel like something to eat—if you wouldn't mind scraping together something for me."

He followed her into the kitchen with a spring in his step that had been missing for some time.

"Sheila, you know that feeling when a heavy weight has been lifted from your mind? There's just no feeling like it."

"So you've solved all your problems, have you?" she said, lifting the pressure cooker out of the cupboard. "It's amazing what a few days' rest can do."

"Not solved them. Identified them. Over the past few weeks I've been used, abused pushed around—just because I've tried to do what I thought was right. I still think it's right, but my credibility now seems to be nonexistent. That means the people who should be doing something are just sitting on their backsides, watching the world go by, and taking no notice of a ranting nut-case. So what's the answer?"

"Tell me," she said cautiously.

"It's obvious: I've got to take action myself."

She looked at him curiously. "It would be helpful if I knew what you were talking about. What action?"

"That I can't tell you. In any case you wouldn't believe me, and you'd start looking at me like all those others." He was pacing nervously up and down the kitchen. There was suppressed excitement in his voice as he went on. "It is crazy, I suppose, but it's the sort of craziness you'll find throughout history—by men who saw a situation clearly while everyone around them was looking the other way, not wanting to face the truth. The anti-appeasement people in the nineteen thirties, for instance, and the ones who had the measure of the Russians in the forties. They weren't popular, and people wrote them off as cranks. But that didn't make them any less right. They stuck to their guns—and that's what I intend to do —literally."

Sheila put the potatoes on to boil. While she timed the pressure cooker she said, "If your problem is to do with work, you've really got nothing to worry about. Everything is quite under control there."

He shook his head. "It's nothing to do with that. In fact, for the next couple of weeks I'll not have time to take any interest in the firm at all. I'll be in and out of the office, but I'll just be using it as a base."

The whisky bottle stood on the kitchen cabinet. Sheila was watching it out of the corner of her eye but he made no attempt to pour himself a drink; indeed, he seemed oblivious of it. There was no artificial stimulant to account for the strange new vitality in his voice as he said, "For the first time in years, Sheila, I've got a clear-cut objective in my life apart from making money. And I'm going out to achieve it."

"I'm not happy about him," Sheila told Tom that evening. "It's not just the things he's saying, although they make little enough sense. It's his eyes. They're too bright —almost as though he's going into a fever again. There's something up with him, Tom, but what can I do about it?"

9

In a committee room in the Edinburgh City Chambers thirteen men seated around an oval table studied a map beamed onto a screen by an overhead projector.

"We've covered every possible route into the city," said the Deputy Chief Constable. "As well as police units, there will be army patrols and continuous helicopter surveillance. We'll have an almost bulletproof corridor from the airport into the city for when the delegates arrive and depart."

A brigadier detailed the antimining precautions the army would be taking and a Special Branch superintendent explained how each delegate would have two personal bodyguards provided by the police. Nationally all forces were keeping special tabs on known political activists and extremists of all persuasions.

"Operation Motherhen," the security program for the Edinburgh Conference, took over an hour to detail. When it was completed, the Secretary of State for Scotland said, "I'm impressed by the amount of planning that has gone into this operation and the high degree of co-operation between every organization involved. Whether our imaginary assassin will be able to find any loopholes remains to be seen, but I can't see any. Can anyone think of any possibility that has not been covered?"

A thin, bald man at the end of the table said quietly, "It's only a minor point, sir, but we in counterintelligence would like some reassurance on it. I saw a copy report some weeks ago about a possible aerial attack."

The Secretary of State's eyebrows went up. "On the castle? That's rather ambitious."

The man went on, "A businessman claimed he'd picked up some information, in East Germany of all places."

"If I can comment on this, sir," Blair put in. "The Internal Security Coordination Office itself has been responsible for the Martin file, as it's known. I can assure you it's all been neatly tied up and put away. The man is clearly unbalanced."

The Secretary of State said, "In that case, perhaps he should be tied up and put away also." When the laughter died away, he went on, "I presume the information he supplied was checked out?"

"With extreme care, sir. That was only one of about half-a-dozen tales he brought back—each equally far-fetched. All have proved to be without foundation."

The Special Branch man said, "On an occasion of this kind, all sorts of cranks come to the fore with fantastic stories and warnings. We know most of them by name."

Blair said with a slight smile, "Our friend Martin is rather a persistent nuisance, I'm afraid. His latest tale is that East German agents set fire to his bed, somewhere in the Home Counties."

The counterintelligence man did not join in the laughter. He said, "All the same, we mustn't overlook any possible security hazard. Is this man dangerous in any way? We have had so many examples in recent years of apparently water-tight security being breached, particularly in Arab-Israeli situations."

"We may discount the actual warnings, but we do take such people themselves seriously," said Blair with ill-concealed annoyance. "We're arranging to have him under continuous surveillance during the conference and for two weeks prior to it."

"I know we can rely on our security agencies to leave no possibility uncovered," said the Secretary of State smoothly. "Thank you for your attendance, gentlemen. As a result of your efforts, it is my belief that we shall have a successful and entirely peaceful conference that will bring nothing but credit to Scotland."

"How are you, my dear friend?" Boulin's voice boomed cheerily over the phone. "I hope you are not telling me you cannot meet the delivery dates."

"You'll get the goods in time." The Algerian order had, in fact, not crossed Martin's mind since before his illness.

"I have a special request, Boulin. And this must be kept completely confidential." He glanced across to make sure the office door was firmly closed.

"Surely all our business is conducted on a confidential level?"

"I'm not talking of commercial security." Martin hesitated, then went on, "I require the services of a pilot and an aircraft as well. For a very special job."

Boulin's puzzlement was evident in his voice. "Surely there are plenty of aircraft charter firms in your country who can supply any size of aircraft, and a crew as well if necessary."

Martin felt himself perspiring. "They cannot provide the aircraft I require. It's a jet fighter."

There was a long pause. Then Boulin said in a matter-of-fact voice, "It is good of you to call me, Mr. Martin, to tell me all is under control. I expect the little problems concerning the order to be sorted out quickly."

Martin was mystified. "I don't—"

"Look, why not let me call you later on today?" Boulin went on smoothly. "Where will you be lunching? No doubt at that pleasant little spot you took me to on the last occasion I was in your country."

"Just a minute, Boulin—"

The Frenchman talked him down. "I do suggest you go there. It is good food, as I recall, and should not be too crowded at midday."

Martin cast his mind back to Boulin's last visit. They had gone out to a pub five miles from the works.

"You mean the—"

"I must go now, Mr. Martin. Have a good lunch."

The line was disconnected and it took Martin a few moments to realize what the Frenchman had been trying to tell him.

He shook his head. "The man's got a security complex. He must seriously think the line is being tapped."

He drove out to the Black Horse in Collington and reached it just before noon. It was a genuine country pub, where the landlord had developed the catering side without losing sight of the fact that his essential function was serving good beer.

The pub was empty when he entered but another hour would see it packed with lunchtime drinkers. He ordered half a bitter and drank it at the bar. His glass was almost empty when a phone rang somewhere behind him.

A minute later the landlord came toward him. "Are you Mr. Martin? There's a call for you." He pointed toward an alcove at the end of the bar. "Sounds like a long-distance one."

He took the receiver and tucked his head inside the canopy.

"I think we can talk more freely now," Boulin said.

"How did you know this number?"

"I took a note of it on the occasion when we were there together. Just in case we ever needed to talk privately."

"You really think my line is being tapped?"

Boulin said seriously, "It is more than likely, in view of the matters you have been involved in recently. And these days any discussions about the supply of military material require the utmost degree of security. When do you require the aircraft?"

"For several days up to and including May the fifteenth."

"Armed?"

"Of course."

There was a pause. "You realize this is not an easy request to meet?"

"I would not have come to you otherwise, Boulin." He waited a moment. "Well—can you help?"

"I cannot give you an immediate answer," the Frenchman said. "I suppose it is wasting my time to ask the purpose for which you need it?"

"That's right, Boulin. Just find me the plane and a dependable pilot. I'll take it from there."

"How much are you willing to pay?"

Martin hesitated. "Can I leave it in your hands to fix a price? I'm not interested in haggling. I'll pay well for a good experienced man. And your commission will be at the usual rate."

Boulin sounded doubtful. "Perhaps you do not realize the scale of the commitment. This could cost some thousands of pounds."

"I'm aware of that."

"Chartering a war plane—it is difficult to establish a market rate for that. They could ask whatever figure they like—if I can find someone willing to make the charter in the first place. Really, the more I think about this—"

"Forget about chartering then. Try and buy me a plane, will you?"

"Are you serious?"

"There are bound to be surplus aircraft for sale in different parts of the world. Governments updating their air forces are usually glad to find a buyer for their old planes."

"But the cost would be enormous," Boulin said. "A jet fighter is a very expensive piece of machinery, even second-hand. I find it hard to believe you are serious about this, Mr. Martin."

"Boulin. Just get this clear: I'm deadly serious. If you don't want to help, just say so. Otherwise get off your backside, go out there, and find me what I want. Leave me to worry about the finance. Now Boulin, will you do it?"

The Frenchman said, "All that I can promise at this stage is that I will make some inquires. I will contact you again tomorrow at a similar time. On this number, of course."

"Don't bugger me about," Martin warned. "I want to know as quickly as possible if you can supply the goods. Otherwise I'll have to try somewhere else. Time is the one thing I'm short of."

Martin replaced the receiver and nodded to the landlord as he left the pub.

He drove straight to Molyneux, where he found Mike in the main hangar, his head buried in the engine compartment of the Spitfire. The aircraft's blue-gray paint was faded and chipped in places, while the perspex of the canopy was scratched and yellowed with age. But the thouroughbred grace which Mitchell had built into the design was still there. Strange, thought Martin, how that shape had not dated at all. It had the inevitability found only in a true artistic creation.

"Over twenty Marks and they never finished ringing all the changes on her," Mike said, watching Martin as he studied the shape of the airframe.

Martin said, "I flew several of them, but not a Mark Eighteen like this. How fast is she?"

"In her prime, just over four hundred knots up to twenty thousand feet," the engineer said, wiping his blackened hands on a piece of mutton-cloth. "It's only a collection of aluminum and iron and copper. But put together in the right way, it takes on a soul, somehow. Anyone who flew or worked on one, they never forget the experience." He nodded toward a gangly youth who was sweeping the floor at the far side of the hangar. "My nephew Harold, there. He's only sixteen but he knows all about the Spit. He worships this one."

"I didn't know you felt so emotional about your work, Mike. But what about the really old ones in the collection —the Avro, the Camel. Even the Bleriot. They were the pioneers."

"True. But they're museum pieces, really. Oh, I know we fly them sometimes on exhibition days. But this one— she can still frighten the wits out of anyone by flying over at nought feet. She's got the looks of a killer, see—even at thirty years of age."

"Is she as fast as when she was built?" Martin asked.

"I doubt it. We daren't put her at full stretch to find out—and we have to be careful with those tight turns. I'd hate to see her wings fold up at this age. By the way, I'm just putting in those compressor cylinders. They arrived this morning."

"Do they fit?"

Mike grinned. "Luckily, yes. Can't say I'd have the nerve to ask you to do them again. It's a good thing for the museum we've got you so handy, Mr. Martin. We owe you a lot."

"It's a pleasure to help," Martin said. "I can't expect you to make some poor sod fly it without flaps and brakes."

"The cylinders feed the supercharger gear-change ram as well, and the radiator shutters. Not to mention the guns, although we don't have them, of course."

Martin said, "I came over to let you know you might be having a new addition to the family shortly. A jet."

The engineer's eyes opened wide. "Is that so? What

101

will it be? Because they can be pretty expensive planes to keep flying."

"I don't know yet," Martin admitted. "It could be a single-seat fighter. I intend to donate it to the museum once I know I can get it. What I want to know, Mike, is the drill for getting one into the country. It's abroad at the moment, you see."

Mike said thoughtfully, "Import licenses, duty, things like that. Could be complicated. On the other hand, the rules may be different for something coming to a museum. I'll make some inquiries."

"I'd appreciate that. But one thing—for the moment don't drop a word to anyone that I'm planning this."

"Keeping it as a surprise for the other trustees?"

"Something like that. I should hear definitely about the plane in a day or so and I'll let you know."

When he got back to the office the company accountant, Gerald Harris, was waiting for him, presumably to continue their discussions on the firm going public.

"How are you feeling, Alec?" the accountant asked, watching him closely.

"I feel all right, Gerald, but I'm not quite well enough to talk about figures. You know how they scramble my mind for the rest of the day." Martin sat behind the desk and smiled as pleasantly as he could. "You've managed to manipulate them all right while I've been away, haven't you? Well, carry on juggling."

Gerald said stiffly, "Believe it or not, it was just a social call. Some of us do take an interest in each other's welfare, you know."

"Thanks for asking. I'm fine, as I said." As the accountant opened the door, a thought crossed Martin's mind. "There's something I want to ask you, Gerald. First, how much is the Boulin business worth—the orders outstanding at the moment?"

"Roughly forty-seven thousand. Why?"

"And the amount he still owes us against previous deliveries?"

"He's a notoriously slow payer. I think it's about thirty thousand. But we'll get it eventually."

Martin nodded. "Seventy-seven thousand in all. Now if I wanted to buy something from abroad I'd have to get all sorts of clearances to do it, using sterling. But there's nothing to prevent me telling Boulin to hang on to the money he owes me and use it to buy these goods for me instead. Isn't that so?"

Gerald closed the door and sat down facing the desk. "What are you up to, Alec?" he asked quietly.

"Asking hypothetical questions, that's what. Come on, Gerald. Could I do it?"

The accountant said, "It depends on whether you're asking from a legal standpoint or as far as the company's own financial system is concerned. The answer in the first case is probably no, and in the second definitely no."

"Why?"

"Legally, because there are things like tax to consider. It would look like a very crude dodge to keep the profits down and so ease the tax liability. From the company's point of view, it can't be done because we just don't do things that way." He held up his hand to forestall an interruption. "That's not the classic bureaucratic excuse for inaction. It's because the bookkeeping system of this company would be thrown out of gear and the auditors would never pass the accounts."

"So what?" Martin said. "The only people concerned about that would be the people owning the company, whose money is involved. And that comes down to me, and me alone."

Gerald suppressed a sigh. "If only life was that simple. Without proper accounts, you've got no credit rating. The banks won't want to know you and your suppliers will insist on cash on delivery. Life would become very difficult indeed."

"But not impossible?" Martin said. "We've enough cash reserves to pay for our supplies on delivery if necessary— and I don't believe for a moment our regular suppliers would do that to us. As for the bank, our overdraft has always been more than covered by the securities they hold in their greedy little hands. No, Gerald, a little unorthodox transaction like I'm talking about would not bring Martin Engineering crashing to its foundations."

Gerald looked heavenwards for patience. "Alec, you're overlooking the most important aspect of all: going public. We wouldn't get within a mile of the Stock Exchange without whiter-than-white company accounts.

Who's going to put their money into a company where the boss casually spends the receipts before they even reach the till?"

Gerald sat back, hands crossed on his lap and his plump face saying, Get out of that one, cowboy.

Martin simply nodded. He swung his swivel chair round and stared out of the window as he said, "No problem there, either. Because we're not going public, Gerald." He waited until the hiss of breath behind him had died away; then he went on, "I've been talking to my solicitor. What you've been saying about going public is quite true—it's a bonanza. For everyone except me." He swung round again. "My former wife, you see, would get half of the proceeds."

There was a pause. Then Gerald said, "I wish you'd told me this earlier. I've been wasting an awful lot of my time."

"I've not thrown out the idea completely. What I'm doing, I suppose, is playing for time."

Gerald stood up. "Just what is this deal that's so important? Oh, I know it was a hypothetical case. But what are the hypothetical goods that only Boulin can get for you?"

Martin said, "It's nothing criminal, Gerald. I'm just trying to get hold of a new exhibit for the Molyneux museum. That's all I can tell you for the moment."

Gerald's expression was one of disbelief. "Seventy-seven thousand pounds' worth? That's one hell of a price for a donation to that old crock's collection. What is it—the Archangel Gabriel's original wings and undercarriage?"

Martin stood up and opened the door. "Let's forget it all for the moment, shall we? I'll talk to you next week."

The accountant was tight-lipped as he went out. As he shut the door, Martin caught a glimpse of Gerald giving Sheila an I-see-what-you-mean expression. Martin went back to his desk and opened the drawer. In it was the map of Northeast Scotland he had asked Sheila to get for him earlier. He put it in his briefcase, pulled on his coat, and said to Sheila as he left the office, "I'm finished here for the day. I don't know if I'll be in tomorrow. If not, I'll see you on Friday. Good night, Sheila."

* * *

At twenty minutes past noon the following day, the landlord of the Black Horse said to Martin, "It's for you again, sir."

Martin picked up the phone.

"I have found an aircraft," Boulin said, "which I think would be most suitable for your needs. It is a Hawker Hunter fitted with Aden machine guns."

Martin said, "That sounds as though it might do. In good condition?"

"It has seen a good deal of service but is well maintained. It has found its way to Tunisia, surplus to a certain country's requirements. The price is one hundred thousand pounds sterling."

There was a pause. "It's a very high price."

"It is an exorbitant price," the Frenchman said bluntly. "But I am in no position to bargain. That would take time, which I understand is a commodity in short supply. You did say price was no object, Mr. Martin."

"I don't think I said exactly that—but listen. I can pay ninety thousand. Can you get it for that?"

Boulin hummed a little. "I will try. That is all I will promise for the moment. But there is another problem. I cannot find a pilot."

Christ, Martin thought, now he tells me. "There must be someone around who can fly the thing. How far have you looked?"

Boulin said defensively, "It is not an easy thing to do, in such a short time. It could take me several weeks to find a person willing to undertake the job. And one other point, Mr. Martin: you find it difficult to meet the asking price for the aircraft, but the amount for the pilot would be on top of that."

Martin thought quickly. "I'll take the aircraft, Boulin. You'll find you owe Martin Engineering thirty thousand pounds at the moment, so you can use that as a down payment."

"Now just one moment, Mr. Martin," Boulin protested. "I was simply acting as your agent in finding this aircraft. I do not agree that my money should be used to finance it."

Martin said sharply, "Look at our conditions of sale and you'll see goods should be paid for within thirty days

105

of the invoice date. You've been getting away with murder for years—you've never paid us in less than six months. You owe thirty thousand, so just pay it and stop arguing, Boulin."

"And the balance? How will that be paid?"

"We're in the process of supplying you with goods worth forty-seven thousand pounds at the moment. Set that against the total and I'll find a way of getting the balance to you as soon as I can."

Boulin spluttered. "That is not acceptable at all. I myself will not receive payment for the parts you are making until they are delivered. You are asking me to loan you this money!"

"Call it that if you like. Come on, Boulin, you make plenty on your commission from us. I'm just asking you to accommodate me on this one occasion. You know you'll get your money."

There was a long pause. Finally Boulin said, "On one condition: you bring forward delivery of the goods now on order to the date I requested at our last meeting."

Martin made a mental calculation. "Very well. In the meantime, you will purchase the aircraft on my behalf."

"Leave that to me. As usual, I shall do my very best for you, Mr. Martin."

Boulin's voice had regained its equable tone. It was clear that early delivery would mean a substantial bonus for him at the other end of the Algeria deal.

When he arrived at the works Martin went straight into Arthur's office.

"The Algerian order has to receive top priority," he told the production engineer. "I want full overtime, evenings and weekends. We've got to save two weeks somehow."

Arthur whistled. "That's going to be mighty expensive, Mr. Martin. Double time at weekends—the lads will love it. But it's really going to eat into your profit."

"I'll worry about that. It's time that counts now, and I want you to save every second you can."

Martin sat at his empty desk and considered his most immediate problem: finding a qualified pilot, able to fly a Hunter and willing to fly it for this particular operation.

He had an extremely expensive commitment on which

he could not progress further until he solved this problem. During his business life experience had taught him that the burden of commitment concentrated his mind wonderfully and somehow forced through a solution. He took out a piece of paper and doodled as he waited for the ideas to flow.

An advertisement in *Flight International* was the obvious thing. That would mean sifting through a pile of letters and interviewing a list of candidates. Apart from the desperate shortage of time, the chances were slim that the successful applicant would be willing to take the job when it was explained to him. And such a man, being in his right mind, would go straight to the police and report that a dangerous psychopath was at large.

The person he was looking for, apart from having the qualifications and willingness to do the job, must be trustworthy enough to keep his mouth shut if he did refuse it.

On the paper he had drawn the rough outline of a Hunter and he found himself pencilling in the RAF roundels, going round and round the outer line until it began to wear through the paper. Such a man would, by definition almost, be a former RAF pilot. The only ones he knew were of his own generation and were unlikely to have any recent flying experience. Colin Raymond, for instance, with his regular commission, had stayed on to reach the rank of air commodore. His operational days would now be well and truly over.

In the old days Colin would have leaped at the chance of something as outrageous as this. During those winter months of 1944–5, when they stormed their way across Europe, Colin's leadership of the squadron had at times bordered on the fanatical. Driving his pilots to their limits was only one aspect of it; he was obsessed with the art of anticipating the enemy's moves, and he cultivated a gambler's instinct. On the barest scrap of information he would commit his resources to a particular area at a particular time. The Spitfire's limited range, save when carrying drop-tanks, was one of his reasons for adopting this approach. The remarkable thing was how often he was right. On the basis of Colin's hunches they intercepted and destroyed dozens of German intruder flights before they even got as far as the Allied front line.

His postwar career in the service had been equally successful. Martin had noted the various stages of this career from the promotions notices in the press, right up to the time twelve months ago when the family name made headlines of its own. Only this time it concerned Colin's son, who, having also taken up an RAF flying career, was being court-martialled. He recalled the headlines: "Son of war hero denies theft charge." The amount had been trivial but enough for him to be cashiered. There had been a girl mixed up in it somehow.

Martin stopped doodling and laid down the pencil. That son—what was his name? Philip. He had been a fighter pilot. Lightnings or Jaguars. There had been some mention of it in the papers. Even if he did not have actual experience of flying a Hunter, such an aircraft would present no problems to him.

Where was he now? Martin picked up the phone and, ringing Directory Inquiries, asked the operator if there was an Air Commodore C. P. Raymond listed in the Hastings area, which had been his home the last time Martin had heard from him. There was, and he dialed the number.

A woman answered the phone.

"My name is Alec Martin. I'd like a word with Colin if he's in, please."

The woman said sharply, "Who did you say you were?"

"I'm an old friend of Colin's. Alec Martin."

There was a pause. "If you're a friend, I'm surprised you didn't know my husband died three weeks ago."

Martin was stunned. "Colin is dead? I'm terribly sorry. I've been ill for a while and I haven't seen the newspapers."

Her voice lost some of its edge. "I see. Well, it was very sudden. Coronary thrombosis. The funeral was well attended by his friends and colleagues." There was a pause; then Mrs. Raymond said, "What did you wish to speak to my husband about? Can I help?"

Floundering, Martin said, "I wanted to contact your son and I wondered if you could let me have his address."

"If you mean Philip, he is my stepson." Her voice had regained its brittle shrillness. "It breaks my heart to think of the anguish that boy caused his father."

"It was a sad business—"

"It was a sordid business. Philip was given every opportunity, all the help his father was capable of. He wanted for nothing. Then, because of that woman, he

108

threw it all away. It's not even as though she was worth it."

There was clearly more to come, so Martin said quickly, "I can see the distress you've suffered, Mrs. Raymond, so I won't cause you any more by asking you all about it. Could you just give me Philip's address? It's a business matter I wish to contact him about."

"Owes you money, does he?" she said with a sniff. Martin could hear her flicking through the pages of an address book. Finally she said, "I only got hold of it so I could notify him of the funeral arrangements. As far as I'm concerned, his address can come out of the book now. Here it is—Marchant's Limited, Solihull Road, Clarkside, West Midlands."

Martin wrote it down. "Is this a business address?"

"I don't know and I'm not really interested. That's where he can be contacted. It's something to do with the motor trade."

"Thank you, Mrs. Raymond. I am very sorry to hear of your bereavement. Colin and I served together at the end of the war and we were good friends."

"Well, if you're hoping to see him reflected in Philip, you'll be disappointed. As for that woman—"

"Thank you, Mrs. Raymond. Goodbye."

He put down the phone and looked at the address. Then he took down the AA book from the shelf and established that Clarkside was not far off the M6, south of Birmingham. It was no good telephoning. This matter needed to be broached face to face, after a delicate build-up.

He went out to Sheila, who was on the phone. She was saying, "Mr. Martin is in, Mr. Harris. I'll just see if he's free—" She saw Martin shaking his head and then said, "I'm sorry. He's busy at the moment. . . ."

She listened for a few seconds and then put down the phone. "He's got to see you immediately and he's coming over now."

Obviously Gerald had heard about the overtime working. "He's not going to find me here," Martin said. "Give him my apologies, will you, Sheila? I'll see you on Monday."

He hurried out to his car and headed for home. Then

he realized that as soon as he got there Gerald would be on the phone, blowing his top about the Algerian order turning the company into a non-profit-making organization. He stopped the car outside the gates, reversed a few yards, then headed in the opposite direction toward London.

10

It was evening as Martin drove into Clarkside. Straddling the main road, it was a small town of undistinguished semidetached houses, leading into terraced houses before the shops—a couple of supermarkets, a co-op, and three betting shops—took over. Beyond them was a redbrick factory building with the words "Clarkside Bicycle Works" picked out in white tiles among the brickwork. At a lower level an orange sign reading "Zelco Plastics" showed that the traditional industries were making way for the new.

There was a pub, the Sportsman, which had a sign depicting an Edwardian gentleman astride what was presumably an early Clarkside bicycle.

Martin drove slowly along the road past the rows of silent houses. There was a cemetery, beyond that was some waste ground, and then a petrol filling station. Among the neon Esso signs surrounding the canopy he saw the name Marchant's and a "closed" sign.

He parked on the forecourt, then walked over to the small bungalow that stood behind the filling station. Sooty gray rendering with faded cream paint on the window frames gave it a run-down appearance.

He rang the bell and waited. The door opened a minute later. There was no light in the hallway and in the gathering dusk he could barely make out the figure of a woman wearing a housecoat.

He said, "I'd like a word with Mr. Raymond, please. It's a business matter."

The woman hesitated for a moment, then stood to one side. "You'd better come in."

He stepped in while she closed the door and then he followed her into the front room.

"Sit down if you like," she said, switching on the light.

The room was furnished with a well-worn leatherette three-piece suite and a carpet square. The walls had been painted a long time ago in pink emulsion that went badly with the brown curtains.

The woman, he was surprised to see, was quite young. In the hall she had given the impression of someone middle-aged, possibly from the way she shuffled along in her loose-fitting slippers. She was thin featured and quite pretty, and the paleness of her face was emphasized by her dark, shoulder-length hair. She had a dispirited look in her eyes that seemed to reflect the atmosphere of the house.

As she went out, Martin looked round the room. If the furnishings of a home were an expression of one's personality, then Philip Raymond was going to be a dull and uninspiring young man. The drabness of the surroundings gave an additional dimension of unreality to what Martin intended to talk about.

However, Philip Raymond, when he came in, was certainly not dull, any more than his father had been. He was wearing an oil-stained coat with Esso on the breast pocket, but his features were very close to those of Colin's thirty years ago. The prominent nose, the square-cut face, the direct, dark brown eyes—and the grin. It wasn't a grin in the true sense but a built-in feature of his facial architecture. Its boyishness had served, in Colin's case, to charm and cajole men to work with and serve him, and to do so with an intense loyalty Martin had rarely encountered since.

"I'm Alec Martin. I was a friend of your father."

Martin offered his hand and Philip grasped it firmly. "Hello, Mr. Martin. I can't say I've heard of you—" He hesitated for a moment. "Unless you were the one he called 'Masher'? From the time you landed in the tented area of a forward airstrip and your prop chewed up the admin office. Dad had a fund of stories about the war years."

Martin smiled. "I haven't heard that nickname for years. Masher Martin. You really remember your father telling you that?"

Philip said, "I remember everything Dad told me about

the war. My future had always been planned for me, you see. And don't think I was one of those repressed youngsters being forced to follow in his father's footsteps, while all the time wanting to paint landscapes or be a ballet dancer. I really wanted to fly. My only regret was that I'd missed World War Two, so I had to experience it vicariously by listening to Dad's tales. And I absorbed every one of them."

His wife came in with a tray of coffee and sandwiches, which she placed on a small table.

Philip said to her, "This is Mr. Martin, an old friend of my father.'"

Martin stood and took the limp hand she offered. She dismissed him with an uninterested glance and said to Philip, "There's cheese and tomato, and meat paste. That's all I can find."

"Fine, Carol," Philip said quickly. "Are you going to have something?"

"I've got my ironing to finish," she replied, in a tone implying Philip had little conception of the burden she was carrying while he was enjoying himself.

When she had gone, Philip passed the sandwiches to Martin and said, "She's not really herself at the moment. We lost the baby, you see."

Martin said, "I'm sorry. I didn't know you had a child."

"We were expecting one. Miscarriage."

They ate in silence for a while. Philip said, "You read about the court-martial. What was the picture that came across to you?"

Martin thought for a moment, then said carefully, "You seemed a foolish young man—irresponsible perhaps—but certainly not criminal."

"I took money that didn't belong to me."

"You intended to pay it back, as I remember. It was a temporary situation—you borrowed it."

Philip laughed harshly. "The excuse of every embezzler who was ever caught. The fact that it was true in my case was not an acceptable reason, any more than it is in theirs. Why are you so anxious to avoid hurting my feelings, Mr. Martin?"

His relaxed attitude had disappeared and there was an intensity in his voice as he stared at the man facing him.

Martin said, "You seem to have hurt them yourself sufficiently already. Maybe it's because I've forgotten about

113

the stringent standards expected of an officer and a gentleman. In business we cut corners all the time."

The younger man nodded, then picked up a sandwich and began to eat. Finally he said, "You have a business proposition you want to talk about?"

"There's a job I want doing. You seem capable of it and I'll pay well."

"My record doesn't worry you?"

"This doesn't involve handling money." He stopped as he saw Philip's sardonic smile. Martin went on, "That was meant to reassure you and not myself. It's a flying job—a one-off."

There was interest in Philip's eyes now. "A charter flight?"

Martin shook his head. "It's a Hunter. It's in the Middle East now and we need it in England at the Molyneux Museum."

"A ferry job. Well, of course, I'd be glad to do it. How much?"

"I was thinking of five thousand pounds."

Philip's eyes narrowed. "Just for a ferry flight?"

"There's rather more to it than that. It's a complex matter and certain details have yet to be worked out. I don't expect a firm commitment from you until I've told you exactly what's involved, of course. But I just wanted to make sure you'd be interested."

Philip got to his feet and strode restlessly up and down the room. There was a new enthusiasm in his voice.

"It's the thing I miss most. I'd worked my way up to Lightnings and I was on a conversion course for Jaguars when the trouble broke. What really hurt was not losing the commission or being booted out of the service—although they weren't pleasant, of course. It was the thought of no more flying that I couldn't bear." He looked hopefully at Martin. "If this goes all right, there could be other jobs, perhaps?"

"I just couldn't say at the moment," Martin said noncommitally. "If it went well it certainly couldn't do you any harm."

"I'll tell Carol," Philip said, going to the door, but Martin held up his hand.

"If you wouldn't mind leaving that for the moment— until things get a bit clearer . . ."

"Oh. All right." Philip looked round the room. "I was

going to suggest we have a drink on it, but I couldn't face that sherry. Come on, let's walk down the road."

He went into the hall and called, "Carol, we're going to the Sportsman for half an hour. Won't be late."

There was no reply as Martin followed Philip out into the mild evening air.

The pub was quite busy as they entered. They found a table in the corner of the lounge and Philip insisted on buying the first round of draft Guinness.

"Carol drinks the bottled stuff," Philip said. "Her mother reckons it's a tonic for the blood and she treats it like a medicine—except she doesn't take it in teaspoons."

"Her mother lives in Clarkside?" Martin asked.

"That's why we came here. Carol wanted to be near her family and they found the job for me with the bungalow thrown in.'" He glanced at Martin. "It's not the tycoon end of the oil business, but it gives us a living—which is something we need right now."

He finished his pint quickly and started on the next as soon as Martin brought it to the table. "Did you see my stepmother at all?" he asked after a while.

"I spoke to her on the phone, to get your address."

"I can guess the tune she played." Philip studied his pint gloomily. "All the same I can't help wondering sometimes if what she says is true. That my disgrace helped to kill Dad."

Martin broke the silence. "I've forgotten the details now. It was mess funds, wasn't it?"

"Not exactly. I was responsible for a cash float that sank without trace. I'd got used to dipping into it and then cashing a check at the end of the month to replenish it. Until one Friday I left it too late and the bank was closed."

"How much was it?"

"Two hundred pounds." He saw Martin's eyebrows rise and went on, "Yes, it was swallowing up a fair chunk of my salary each month. I was always a poor manager and Carol didn't have much idea." He took a long drink and looked directly at Martin as he said, "We had to get married, you know."

There was a pause and Martin said, "It happens."

"It didn't help my promotion prospects, either, marrying into the ranks. It's not the sort of thing permanent commission people do. I didn't give a damn what anyone thought, and Carol's a very attractive girl."

"I can see that."

"Once she was pregnant she had to leave, of course. We didn't have married quarters, and so we rented a house. It was a big place—stupid, really, because I couldn't afford it. Not on top of the car and everything else. I was off flying pay at that time, you see. But we still reckoned we were entitled to enjoy ourselves."

"So that's how the money went?"

"And my career with it." Philip leaned back in his chair and looked around at the now crowded pub. "The sign of a mature man is adaptability to circumstances. As you can see, I'm adapting like mad."

Martin brought him another pint. As he placed it on the table he said, "I hope this job I'm talking about can be of some help to you. But I think I'm going to have to lay my cards on the table before we go any further."

Philip studied him over the top of his glass. Then he smiled knowingly. "Bit near the wind, is it? I wondered why you should search me out for a job like this, if it was as straightforward as it sounded. What is it—tax dodge?"

Martin took a deep breath. "I'm going to tell you what happened to me a few weeks ago, and about various things that have happened since then. I don't want you to interrupt. Wait until I've finished and then tell me what you think of it all. And let me first of all assure you that every word of it is the truth."

He related everything from his visit to East Germany up to his decision to come to Clarkside. When he finished there was a long silence. Then Philip lifted up his glass, which had remained almost untouched during the telling of the story, and took a long drink. He put down the glass and his fingers drummed on the table as he stared at Martin thoughtfully.

Finally he said, "I believe you all right, Mr. Martin. When you think of the attack on the Olympic village, kidnapping the OPEC ministers in Vienna, the Entebbe raid—anything seems to go these days. And this seems to me to make sense from the PFF point of view, if from no one else's."

Martin said, "Then if you can accept it, can you tell me why the security services should find it so unbelievable?"

116

"There is one difference between them and me," Philip said. "I know you and I know the sort of person you are."

"That's a rather arrogant assumption," Martin observed mildly.

"It isn't. I told you how much I absorbed from my father. He was a man who trusted his own judgement, and it paid off. I think I have some of his ability in that respect." A smile developed on his face. "Dad certainly had tremendous faith in you—or rather in your luck."

"It isn't a matter of luck—"

"But so often it is. You proved you had it, and Dad benefited from it. Remember New Years' Day nineteen forty-five?"

Martin remembered it very well: that day in Holland when the Luftwaffe appeared from nowhere, in a mass of strength no one at that stage of the war suspected it was capable of, and devastated the Allied air forces on the ground. Within a mere thirty minutes on that morning, the German air fleet was on its way back to base, leaving behind the burning wreckage of hundreds of British and American planes.

His own squadron was one of the few to survive intact, thanks only to the fact that Martin had taken up his Spitfire after a radio change. Twenty miles out from base, after finding the new set was not operating, he had spotted columns of black smoke rising from the forward airstrips and had guessed what was happening. He had rocketed straight back to his own strip, leaped from his cockpit almost before the aircraft had halted, and had sounded the alarm.

The squadron was literally in the middle of its take-off as the Luftwaffe vanguard roared over the hedgerows toward them. Not only did the squadron survive, but it succeeded in downing six of the enemy.

On such a black day, their action stood out like a beacon as the grim picture was pieced together. It was inevitable that, as the brass in sheer desperation looked for somewhere to bestow gongs, the squadron would benefit.

"I'm going to stick closely to you, Masher," the squadron commander had told Alec Martin. "You may or may not be the devil's own, for all I know, but you've certainly got his luck—and some of it could brush off onto me. In fact," he added, glancing at the bar to his DFC, "it already has."

11

The barman was calling for last orders. Martin looked at Philip's glass but the younger man shook his head.

"When this place starts looking bright and cozy, and the people all seem pleasant, I know I've had enough." He leaned back in his chair and produced a pipe from his pocket. He glanced at Martin and said, "Carol doesn't like me to smoke this at home, so I have to make the most of it." As he filled the pipe he went on, "I believe my father's assessment of you was right, Mr. Martin. Certainly he learned to trust you, and I'll do the same."

"I'm glad," Martin said. "But I'd like to think you're joining in this enterprise on the basis of a clear decision, arrived at rationally. My so-called luck doesn't enter into it."

Philip nodded as he put a match to the pipe. "Fair enough. Let me put it this way then: your story convinces me, and I know enough of your character to want to go along with you in whatever you intend to do. I assume you are planning to frustrate the Palestinian attack in some way. Where do I fit into things?"

Encouraged by Philip's apparent confidence in him, Martin went on, "The most effective and, in many ways, the simplest means of frustrating the attack is to make sure no one is in the castle at the time. There would be damage, but no casualties—apart from the crew of the plane. And the way to get the people clear is to frighten them out of the place."

"A bomb scare? Telephone a warning to say you've planted one?"

Martin shook his head. "There have been so many

hoaxes along those lines that now there's a basic rule: if a place has been thoroughly checked and kept under continuous guard, and everyone entering it has been searched, then any call about a bomb has to be a hoax. You need to apply some common sense to it; otherwise one nut-case could bring everything to a halt."

"And those conditions will apply to this conference?"

"It's being staged under the cover of the biggest security operation ever organized in this country outside wartime—so the papers tell us. One telephone call isn't going to be allowed to disrupt it. No, we have to scare them out with something much more tangible and immediate—such as an attack from the air."

Philip said thoughtfully, "The very thing which no one will believe is going to happen?"

"An aircraft—our aircraft—flies in very low, twenty minutes before the Palestinian attack is due. It starts buzzing the castle. Apart from the disruption to the proceedings caused by the noise, I'm hoping it will make the security people recall my warning. They'll realize that an air attack really is in the cards—and with luck they'll decide it's best to adjourn the proceedings for the time being."

"So everyone is clear of the place when the real attack comes?" Philip thought for a moment. "You're making an awful lot of assumptions. They may just tell everyone to sit tight until the interruption is over."

"In that case there's only one thing left to do. That's why I'm using a jet fighter plane, which is going to be armed."

Philip stared at him. Then he said slowly, "Go on: say what I think you're going to say."

"We've got to stop the Palestinian plane from making its attack: that means intercepting and destroying it."

The barman came over and swept the empty glasses off their table, emptied the ashtray into a box, then flicked a damp cloth over the surface.

"Drink up, everyone, if you please," he called as he moved on.

Philip said, "That's what I call a desperate remedy."

"It's a last resort. Can you suggest anything else?"

"No." Philip shifted uneasily in his chair. "So that's to be my job." He absently tapped the ashes out of the pipe.

"This is a bloody big thing you're asking me to do, Mr. Martin. I never imagined . . ."

"I can't do it myself, or I would. I can't fly a jet, so I have to use someone who can. He's got to be able to do the job—and he's got to be willing."

The pub was starting to empty now, and Philip glanced at his watch. He said slowly, "It's not an easy decision. It needs thinking about for a day or so. There's so much involved. . . . Look, if I did destroy that jet over the center of Edinburgh, there's going to be lots of bits and pieces flying around. Someone on the ground is bound to get hurt."

"If it happens over the city, yes," Martin admitted. "But it's the lesser evil to hundreds of people being blown up. Anyway, I'm hoping it won't come to that, and that the buzzing will be sufficient to do the trick."

"Even so, there's going to be big trouble in it for me. The buzzing of the castle by itself will bring the wrath of the civil aviation boys down on me so much that I'll never get another pilot's license."

"The Palestinian attack is going to take place immediately afterwards," Martin said. "Who's going to blame you for your action in saving all those lives?"

"That's assuming the attack does take place." Philip stopped and looked at Martin. "No, don't get me wrong. But say their plans don't work out for some reason? So the only attack that takes place is mine? I'm in it up to my neck—you as well. And there'll be no one to bail us out."

Martin felt a bitter stab of disappointment. It wasn't just the fact that his plan was now in jeopardy, but the thought that Colin Raymond would have shown no hesitation in taking on such a challenge, if he believed the cause was just. Physically, Philip might have been cast in the mold of his father; missing was that indefinable spark, the spirit of the adventurer, that had sustained the squadron in 1944.

However, he was calm when he said, "I'm sorry I can't offer you any reassurance. If the whole thing was risk-proof, I could have found dozens of people to do it for five thousand pounds."

Philip leaned forward and said awkwardly, "But—well —you might not be in a position to pay up afterwards if

121

anything went wrong. What I mean—it's the bird-in-the-hand business. . . ."

Disappointment suddenly turned to surprise, and then relief. So it was the money. Well, a mercenary hero would serve his purpose just as well as one motivated by humanitarian zeal.

"I'll send you an open check tomorrow for the full five thousand," Martin said. "You can cash it right away."

Philip's reaction was a mixture of enthusiasm and embarrassment. "Well, in that case I'll be happy to do it. It's not just the money—but I do have commitments, and things aren't too easy at the moment."

"That's perfectly understandable," Martin said. "So we can consider the matter settled." He held out his hand and, after a second's hesitation, Philip shook it. "The next thing I have to do is get the aircraft itself fixed up. I must be on my way."

They made their way into the street, Philip's step noticeably jaunty as they headed for the garage.

"This is one hell of an exciting prospect, Mr. Martin. In the service everything we did was by the book. You went where the flight plan and ground control told you, and you made your attack looking at the instruments and the radar screen. Most occasions you never got a visual on the target. But this—well, it's real seat-of-the-pants stuff, isn't it? Find your target, straight in, and wallop! Just what it must have been like in your time."

"It won't be straightforward," Martin warned him. "No doubt the RAF will come sniffing around you as soon as you appear on the radar. You've got to get past them somehow."

"From what you say, they won't chance shooting down the Palestinian plane even when they can see where it's headed. They're hardly likely to do anything drastic to a private plane that's simply strayed off the course."

As they walked up the path to the bungalow, Philip glanced several times over his shoulder toward the road. He opened the door with his key and said, "That's funny—"

A shrill voice echoed along the hall. "I suppose you've had a skinful again! Well, you can go in the other room tonight. I'm not having you breathing your stinking beer fumes all over me."

Even in the yellow light of the hall, Martin could see the pink embarrassment on Philip's face.

He said quickly, "I'm sorry, we've obviously woken your wife. Nothing more annoying when you've just dropped off to sleep. It's time I was off, anyway. I have to get on with some work first thing in the morning." As he headed for the door, Martin added, "You were just saying something was strange."

"What? Oh—yes." Philip opened the front door. "There's a car parked along the road, just past the filling station. I noticed it was there when we went out. I'm sure there are a couple of people in it, but I can't see why they've stopped in that particular spot. A courting couple would find somewhere off the road."

Martin had no doubts about who the occupants of the car might be and swore under his breath. "I might have guessed they'd be following me. Look, do you have a car I could borrow? I'll leave mine here with you."

"Sure. It's just behind the office. We'll go out the back door so they can't see us."

It was a large Humber Snipe, about fifteen years old.

"I use it for taxi work," Philip said. "It's largely held together with fiberglass filler, but it moves all right."

"This will do fine," Martin told him. "You can use mine as you wish. We'll swop them back the next time I see you."

"Won't do the business any harm for me to be seen with a Rover," Philip said with a grin. "I'll tell you what: I'll take yours now and drive a mile or so up the road. See if they follow me. It'll give you a chance to drive off in the other direction."

"As long as you don't mind. But listen—they're dangerous people. Don't try any funny business with them." As they exchanged keys, Martin said, "I'll keep in touch with you, but I can't trust private phones. Are you in the Sportsman most evenings?"

"Between eight and ten."

"I'll ring you there if I have to." Might as well take a leaf out of Boulin's book.

Philip switched on the Rover's engine, put the headlights on full, then drove at speed off the forecourt and swung onto the road. The headlamps briefly illuminated a yellow sedan parked without lights on the grass verge.

123

Martin could only marvel at Philip's eyesight: he wouldn't have spotted it at all. As he watched, the yellow car's lights came on and it pulled onto the road to follow the Rover.

Martin climbed into the Humber. Everything seemed awkward and heavy after his own car, but the engine started first time. The body vibrated, and a hollow booming sound, which shattered the night air, gave every indication of a corroded exhaust.

As he drove down the forecourt, a window of the bungalow was thrown open. In his mirror he saw a curler-wrapped head mouthing violently after him. Clearly Carol Raymond wanted to know where her husband was driving to at this time of the night.

He turned onto the road and headed for Clarkside. It was up to Philip to offer an explanation to his wife. Not, he imagined, that any explanation would be acceptable in her present frame of mind.

Clarkside was deserted as Martin drove through the main street, pushing the Humber up to its maximum speed, which revealed itself to be sixty miles per hour. He kept a constant eye on the mirror. If Koster's men were in that car, they could be after him in a very short time once Philip's bluff was revealed.

But the mirror remained comfortingly dark, and by the time he reached the M6 he knew for certain he was not being followed.

The Humber chugged along the inside lane, its exhaust rattling and worn shock absorbers causing the car to pitch and sway each time it passed over a bump in the road. The tank was full, however, and he was able to pick up the M1 and get through London without stopping.

The exhaust noise became worse as time went on. Leaving London on the A2 he could hear the pipe banging against the underside of the car. He had travelled two miles along the road, with twenty to go, when the exhaust fell off altogether. There was a clattering, screeching sound and a shower of sparks spread out across the road. He braked and the sound stopped abruptly. He got out and found the exhaust and silencer unit lying in the road behind the car. It was rusted through and beyond even a temporary repair.

Martin kicked the metal into the ditch and went to study the car. The engine was still running and exhaust fumes were drifting from all round the body. He couldn't hope to complete his journey in it without risking carbon-monoxide poisoning. The headlights picked up a sign indicating a lay-by half a mile ahead. He climbed in and drove to it with all the windows open.

By the time he reached the lay-by he was almost choking and suffering from a feeling of nausea. Gratefully he turned off the engine.

He walked up and down the lay-by until the sickness diminished and then he applied his mind to the problem of getting home. There must be a telephone box or a farmhouse somewhere in the area.

Hearing the sound of a car in the distance, he put his headlights on full beam, then stood waving his arms in the light as the car approached. At the last moment a thought of sickening irony came to him: what if the car was yellow?

It turned out to be a red Volkswagen driven by a young man, who opened his window and called, "Can I help?"

"Not with the car, I'm afraid," Martin said. "It's beyond hope. But I'd be glad of a lift."

The young man was on his way to a job interview in Maidstone. He insisted on going out of his way to drop Martin at his house and they reached it in half an hour. Wishing him well for the next day, Martin watched him drive off and then walked up the silent path to his house.

Consumed by weariness, he went straight to bed.

The ringing of the telephone took some time to register in his consciousness. As he reached for it, he looked at the alarm clock. Two-thirty.

It was Philip. "The characters in that car—they were after you. I led them a dance for a few miles until they caught me."

"Caught you?" Martin was wide awake now. Philip seemed to be consciously keeping his voice low but he spoke in a tone of suppressed excitement.

"They were pretty bright in the end. When we came to a roundabout they went round it the wrong way and cornered me before I could come off it. Your car took a bit of a knock, I'm afraid. Only body damage."

"What happened?"

"Well, I was stuck with my front wheels on the round-about itself, and three of them jumped out—not two as I thought. I couldn't believe my eyes when I saw one of them had a gun. If I needed any convincing about the truth of your story, this was it. They came toward me and one of them pulled my door open. That put the interior light on, of course, and they stopped in their tracks when they saw my face. One of them—a fellow with a thin, sharp face—said, 'Where is Martin?' I told him I didn't know what the hell he was talking about. I'd just taken this car on trade-in from a bloke named Washington and I wanted to know what he was going to do about this damage. I don't know why I picked Washington. It just came into my head."

"How did they react?"

"One of them looked as though he was going to take a swipe at my face with his gun, but this little guy stopped him. Never said a word. Just led them back to the car, then they turned and headed back the way they'd come."

Martin felt unease in his stomach. "How long ago was this?"

Philip's voice was apologetic. "It must have been just over a couple of hours. I would have called you sooner but—well, when I got back to the bungalow I had a lot of explaining to do to Carol. Not the truth, of course," he added hurriedly, "but something to convince her. We had one of those long, long wrangles—you know. Anyway, I couldn't phone you until she'd gone back to bed and I was sure she was asleep. Then I had to get your number from Directory Inquiries—"

"Thanks," Martin snapped, slamming down the phone as a car changed gear on the road outside. There was a crunch of gravel as it turned into the driveway.

In one sweep he grabbed the clothes he had thrown on the back of a chair, put his feet into his shoes, picked up his watch from the bedside table, then headed for the door. He had reached it when he turned back and quickly pulled the sheets straight on the bed.

The car came to a halt at the front of the house as he raced down the stairs in darkness. He was heading for the kitchen door when he heard feet hurrying to the back of the house along the path at the side. He stopped in the hall and looked round desperately. A key was being inserted into the frontdoor lock.

Under the stairs was the junk cupboard. It had a full-size door, but inside the ceiling tapered as the stairs came down. He stepped into the cupboard, pulling the door shut behind him as they came into the hall. He tried to remember what he had seen with the help of the moonlight coming through the window during the two seconds the cupboard door had been open. The vacuum cleaner straight ahead, some wine bottles on the left, and at the back, the old carpet that used to be in the bedroom.

Doors were being opened and someone hurried up the stairs above him. He could make out Koster's voice snapping instructions. It could only be a matter of minutes before they checked in here. Moving very slowly he made his way to the back, crouching lower as he went. He felt the carpet and eased it out. On his knees now, he crawled beneath it, pushing his bundle of clothing ahead of him. Once he was sure the carpet covered him completely, he lay flat on the floor hoping there would be no obvious bulge.

In a short time he found it difficult to breathe. He also realized he was so completely covered that he would not be able to tell when they opened the door of the cupboard. He solved both problems by moving the carpet so that there was a slight gap by the side wall.

More feet were moving rapidly up and down the stairs. They were clearly determined to root him out if he was in the house. And this time, Martin knew, there would be no warnings or attempts to frighten him. Only his death would satisfy them now.

He seemed to have been waiting for so long, it was almost a relief when the door of the cupboard opened. Koster's voice came from the direction of the kitchen.

"Dieses Haus ist seine einzigste Zuflucht." . .

Something about the house being his only sure refuge.

A voice much closer, obviously the man who was looking in the cupboard, said, *"Da der Wagen nicht hier ist, ist er noch nicht zurückgekommen."*

As there was no sign of the car, they assumed Martin could not have returned yet. The door closed again as Martin silently offered thanks for a rusty exhaust system.

After waiting another ten minutes, Martin finally pulled

himself out from beneath the carpet. Pressing his ear to the wall nearest the hall, he could hear Koster's voice. The German was spelling out rapid instructions. Martin's stomach sank as he gathered the gist of what was being said. They were going to sit tight in the house until Martin returned, no matter when that should be.

He sat on the carpet with his back to the outer wall and wondered what the hell he could do now. Wait until they were asleep, and then slip out? One thing was for sure: they hadn't come here to sleep. They would be listening and watching continuously for the slightest noise or movement.

The initial rushing-about seemed to have stopped. The front door opened and closed, and his heart lifted for a moment. It fell again as he heard the car being backed into the garage. They were going to install themselves properly, so no clue to their presence would be visible outside.

The cold was now penetrating the thin cotton of his pyjamas. He started dressing, moving with deliberation so as to avoid the chance of making any noise. He bundled the pyjamas under the carpet and sat down again to await—what? His mind roved over every possible means of getting out of the house. Some were more practicable than others, but all carried an unacceptable degree of risk.

What the hell have I got myself into, he wondered, that makes me a prisoner in my own home? Am I really crazy?

How would an objective outsider view his actions? Sheila, who, with all her faults, was not lacking in loyalty, had a half-formed impression that he was mentally deranged. Yet everything he had done up to now had a rational basis. There was nothing crazy in trying to forestall an attack which could kill hundreds of people. But that begged the question: how sound was the basic premise? Greta's warning had been the start of it all, confirmed by Lukas—and they had both given their lives in consequence. But the ultimate confirmation was the presence of those men in his house. They intended to kill him, there was no question of that. Hadn't Koster said, on the night of the fire, that his death would no longer be an embarrassment to them? Somehow they knew that the British security services were discounting all his warnings, but they must have decided to make sure of it by removing him from the scene completely.

They were moving about in the kitchen now. He heard the fridge door open as they helped themselves to food, and from the voices he picked up one word. *Wein*. Well, they wouldn't find any wine in his fridge. . . .

In an instant he had thrown himself back beneath the folds of the carpet. Seconds later, the door was flung open. A hand picked up each of the empty bottles and dropped them one by one on the floor.

"Sie sind leer."

The door slammed shut again. The sweat was pouring down Martin's body as he crawled out from beneath his cover. His idiotic complacency had almost cost him his life. He simply dare not relax for one moment. He pulled back sharply as his knees found the pieces from one of the bottles that had broken, and he carefully swept them all to one side.

In his pocket he found his cigarette lighter and he used it to look at his watch. Half an hour had passed since they entered the house.

How he was going to survive the night, he had no idea.

His mind seemed to slip away from the confines of his body as the hours dragged by. The solid darkness contributed to this, as did the need to try to ignore the cold cramps that gripped his leg muscles.

The disembodied feeling was something he had not experienced for many years. He probed his memory for the last occasion. The war . . . flying . . . the time his oxygen mask became disconnected at twenty-nine thousand feet. But that had been a feeling of euphoria, when he knew he was capable of achieving anything he wanted. He decided to test his Spitfire to destruction and put it in a vertical dive at full throttle with the cold, analytical approach of the scientist. It was only at three thousand feet that sufficient oxygen was drawn into his bloodstream to seep into his brain. The airframe was vibrating like a dozen road drills and he had a genuine fear the wings would fold up on him as he fought to pull the plane into level flight.

This feeling was different. It was more akin to watching himself in a dream. He was unimpressed by what he saw. A middle-aged, short-tempered man, inclining to plump-

129

ness, very much out of condition, and with an undistinguished forty-nine years of life behind him. A man who had made a mess of all his personal relationships and without even a wife or children to show for his efforts. A hard worker, yes, but even here was failure, with control of his own business in danger of slipping from his hands.

A shiver ran through his body and he sat up sharply. He had drifted into sleep despite himself. He was shocked, on checking his watch, to see the time was seven o'clock. He could hardly believe it, until he recalled that it was the sound of the letter box that had woken him: presumably the postman with the morning mail.

As he moved away from the wall he was finally convinced. That stiffening of the lumbar muscles could only be the result of sitting in the same posture for several hours. Footsteps came down the stairs and stopped by the front door. That would be his mail being examined.

Minutes later voices came from the direction of the kitchen and he pictured the men preparing breakfast. They wouldn't wax fat on the amount of food in his larder, but right now he would have been glad of a piece of baconrind.

His empty stomach was not the only discomfort he felt. There was a more pressing and immediate demand that had to be met. One of the wine bottles proved an adequate receptacle, and he carefully placed it well to the rear of the cupboard, where there was least danger of its being knocked over.

How long did they intend to stay in occupation? God knew, but the fact was he himself couldn't tolerate the prospect of staying here very much longer.

The obvious thing to do was to get out under cover of darkness. But what if they had the lights on all night? Well, he could pull out the fuse of the lighting circuit. How? By lifting the cover off the black service unit that was fastened to the wall just eighteen inches from his own fat, stupid head.

In the darkness he sat and described himself in every derogatory term he could think of for a full minute. The only excuse for his stupidity was that maybe the intellect became paralyzed by fear.

Using the cigarette lighter he examined the row of fuses. The one marked "lighting circuit" was the second along.

130

He looked at his watch again. Nine o'clock. They wouldn't have the lights on now. He pulled out the fuse and examined it.

It was the straightforward bridge type with a wire running from one screw across to another. All he had to do was break it. The car key in his pocket would do the job . . . but not yet. He would wait until after dark. They must be plunged into unexpected blackness just long enough for him to get out of the house. They were not slow-witted and the most he could allow himself was half a minute before they came down to examine the fuse box.

But even then there must be no reason to suspect that he had been there: they would search the grounds of the house thoroughly without delay if there was the slightest chance of that. The fuse must look as though it had blown accidentally. After a while he saw that the answer lay in his hand. He held the cigarette lighter so that the flame was directed against the fuse-carrier behind the wire. Soon there was a brown mark on the white porcelain that could have been caused by a flash. It was as much as he could do for now. He replaced the fuse and settled down to count off the weary hours of the day.

By the time evening came, Martin felt as though he were suffocating. A slight gap beneath the door was the only source of fresh air and to gain any benefit from that he had to lie flat on his stomach, a position he found too uncomfortable to hold for anything but short periods.

He had planned to leave his escape until the early hours of the morning, when their vigilance should be at its lowest ebb. But by 10:15 he felt he could not face another two or three hours in this foul-smelling trap. He picked himself up, flicked on the lighter, and took hold of the fuse. The fuse carrier came out easily but, Christ, how could he break the wire without a free hand? He dropped the lighter into his pocket and levered the key under the wire. It snapped easily and he went to replace the fuse carrier. Where was the damn box? The lighter. Of course it wouldn't bloody-well light the first time. There. Shove the fuse back. Now to get out.

There were feet moving about upstairs as he picked up the neck of the broken bottle and opened the cupboard door. The air made him light-headed and his limbs felt detached. The footsteps were at the top of the stairs and the beam of a torch sliced down into the hall.

Martin pushed open the door into the kitchen and blinked at the moonlight shining through the glass of the door leading into the back garden. But for that he would not have seen the stool that stood in his path. He made his way round it and grasped the handle of the back door. The thought flashed through his mind that here were two dangers: he might be heard unlocking it, and he had no way of relocking it once he had gone out. But Koster's men had simply left it on the latch. It opened as soon as he pushed down the handle.

The footsteps had reached the hall as he stepped into the garden and silently eased the door shut behind him. He ran swiftly across the grass to the bottom of the garden, sheltering in the shadow of the rhododendrons that marked the border of the garden. He glanced back at the house. No shouts. No doors opening.

He hauled himself over the fence that led into the meadow belonging to Askew's farm, then walked swiftly round the perimeter until he reached the gate leading to the road.

As he stepped onto the firm asphalt, he glanced back in time to see a light come on in the house.

As he walked into the Greyhound, Martin was surprised to find it was still open and busy.

He stood in the small lobby that connected the bar with the lounge, conscious of his dishevelled appearance and so hesitant to enter either. He was relieved to see Michael coming down the stairs into the lobby.

"Evening, Mr. Martin," the landlord greeted him. "Haven't seen you for a while."

"I've come to ask a favor," Martin said. "It's difficult to explain, but my house is uninhabitable at the moment. Can you put me up?"

"Surely." He looked at Martin more closely. "You seem a bit the worse for wear, if you don't mind me saying so. Why don't you go and have a wash—second door on the left upstairs—then come down and have a drink. I'll get the good lady to cook a meal for you as well."

"Marvellous," Martin told him. "You've singled out the

132

three things I'm desperate for—and in the right order." He was experiencing a small glow of triumph at the way he had outwitted Koster.

When he came down again, washed although still unshaven, Michael met him in the lobby.

"I'll be throwing everyone out in about five minutes, but you can relax. By the way, Mr. Martin, remember the other week when you were in here with poor old Fred and I was telling you about those foreigners?"

"What about them?"

"I thought you'd like to know one of them is in the lounge right now. Perhaps you can ask him why he was nosing around the way he was."

Martin's throat was tight as he said, "Where exactly?"

"Far corner beyond the fireplace. Drinking gin and lemon."

They were standing just short of the open door to the lounge. On the wall inside was a large mirror advertising Bass. It gave a good view of the interior of the room.

Martin turned back toward the staircase and said quietly, "Look, Michael, would you bring a drink up to me in my room?"

"What about your meal?"

"That too, if you wouldn't mind."

He went upstairs leaving a puzzled Michael looking after him. In his room he shut the door and then sat on the bed. His heart was beating fiercely and his whole body was damp. He had been within seconds of walking into that lounge, straight into Koster's view. What the hell was he doing here? Surely he hadn't discovered Martin's escape from the house already and . . .

Calm down. They didn't know he had ever been in the house. But they had reason to believe he would be coming back, and that was what it was all about. Not only did they have the house staked out, but they were watching the pub he was known to use, just in case he came here first.

When Michael came in with a bottle of whisky on a tray and a glass, Martin said, "You gathered I don't want to see that character downstairs. If he should ask you, would you tell him you haven't seen me?"

"He's already asked."

"What?"

"Before you arrived. I told him we hadn't seen you for some time. But I'll remember, Mr. Martin. Your presence here is confidential to me—and the wife, of course. She'll be up in a minute with some liver and onions. That all right?"

"Couldn't be better. Then I'll get myself to bed. I'm just about ready for it."

He wolfed the meal and restricted himself to three double Scotches, despite the temptation to finish the bottle.

When he climbed into the large warm bed, sleep came almost immediately. He awoke the next morning at seven with a clear head and a feeling of general relaxation.

Then he applied himself to the problem of what he should now use as his base. Not only his house but the pub was out of the question now. What about the works? There must be an obscure storeroom where he could rig up a camp bed. But he wouldn't be able to keep his presence there a secret for long. It had to be somewhere else.

He looked at the date on his watch. The first. Just fourteen days to go.

12

The lorry drove in through the gates of the Martin Engineering works. Only when it was parked behind the office block did Martin part the tarpaulin screen covering the back and jump to the ground.

"Thanks, Harry," he called to the driver.

"You're welcome, Mr. Martin." The mystified driver watched him walk into the offices.

Sheila looked at Martin uncertainly as he walked past her.

"Are you in today?" she asked.

"In?"

"To callers, I mean. When you phoned for the lorry to bring you here from the pub, I thought you were going to pick up the reins again."

He shook his head. "Not for the moment. Everything's going smoothly enough, isn't it? Well, we'll let things carry on that way."

"It depends what you mean by smooth. Mr. Harris is doing his nut about all this overtime. He's been pestering the life out of me to tell him where you were. I said I had no idea." She added pointedly, "And for once I was telling the truth."

Martin flicked through the papers on his desk. One of the telephone messages read "Call Boulin."

"He's been on several times," Sheila said. "As well as another chap who wouldn't leave his name. He's rung about four times."

"What did he sound like?"

"Young. Fast-talking. Said it was to do with your car."

Philip. He must be worried at not having heard any-

135

thing since warning Martin about Koster's coming. At that moment the phone rang.

Sheila answered it, then looked at Martin. "It's Boulin."

"Tell him I'll call him back as soon as I can," Martin said. "Later this morning."

As he walked out of the office, she put down the phone and called after him, "Where will I be able to contact you?"

"You won't need to," he told her. "I'll do any contacting that's necessary."

He headed away from the main gate, toward a smaller gate in the perimeter fence; it was always locked, but he had a key. Once outside he took the footpath that led across the fields to the housing estate at Bidwell. After five minutes he turned off the path and headed across the field, walking parallel to the main road. Finally he completed the square by turning toward the road and coming out opposite the entrance to Molyneux Grange.

There was no one in sight as he crossed the road and followed the tree-lined gravel path that wound its way to the house and to the hangar beyond.

His eyes searched the interior gloom but there was no sign of Mike Lowe. There were three aircraft in residence —the Camel, the Spitfire, and the Tiger Moth. They stood silent on the oil-stained concrete and what struck him, not for the first time, was their look of incredible frailty . . . the frailty of a timid-looking girl who, when provoked, could reveal a whiplash tongue and a steel-like strength.

He was about to try the office that led off the hangar when he saw a movement in the rear cockpit of the Moth. Mike was doubled up and his overalled posterior poked above the edge. As Martin approached he heard a stream of muttered, calculated curses pouring upwards.

"Looking for the sky-hooks, Mike?"

The engineer struggled into a normal position, pushing the long black hair from his eyes.

"Hello, Mr. Martin. These bloody rudder bars. I'm trying to fit new ones but the problem is getting the old 'uns off first."

Martin said, "Made to last, obviously."

Mike lowered himself to the ground. "Be no fun if it

136

was too easy, I suppose. How are you keeping, Mr. Martin?"

"Not too bad. I'm thinking of taking a break from work, as it happens."

Martin walked slowly toward the doorway and Mike fell into step alongside him.

"Oh, yes? Holiday abroad?"

"Nothing like that. Just leaving things alone for a few days. You live in the Grange, don't you, Mike? Do you have much space to spare in there?"

"We've got a flat at the back. The rest of the house is empty."

"That's what I thought. Look, would it be inconvenient for you if I was to move into the house? I'm thinking of taking just one room for a couple of weeks. It shouldn't interfere with your domestic arrangements, but I thought I'd mention it out of courtesy."

They were in the open now and Mike was looking at him curiously. "None of the rooms are furnished. They're not really fit for living in as they are."

"I realize that. I'll be bringing a camp bed and things."

"How about food? You're welcome to eat with us. Two snacks and one meal a day. Wife's a fair cook."

"I didn't intend to cause any trouble—"

"No bother. Make a change to see a different face across the table. What's going on, Mr. Martin?"

Martin had prepared his answer during the walk across the fields. "I've a few problems at the moment. Business and personal. A lot of people are bothering me and I want to get away from them while I sort things out in my mind."

"I understand," said Mike, who didn't but had the NCO's instinctive knowledge of when not to probe too deeply into a superior officer's affairs. "That means you won't want anyone to know you're here?"

"That's right."

"How about your secretary?"

Martin shook his head. "I'd rather no one but you and Mrs. Lowe knew about it."

Mike nodded and started walking toward the house. "May as well go and tell the wife."

Eileen Lowe was a small, pink-cheeked woman whom

137

Martin knew slightly from the occasions when she served afternoon tea at the trustees' meetings. Her cool gray eyes showed no surprise when Mike told her of Martin's proposal.

"You're welcome to share our meals, Mr. Martin," she said in a slight Scots accent. "The first thing, though, is to sort out a suitable room for yourself."

She led him up the stairs to the south-facing wing of the house. At the end of the corridor she opened the door into a large bare room with a window looking out onto the back of the house. There was a fireplace that had clearly not been used for many years.

"You'll be better off at the back of the house," she said as she walked over and opened the window. "Mike starts work early in the mornings, you see, and if he's testing an engine it can be noisy. Now about your sleeping arrangements: we do have a camp bed, which you're welcome to."

"That would save me the bother of buying one," Martin said. "Thanks a lot."

"Bedding. I can lend you that as well. We keep it for when our son Alfred comes to stay in the summer."

"I'm putting you out, I'm afraid. You must let me pay for this, of course."

"We'll settle that at the end of your stay," she said. "Lunch is at one—only a snack. The main meal is in the evening."

Martin nodded. "I'd also like to use your telephone if I may. I'll note all the calls I make and reimburse you for them."

"The easiest way is to ask the operator to advise duration of call," she said as she led him downstairs. "That way there can be no misunderstandings."

Clearly Mrs. Lowe was level-headed when it came to money matters, and it was an approach that suited Martin.

She left him in the lounge with the telephone. "I'll give you a shout when lunch is ready," she told him, then carefully closed the door as though to emphasize he need have no worries about eavesdropping.

Boulin sounded relieved to hear from him. "No one

138

knew what had happened to you, my friend. I was a little worried, I have to say. You are all right?"

"I'm all right, Boulin. Have you any news for me?"

"Are you calling from your office?"

"No. This phone is safe."

"The deal is completed. The aircraft is standing by on a civil airfield in Tunisia, fuelled and ready to fly."

Martin gave a whistle. "Boulin, you're a genius. I knew you could work quickly when you had to, but this is your best performance yet. Now there must be some paper-work we have to do—"

"That also is complete. It cost a little money, which I will add to your bill. But it means that all you need now is a qualified pilot. Did you manage to find one?"

Martin told him about Philip and promised to call again with final confirmation of the date and time the air-craft would be collected.

Before ringing off, Boulin said, "My friend, you sound as though you are under much strain. I do not know what you propose to do, or why you are doing it. But I know your motive must be a noble one, so God will be with you."

Boulin rarely did anything without first pinning a price-ticket firmly to it. It was curiously moving to hear what seemed a note of genuine concern in the Frenchman's voice.

Next Martin called Philip at the garage.

"You said you'd be in touch," the pilot said accusingly. "You also promised to send a check."

"I'm sorry about that. It will definitely be in the post today. How soon can you travel to Tunisia and pick up the aircraft?"

Philip was still disgruntled. "A deal is a deal, and this was cash in advance."

"You'll get your money. Tomorrow morning, I prom-ise," Martin said wearily.

"That's good enough for me, Mr. Martin. Tunisia, did you say? I'm ready to go whenever you like. You want it delivered to the Molyneux place?"

"That's the idea. The flight plan and customs clearances will be ready and waiting for you in Tunisia. Tell me how soon you can leave, and I'll book an outward flight."

"Tomorrow, if you like. Can I use your Rover? I can reach Heathrow in a couple of hours with that."

"All right. By the way, I'm having a new exhaust fitted to your car. It gave up the ghost, I'm afraid. I'll call you back in half an hour."

He then telephoned the agency that Sheila used for his overseas trips and made a one-way booking to Tunis for the following day. The cost would, as usual, be charged to the Martin Engineering account.

"That's fine," Philip said when Martin rang back with the details. "I'll start packing immediately. I must say I'm looking forward to a bit of sunshine. Thanks for the opportunity, Mr. Martin."

After confirming with Boulin the time of Philip's arrival in Tunisia, Martin rang Sheila at the office.

"Can you get out one of the emergency checks," he said. In a locked drawer she kept half a dozen blank checks already signed by him. "Make it out to Philip Raymond, and send it to him at Marchant's Garage, Solihull Road, Clarkside, West Midlands."

There was a pause, then Sheila said coldly, "That's not a very satisfactory way of doing things, especially for someone I've never heard of. How much is it for?"

"Five thousand pounds."

The pause this time was much longer. Then, in a choked voice, Sheila said, "I'm responsible for the safe custody of these checks. How can you ask me to make one out for an amount like that?"

"I'm not asking you, Sheila," he said shortly. "I'm telling you. Five thousand pounds. And get it in the post today." He slammed down the phone.

What annoyed her, he knew, was not the amount of the check but the fact that she didn't know what was going on. Recent events and a lack of explanation for them must have left her boiling with frustration.

There was a knock at the door and Mrs. Lowe told him it was time for lunch.

Over a cheese salad, Mike said casually, "I suppose the other trustees know about your staying here?"

"This is an informal arrangement," Martin said. "As I explained, you're the only people who need to know about it."

140

Mike and his wife exchanged glances. "Not even Mr. Henshaw?"

Martin said evenly, "There's no need to bother him about a trivial matter like this." After a moment he added, "I'll probably mention it to him at the next trustees' meeting."

Mrs. Lowe had already made up the camp bed in his room and that night he lay awake, turning matters over in his mind. Over the next ten days he and Philip had to work out with extreme precision the final details of the operational plan. Timing was crucial. He knew the ETA of the Palestinians. The problem was deciding which airfield the Hunter should use and devising a schedule which would take it over the castle at, say, thirty minutes before the attack. Armament? Boulin had said that was included. It would need to be checked out carefully once the Hunter arrived at Molyneux. And what would Mike Lowe have to say when he found his latest exhibit was carrying live ammunition? Martin sighed. He would worry about that when the time came.

Boulin had commented on the strain he seemed to be showing. Martin put it down to tension, the feeling that developed during the buildup to a wartime op. The adrenaline wasn't flowing yet but it was there, ready to be released when the time came.

He slept soundly, and part of the next day he spent exploring the grounds of Molyneux. The wooded acres surrounding the airstrip were barred to the public, even on open days, and they teemed with wildlife that had adapted happily to the noise of aircraft engines. It was hard to recall the last time he had felt such a sense of personal freedom, even temporarily. Normally he would have been concerned about some aspect of the business, even when things were going well.

Now he found it difficult to relate to Martin Engineering in any way at all. In fact, he surprised himself by realizing that he would be quite happy never to see the inside of the place again. Recent events had brought a new sense of perspective to bear on his life. Twenty years he had spent building up a business that had him working harder now, with more worries, than when he started. As the years passed, the need to run faster in order to stand still was so pressing that there had never been time to take stock of the surrounding treadmill.

His vanity might be appeased by the upward climb of production and profit graphs, especially in view of the pessimistic prophecies that had been showered on him when he started. What else was there? Money? He could sell out tomorrow and have more than enough capital for the rest of his life. Job satisfaction? That only came with a job well done, and he never seemed to be finished with the bloody job.

Walking through a clearing in the ash trees with bracken up to his knees and a scuttling bright gray sky above, he had the feeling that comes on leaving a sickbed after several weeks. The legs are weak, but the world has a newly washed look that almost blinds eyes conditioned to the shaded patterns of bedroom walls.

Logically, he saw that, once this fleeting euphoria passed, he would eventually be drawn back into the company that represented an investment of two decades of life. But things would never be quite the same again: the dedication had diminished and work would more obviously be a burden.

Philip telephoned from Tunis the next day.

"I won't be leaving today. The red tape hasn't all been unravelled yet." His voice sounded cheerful on the crackling line. "With luck it could be tomorrow. In the meantime they've put me up in a quite decent hotel."

"If you don't seem to be getting anywhere, let me know," Martin reassured him. "I might be able to pull some strings through our French agent."

The news came as no real surprise to him. If there were going to be snags they would most likely occur at that end, where he had no personal contact or control. He was not unduly worried. Such complications were endemic in the Middle East and often were finally resolved by some time-honored palm-greasing. He would have to rely on Boulin's agents to come up with the right prescription.

The following day he rang Sheila. "Has Boulin been trying to contact me, about some snags with one of our Middle East contracts?"

Sheila almost exploded. "So there you are! No, Boulin hasn't been looking for you, but every policeman south of Birmingham has. Where on earth are you? I'm sure they think I'm lying when I say I don't know your whereabouts."

"Calm down for a moment," Martin cut in. "What police? Why do they want me?"

"Ask them yourself. They don't confide in me any more than you do. It's the West Midlands police, that's all I know. Here." She scrabbled for a piece of paper. "Detective Sergeant Langley at Bilsden two-two-nine-two."

"I thought you said the West Midlands police."

"They've asked the local police to pick you up. Isn't it about time you came down to earth, Mr. Martin, and told us what you're up to? It's not fair on the person who has to cover up for you all the time."

"There's nothing to cover up, Sheila, and I hope you haven't been giving the police that impression. I'll speak to them now and sort things out."

It was probably the abandoned Humber they were checking on. He'd forgotten all about that until he had spoken to Philip. But it was outside the West Midlands area that he had left it. And wasn't Langley with Special Branch?

When he phoned he said to Langley, "I'll come down and see you at the station now, if you wish."

"If that would be convenient," the sergeant said with exaggerated politeness. "I'll be waiting."

Transport was the problem. His own car was at Heathrow and he had no intention of going to the works to pick up one there. Finally, he asked Mike, who willingly gave him the use of his old Morris 1100.

He saw Sergeant Langley in a small, bare interview room, furnished only with two chairs and a battered table. In the center of the table there was a tin ashtray that had been used for years but never properly cleaned. The room itself gave the same impression.

"We've been looking for you over the past two days," the sergeant said as he sat on the other side of the table and opened a notebook. "You don't seem to have been at home."

Had there been any trace of the Koster occupation when they called at the house? "I've been around and about," he said. "When did you go to the house?"

"The first time was seven o'clock yesterday morning.

The constable reported no sign of anyone being in residence."

"You start early in the day. Yes, I was away the previous night. In my business I travel around a lot."

Langley nodded, then said, "You know a Mrs. Raymond, of Solihull Road, Clarkside?"

"I've met her, but it's her husband I know. Why?"

"She reported to the police that, in the early hours of yesterday, three men broke into her home and threatened her. They wanted to know where her husband was."

Martin's mouth had gone dry. "Did she tell them?"

Langley studied him pensively for a moment. "Was there any reason why she shouldn't?"

"I don't know. Mr. Raymond is working for me at present, as you no doubt know."

"Mrs. Raymond told us that you had sent him abroad. Tunisia."

Martin said, "Did she tell them the same?" The detective nodded. "How did she describe the men?"

"I have no details on that. The West Midlands police simply asked me to check out this one aspect."

Martin took a deep breath. "I've very good reasons for thinking these are the same men who assaulted me on the way from Heathrow."

"The German agents?" Langley pronounced the words distinctly as though in inverted commas.

"It fits in with everything I told you. The business I'm involved with—they wanted me to leave it alone. Clearly, they assumed Philip Raymond was concerned as well . . . and they were going to give him the same treatment."

"Is he concerned with the matter you were talking about?"

Martin hesitated. "He's simply gone to collect an aircraft for the Molyneux Museum. But they're suspicious of everything involving me. I think I should tell you they were at my house again last week." The detective remained silent and Martin went on, "They occupied the house, in fact, waiting for me. I hid from them in a cupboard and then I slipped away."

The long silence that followed was finally broken by Langley. "You didn't report this incident to the police?" There were the inverted commas again, around the word "incident."

144

"What was the bloody point?" Martin's fury boiled in his voice. "You've never believed a damn thing I've told you up to now. Is it any wonder that I've washed my hands of you and your flat-footed, Gilbert and Sullivan police force?" He glared at the sergeant. "But when some woman in the West Midlands makes a complaint about three men asking questions, you start running about like blue-arsed flies."

Langley said, "When a woman is roughed up by men breaking into her home, we do take it seriously. Even to the extent of questioning her husband's employer."

"Why? You don't think I did it?"

"If the husband is sent away suddenly, leaving the coast clear for these men, we want to know why. At least we want to make sure it's a genuine errand." He smiled slightly. "Although I think our Midlands colleagues are taking things too far. Such an elaborate setup wouldn't be justified by the proceeds from a run-down filling station."

"They weren't after money—"

"They were. They took"—Langley consulted his note-book—"forty-seven pounds away with them, representing the day's takings of the filling station. They were straightforward criminals, Mr. Martin, with no other interest except acquiring money—which they did." He wrote briefly in the notebook. "Anyway, you can confirm that you did arrange for Mr. Raymond to go away for a few days on business. That it was a genuine errand and"—the glint in his eye contradicted the solemnity of his voice—"you did not arrange thereupon for three men to force their way in and rob Mrs. Raymond of forty-seven pounds."

"I don't suppose Mrs. Raymond thinks it's funny," Martin said sullenly.

"Nor do I, Mr. Martin." He closed the notebook. "Thanks for coming in. I'll pass this information on to West Midlands, and I don't think you'll be bothered any more."

Martin didn't linger. A feeling of unease was growing in his mind. Taking the money had just been surface dressing for the benefit of the police, he was sure. He drove as fast as he could out of the town, deciding on impulse to head for the office. If what he feared was in fact happening, there was no point now in lying low. Philip

145

would almost certainly have given his wife an outline of what he was doing.

"Get hold of Boulin!" he barked to Sheila as he strode into the office.

She held up the receiver. "He's on now, trying to get hold of you."

He slammed the door of his office shut and picked up his own receiver.

The Frenchman was not his usual ebullient self. "I have some bad news, my friend."

"I suspected as much," Martin said grimly. "Let's have it."

"The aircraft finally made its take-off three hours ago. It was just crossing the coast and gaining height when it exploded. Several witnesses have testified to it."

"He's dead?"

"My agent is positive. I am very sorry."

He saw Philip only in terms of that bungalow and the grimy lounge of the Sportsman. It was hard to visualize him climbing high over white sand and Mediterranean breakers, then being torn apart by an exploding turbine. It had always offended him when, during the war, people talked about a "clean" death, as though the violent separation of spirit from body could ever be anything but filthy and detestable. Yet it had to be preferable to an eternity telescoped into minutes as one fought desperately and vainly to escape from a burning aircraft hurtling earthwards.

"You're a bloody crook, Boulin. I paid you top money for that plane, and you come up with a flying rubbish heap. That man's death is on your slate."

"The aircraft was in first-class condition and I have the documents to verify that," Boulin replied. "This matter distresses me as much—"

"Documents! You said they were all taken care of, but Philip was delayed for two days. Why was that, Boulin? Come on, let's have the alibi!"

The Frenchman's voice was soft. "I understand your emotion, and I share it. As to the reason for the delay—well, there I am at a loss. Everything—I swear to this—everything had been taken care of. Yet for some reason certain alleged complications arose. I say alleged, because my agent tells me there was no real basis for them. He cleared them up, but it took that much extra time to do so. That is all I know at the moment."

Martin could find nothing more to say. There was no anger, no bitterness left. Only an intense depression and a feeling of futility that swallowed every other emotion.

"Thanks, Boulin."

He carefully replaced the phone and stared at the wall. The office now had a constricting, claustrophobic atmosphere in relation to the bizarre adventure—no other way to describe it—in which he had become involved. He tried to be honest in his self-analysis. In the beginning, circumstances had driven him into this role, to which he was ill-suited and which he was reluctant to adopt. Why, then, did it now absorb him so much? Because it was a straightforward personal challenge, of the kind he had faced in business for years, but with a much greater reward: credit for saving several hundred lives, no less.

Or was it that? Wouldn't the saving of those lives simply be a bonus on top of the basic satisfaction of inflicting a defeat on Koster and the people he represented?

I'm a selfish, arrogant bastard. What about Philip? That poor sod has given his life for this. And his widow —what must she be feeling?

Oh, God, she won't know yet. Someone's got to go and tell her.

13

"Let me get this straight," said Blair in genuine puzzlement. "You hired a pilot and a jet fighter to carry out a dummy attack on the castle—at the start of the conference?"

"It's a measure of my desperation," Martin said, mustering all the sincerity he could into his voice. "When a man sacrifices his money and his business to carry out an operation like this, doesn't it prove something about his motives?"

Blair knocked the tobacco out of his pipe. "No one's ever questioned your motives, Mr. Martin. Only your judgement."

"But can't you see this latest development only confirms my judgement?" Martin almost banged the desk in his frustration. "I've told you of all the efforts made to persuade me to keep out of the matter. All right, you can put them down to coincidence, imagination, even drunkenness—whatever you like. But now there's a dead man in the picture. Philip Raymond was killed, blown up in his plane. Why?" He waited, but Blair carried on filling his pipe in silence. Martin leaned across the desk. "Because he was the man who was going to frustrate the Palestinian attack."

Blair put a match to his newly filled pipe and said, "So these—East German agents knew what you planned to do?"

"Obviously. At least they must have guessed what we were up to."

Blair shrugged. "Even we never imagined you could be planning anything as outlandish as a pre-emptive strike, I

148

suppose you'd call it. You're crediting your German friends with a remarkable degree of prescience."

Martin gave a snort. "I'm crediting them with nothing more than a normal degree of common sense. They knew I'd been to see Philip Raymond. They found out he was a pilot and that I'd sent him to Tunisia to bring back a plane at my own expense. Even if they couldn't guess precisely what we were planning, they deduced it was meant to interfere with their own plans. So they took the necessary steps. It would be no problem to them to arrange the sabotage of that aircraft. Not only does that remove Philip Raymond from the scene, but it wipes me out too, financially."

Blair stood up and walked round to the other side of the desk so that he stood directly in front of Martin. Any trace of geniality was now gone from his features.

"It's clear now, Martin, that you're not just unbalanced. You're dangerous. On the basis of what you've told me about your lunatic scheme, I could have you prosecuted for conspiracy. I'm not going to, simply because it would be a messy business and we have more important matters to concern us." He walked over and opened the door. "Just get out, will you? And if I'm pestered by you again, or hear you're trying to organize any other stunt to interfere with the conference, then I won't hesitate. You'll be locked up, at least until the conference is over."

Martin's eyebrows went up, but Blair hadn't finished. "We could bury you alive for months if we wanted and never cause the slightest comment. As it is, I'm doubtful as to the wisdom of letting you go now. You'd better be on your way before I start thinking seriously about where my duty lies."

Martin stood and walked silently out and into the corridor. He turned as Blair was closing the door and said, "After next week a lot of people will know where your duty lay—and how you were too blind and stupid to know it for yourself."

Blair closed the door with the nearest to a slam that a civil servant could manage and still retain his dignity. Martin made his way to the street with disgust and anger boiling inside him. Philip had died in a blazing explosion under the Middle Eastern sun, and those shiny-suited bastards just wrote him off as a crank. What would it take to convince them?

"I've done all I damn well can," he said aloud, gaining a suspicious look from the doorman, who had not been happy about him from the start. If the people who were paid to protect the country refused to move off their backsides, how could one man do anything? He'd tried every possible thing he could think of. But there had to come a point when there was no option but to face defeat and accept it. He had reached that point now.

The realization should have brought some degree of relief with it. But calling on Blair on his way to collect the car from Heathrow had, he realized, been a subconscious excuse for delaying the worst part, which was yet to come.

He climbed into the Rover and headed toward the M1 and Clarkside.

The car ahead of him moved off the forecourt and Martin edged forward.

"How many?" asked Mrs. Raymond.

"Fill it up, please. It should take ten."

She showed no sign of recognizing him as she held the nozzle in position. Martin had called in at the Sportsman and downed two stiff whiskies, but they weren't doing him much good.

He waited until she had finished. Then, as he handed her the money, he said, "We met the other evening, Mrs. Raymond. I'm Alec Martin."

She looked at him in surprise. "Oh—you arranged that job for Philip."

"That's right. I have something to talk to you about."

"I had to go to the police, you know," she said accusingly. "These men came and pushed me around. It was to do with that job—they knew Philip would be away."

"I heard about that and I'm sorry. But there's something else. Could we go inside and talk?"

"I can't leave the pumps," she said. "You'll have to talk here."

There was an office, not much bigger than a telephone box, on the island between the pumps. She sat down on the stool and looked at him.

"It's bad news, I'm afraid," he said after a while. "Philip has had an accident. He's dead."

150

She stared at him. "Are you sure? When? What happened?"

"It was a flying accident. Early this morning."

"Oh, no." She seemed to slump on the stool, her eyes on the ground. "Poor Philip."

He said, "We'd better go inside. I'll make you some tea."

Later she silently sipped from the cup as he explained that the aircraft Philip was flying had gone out of control, for a reason that had not yet been established. There had been no chance of his escaping and death had been instantaneous.

"You'll want to know about compensation," he went on. "It's difficult to say yet what that will amount to, but certainly it will be substantial."

It really amounted to how much he could raise himself. Mrs. Raymond showed no reaction to what he was saying. Her eyes were dry although they seemed out of focus. She sat upright in the armchair, nursing the tea cup with her hands.

After a while she said quietly, "We loved each other, Philip and I. You might not have thought so, Mr. Martin, but we did."

"I don't doubt it."

"That doesn't mean we were happy. We should never have got married, you see, but for the baby. . . . Philip didn't belong to a place like this. You must have realized that."

"He seemed determined to make a go of this business. He knew you can't have all you want right away. You have to work for it."

"I don't mean just the filling station. I mean this place, my family, even me. His background was so different and this must have been a come-down for him. We should never have come here. He should have left me and gone back to the things and places—the people he really knew."

Her voice was more firm than it had been when he heard her speak to Philip. The deadness had gone from it and there was a new, purposeful strength in her manner.

She turned and looked directly at Martin. "I'm glad it happened this way, though. It broke his heart when he left the service and I always hoped he would go back."

Martin nodded. "I think he might have done, some-day."

"Well, it was almost the same thing, wasn't it?" she asked with a knowing expression. "I don't pretend to know about this top secret business, but I could guess what was going on."

"Could you?"

"It was the things he didn't tell me, as much as any-thing. It's pretty clear now. You've given me the official version, but I wouldn't expect to be told any more."

Nervously, he said, "The next thing I have to do is tell his stepmother. I'd better be on my way as it's quite a distance."

As he stood up she asked him if he knew Mrs. Ray-mond.

"I've spoken to her on the telephone."

"She's a difficult woman. If you want, I'll tell her."

"Really?" he said, surprised. "I thought you and she were . . ."

"We're not friendly in any sense of the word. But I think this news would be better coming from me. It will give me the chance to make quite clear to her how things really were between Philip and me."

His relief was immense. She followed him to the front door of the bungalow.

As he stepped out, he asked, "Are you sure you'll be all right now, Mrs. Raymond?"

"If you mean financially, yes," she said. "And in the long term I'm not worried because I know the service takes care of its own in matters like this. As for myself—well, when you've gone I'm going to cry a great deal. But it will be from pride as well as sorrow. Goodbye, Mr. Martin."

He should have felt like a fraud as he drove away. Ex-cept that everything she assumed could in fact be said to be true, in that Philip had died for his country—plus five thousand pounds.

What did seem unrealistic was her instant adoption of the role of the woman left behind, stoically receiving the half-expected news of her lover's death at the front. It was a portrayal she must have seen in scores of films, so she knew immediately the right words to say and the correct amount of controlled grief to display.

By the time he neared his home, Martin had found himself guilty of cynicism. She wasn't acting. She really did feel grief and the way she reacted was simply proof that clichés become so because of their basic truth.

She had never mentioned money, and she had volunteered for the unpleasant task of facing the stepmother. Carol Raymond had guts and he, Alec Martin, was a patronizing fool who never had understood women.

Would it be safe yet for him to return home, he wondered, as he picked up the A2. Surely Koster must know that Martin was now no possible danger to him. On the other hand, he rather liked living at Molyneux. Not only was Mrs. Lowe's cooking in a class of its own, but the easy, undemanding company the couple offered was something he really valued.

He drove on to Molyneux, reaching it just after midnight, and let himself in the back door with the key Mrs. Lowe had given him.

He was awakened at seven o'clock by the coughing roar of an aircraft engine warming up. He dozed off once more until it was joined by the sound of more engines. Then he remembered that this was one of the Molyneux open days. There would be aircraft warming up from now until eleven, when the public arrived and the flying started. Further sleep was out of the question.

He and Mrs. Lowe were alone at breakfast.

"Mike has to be out on the field before dawn on days like this," she explained. "It takes a lot of work to get all those aircraft up, even with the voluntary helpers he has."

"How many will fly today?"

"The whole collection, if possible. Haven't you ever been to one of our open days?"

"I'm like the Londoner living in the shadow of Westminster Abbey. I'll get round to visiting it one of these days."

"Why not today? You don't seem that busy."

"That's true. And being on the premises, I'll avoid the admission charge! I'll call in at the office first, but I'll be back here for eleven."

As it was Saturday, the works were closed, but he had

his bunch of keys. Sitting in his office he wondered why he had come here, and supposed it was an attempt to pick up the threads again. He could catch up with the paperwork and be ready, when Sheila came in on Monday, to resume the role of a dynamic executive.

The calendar still showed Friday's date. As he tore it off the leaf he made the calculation automatically: in a week's time the Edinburgh Conference would begin. At 11:00 a.m. the pilot of the Palestinian jet would aim his aircraft at the crowds gathered on the esplanade and utter a prayer to Allah as he opened the throttles wide. At 11:02 it would be all over. There would be a news flash on the radio within minutes, a garbled, hysteria-filled voice promising more details as they came in. He, Alec Martin, would sit here with his transistor radio in one of the greatest "I told you so" situations in history. But smugness was not one of his vices, and it would give him no satisfaction at all to know that people like Blair would be feeling sickness in their stomachs.

He would be feeling the nausea, too, combined with the full flowering of a conscience-rooted thought that had been developing in the recesses of his mind. Had he really done all he could?

He'd tried hard enough, in his blunt fashion, but was there another way, a different approach?

In any case, it was all academic, because the moment had passed, and there was no point in speculating on what might have been. He was so discredited that no one would listen to him now.

He started turning over the papers on his desk. The second one he came to was a telex from Boulin which read:

I did not have time to mention it but I arranged insurance on your employee before the accident. It was with Occidental Fidelity and the premium will be included in my invoice. I am not popular with my brokers at the moment.

The service looks after its own, Carol Raymond had said. Her faith would be vindicated when this money came through. Thank goodness for Boulin's shrewdness

154

and business sense in seeking a commission at every possible turn.

He threw all the papers into the tray. Somehow that telex lifted much of the grayness that had been surrounding him. There no longer seemed to be the need to sedate his mind with work.

He'd go and watch some real airplanes flying.

Encouraged by the clear sunshine, the crowds were pouring in steadily when the display began. Martin stood by the hangar and watched the Tiger Moth bumbling its way across the field at a hundred feet while the commentator's voice echoed through the amplifiers.

Mike and his volunteer assistants were dashing around, making sure the next plane but two was lined up and ready to roll when its time came. Molyneux prided itself on the slickness of its flying program. Henshaw, who produced it, sat in the control caravan and was on the field telephone practically nonstop during the entire show, chivvying everyone along in his brusque, no-nonsense voice.

Martin made his way to the roped-off enclosure reserved for special visitors and sat in one of the collapsible wooden chairs. The sunshine warmed through his clothing and he took off his jacket, consciously relaxing. The distant drone of engines, mingling with the snatches of conversation from passers-by, the shouts of fractious or excited children, and the wind rustling through the trees took him right back to those prewar boyhood days at the Hendon Air Pageants. He was a short-trousered fanatic then, obsessed with airplanes in every possible way, from registration letters to performance statistics. Even now he could quote from memory such arcane information as the stalling speed of the Albatross and the wingspan of the Dragon.

The obsession had stayed with him right through his pilot training and his operational service. Then, after he left the RAF, it had gradually diminished. In the same way as the railway enthusiast's interest waned once steam locomotives disappeared, Martin's joy in flying faded out with the propeller. The jet was too bland, too slickly efficient compared with the basic earthiness of the reciprocating engine. The noise, the vibration, and the prop corkscrewing away in front were all part of the magic he had absorbed in his boyhood; flying just wasn't the same without them.

The Tiger Moth bounced in to land and popped its way toward the dispersal area, making way for the Spitfire. The roar of the Griffon engine brought, as ever, a tingle to Martin's spine. The other, older aircraft taking part could be regarded as curios now, fun-objects not to be taken too seriously. But the Spitfire had lost none of its unique combination of beauty and menace as it soared above the trees, wheels seeking their recessed slots in the wings. On the ground its look of faded fragility had been entirely appropriate to a museum. In the sky it was transformed, like a seagull that paddles awkwardly about a beach but on the wing displays an effortless mastery over the element for which it was created.

Climbing in a straight line it dwindled to a speck in the clear sky. The commentator directed everyone's attention to the south, from where it would make its low-level run over the field. Martin's eyes watered and he lost the speck for about a minute. Then he saw it in an eighty-degree dive about a mile away. Down it came until it was lost beyond the row of trees that formed the boundary of the estate. There was no sound. The voices of the crowd were hushed.

Heralded by a sudden five-second burst of sound, the Spitfire appeared above the belt of trees. As it roared over at four hundred miles per hour, a thousand heads instinctively ducked, then swung to the light, following the line of flight as the plane arched into a sharp climb at the end of the field.

The noise was shattering, but to Martin it was a solid, comforting sound, more masculine than the banshee wail of a jet. One could visualize the pistons pounding up and down, valves bouncing open and shut, crankshaft whirling, in a fantastic orchestration of mechanical power.

At three thousand feet the Spitfire flipped over and then dropped like a rocket-propelled stone toward the crowd below. The noise was with them all the way this time. It grew in volume and intensity, cracking and bouncing off the ground as the blurred propellor grew larger, holding everyone's eyes like a hypnotist's gold watch. The Spitfire levelled out at five hundred feet, but to the people watching, it was skimming their heads. As

156

the Spitfire tore across the field, performing a slow roll, Martin reflected that in this aircraft the ultimate in visual aerobatic agility had been reached. The jets might fly in complex formations, puffing out their pretty colored smoke, but they were so damned fast that they needed a vast amount of sky in which to display their maneuverability. The immediacy just wasn't there.

As the Spitfire dwindled into the atmosphere, gaining height for its next pass, a voice said, "She's never aged, has she?"

Wing-Commander Beacham was in the next seat and watching the aircraft intently.

"That's an example of pure design," he went on. "Its beauty lies in the fact that it's a utilitarian object, without frills, that does the job it was built for superbly well."

"Makes my hands itch just to watch it," Martin agreed. "That Griffon engine and the five-bladed prop make it much more formidable than the Merlin-engined job."

For its next pass the Spitfire went into the inverted position. It thundered past the crowd, then flipped over in a quick half-roll. It made two more low-level passes, and as the plane came in for its landing five minutes later, there was a spontaneous burst of applause from the crowd.

"You know why that aircraft has such style?" Beacham asked. "Because it was designed by one man, not a committee."

"Mitchell, you mean."

"It was the same with Camm and the Hurricane. You know, both those aircraft, which won the Battle of Britain, were works of art, because they had that individuality . . . one man's dream brought to reality."

"No thanks to the RAF," Martin said pointedly. "They pinned their faith to the biplane, right up to the nineteen thirties."

"And those two planes were designed almost despite the Air Ministry?" Beacham gave a slight smile. "Well, there's some truth in that tale. Although it's not quite as black and white as it's often painted."

As the Spitfire taxied toward the display area, where people could examine it in closeup, Beacham said pensively, "It always comes down to one man in the end, when you think about it."

"Designing airplanes?"

"Decisions—the important ones. If you could analyze all the historical landmarks, it would show that, behind the governments, political groups, committees, you ultimatley come to one man who impressed his views on the others.'"

To Martin this was a truism, but he nodded politely. "You're a student of history?"

"I've always been interested in the subject," Beacham said. "And it's why I enjoy my present post at the Ministry so much, although some people might regard it as a backwater. I'm in the Air Historical Section. I regard it as an interesting bonus, keeping in touch with establishments such as this. Although we do have our own museum at Hendon. Have you ever been there?" Martin shook his head. "I'm sure you'd find it fascinating. Perhaps I can fix up a visit for you?"

"That's very good of you," Martin said. "I don't know when I'd be able to manage it, but I'll keep your invitation in mind."

There was a break in the flying program and Beacham stood up. "Care for a drink? The beer tent isn't too full and we can continue our chat there."

"I wouldn't mind—"

A hand tapped Martin on the shoulder. It was one of the youngsters who assisted in the control room on open days.

"Thought it was you, Mr. Martin. We were just going to put it out over the Tannoy. Gentleman wants to see you up at the house."

"Sorry about this," he said to Beacham. "We'll have that drink another time."

"I'm here for the rest of the afternoon," Beacham replied. "Come over when you've finished your business."

The last person Martin expected to see waiting for him at the front of the house was Boulin. The Frenchman was pacing nervously up and down the gravel path, his faded raincoat buttoned up against the mild breeze.

"My friend!" he called with relief in his voice, rushing forward to grasp Martin's hand. "I have been so worried about you. Tell me, how are you?"

"I'm all right, Boulin. What brought you here?"

Boulin held Martin's arm and led him away from the house, glancing over his shoulder as he did so. "One

158

needs to be so careful. I do not think I was followed, but it is possible."

"I know the feeling," Martin said. "When did you first get it?"

"From the time of our meeting in Paris. I have been constantly watched since then." He shrugged. "That does not worry me, as I have people who protect me. But I do not want them to use me to find you. You are hiding here?"

"Not really. I think the interest in me has diminished since the plane crashed. I'm no real danger to them now."

"The crash. I am heartbroken about that." Boulin did look as though he would burst into tears. "A fine young man, I believe, and a gallant one."

He paused, then went on hesitantly, "However, there is no way I can avoid the financial commitment I entered into on your behalf. I have tried, my friend, please believe that. But the crash occurred after the aircraft had been taken over. The people who sold it take no responsibility for what happened."

"It's as I expected," Martin said. "Don't worry, Boulin. I'm keeping to my end of the bargain."

"I was not worried at all," Boulin said, the relief in his voice belying his words. "You are a man of honor, whose word is sacred. I am only sorry that what I arranged for you should end so tragically. Now tell me, what is your next intention?"

"Intention?"

"How can I express it? Your alternative plan of action. You have been working something out?"

Martin looked at him. How much did Boulin know?

The Frenchman went on, "I was in the hospital room when you were talking to Lukas for the last time. Remember? I gained a general impression of what you believe is going to happen, in connection with the Edinburgh Conference. An attack of some kind. Is that right?"

"It may be."

"You were planning a retaliation—or rather a preventive action, using a jet fighter," he went on carefully. "I will not press you to tell me what the actual plan was, because it was clearly a dangerous matter for anyone to be involved in. But you need to have an alternative course of

159

action, as I say. It is my wish to help you in any way I can."

They were at the edge of the field now, where the crowd was enjoying the antics of an alleged novice doing circuits and bumps in the Avro.

"There is, I think, a period of just seven days to go before the conference," Boulin said, as though prompting him.

The biplane touched down with a hop, skip, and jump, and then swung round for another circuit. Only a master pilot could ape a pupil with such wicked accuracy.

"I'm not a bloody superman," Martin said. "I don't have any alternative course of action, as you call it. I've washed my hands of the whole damn business. All I've achieved is a reputation, in the highest quarters, for being an unbalanced, obsessed, dangerous fanatic. So to hell with them. And to hell with you, Boulin, if you've come looking for commission on another crooked undercover deal."

Boulin looked at him sharply. After a few moments he said quietly, "That was an unjust thing to say. I came here not looking for business but to help you if I could. You do not require help, so let that be. But you also imply my dealings with you on the aircraft were not honest. I have never cheated you, Mr. Martin. We have made tough bargains, but always you have received value for money . . ." He paused. "When I realized how deeply this matter affected you, I did all I could to meet your requirements. My commission on the purchase of that aircraft was nil. I used my own money to complete the transaction quickly. Because I sensed that a man I regarded as a friend had deep troubles, and I hoped this would help. Yes, I failed, and no one is more sorry than I. But there was nothing crooked in what I did."

"You're a bloody paragon, then," Martin snapped. "But it doesn't alter the fact that your journey here was wasted. I've nothing more for you."

"You have given up entirely the idea of preventing the attack?"

"My God, you make it sound as though I had some sort of choice in the matter. I'm broke, cleaned out—not only of cash but ideas too. Boulin, there's damn-all else I can do. Does that get through your thick Gallic skull?"

160

The volume of his voice made several spectators turn round, even though they were fifty yards away.

Boulin held up his hands. "I shall trouble you no more. And please do not think I have wasted my time making the journey to this country. I have other business matters. Goodbye, Mr. Martin."

He turned and walked away toward the car park. Martin watched him climb into a rented Citroen and drive out through the main gateway, giving Martin a final wave before he disappeared.

As the Avro made its landing, the Bristol Fighter took off.

All of a sudden the whole thing was a bore. Martin turned away and walked to the house. He went up to his room and lay on the camp bed, staring at the ceiling, as the sounds of the display drifted in through the open window.

What had made him overreact to Boulin's remarks? Because they were so damn stupid, that was why. To Boulin, it was all so easy. All you had to do was shoot down the Palestinian plane. Which showed how out of touch with reality he was. Even as a desperate last resort, which Philip would have adopted if the original plan had failed, the chances of destroying the plane were remote. How could you tackle a 500-mph jet without air-to-air missiles as well as the full backing of radar control?

All right, you knew the ETA of the jet and the possible line of interception as it approached the castle. And it was true that the Hunter, with its 30mm Aden cannons, could destroy it with one burst. But there was no Hunter. And even if he acquired another aircraft, where was the pilot to fly it? Finding Philip in the first place had been an incredible stroke of luck: a young man with the necessary skill, the motivation (even if it was money), and most vital of all, faith in Martin and what he was trying to do. There simply wasn't another Philip to be found anywhere.

The loudspeakers outside were marking the end of the flying display with a scratchy record of the RAF March Past. Old Beacham's words came back to him . . . one man believing in something so strongly, he could affect the course of history. Yes, but that was belief in something that was actually achievable.

161

He found himself pacing the bedroom floor. He stopped at the window and watched the homebound spectators streaming away. In the distance the Spitfire was being towed to the hangar. A momentary image flashed through Martin's mind. In 1940 that aircraft had gone out to meet and destroy the people who were intent on destroying Britain.

The image developed further and became ridiculous. A museum piece. One that flew well, but a neutered, super-annuated curiosity nonetheless. The idea was laughable. How could such an aircraft match the speed of a jet? Not a hope, certainly in pursuit. But for interception, speed wasn't so crucial. It meant lying in wait on the precise route and seizing the one fleeting moment when the jet passed through one's sights. . . . No. Even if it was possible to acquire guns—and fit them—how did you get the trustees to agree to that?

So you just did not tell them. . . . You simply did it all in partnership with Mike, letting him think it was part of the authenticity bit. But then you had to find a pilot. And you just couldn't hire Spitfire pilots off the street who were willing to go up and destroy another aircraft at your request.

Unless, the situation being so desperate, you used a man who last flew a Spitfire thirty years ago. . . .

Martin stood at the window watching the hangar doors being closed. His fists were clenched and damp with perspiration but he barely noticed.

14

On the Monday, instead of leaving for the office, Martin made his way down to the sheds. He had spent the previous day in his room, studying maps, working out figures, and trying to play down in his mind the magnitude of the odds against what he was planning.

In the main hangar Mike was lecturing his teenage nephew, who had the task of washing off the mud that spattered the lower wings of the Tiger Moth.

"You're not scrubbing a concrete floor, Harold. Treat it like a butterfly's wings. It's delicate, you understand?"

He turned to Martin. "They see it being thrown around the sky and think it's made of solid stainless steel. Did you enjoy the show, Mr. Martin?"

"Especially the Spitfire. There's something I want to discuss with you, Mike."

He led the mechanic away from Harold, who was now dabbing at the Tiger Moth as though it were crystal.

Martin had prepared his approach. "The only way that Spitfire is lacking in authenticity," he began, "is in the obvious area." He paused and Mike looked at him questioningly. "What's the purpose of that aircraft, Mike? What was it built for?"

"As a fighter. To destroy other aircraft."

"Wrong. The guns did the destroying. The plane simply carried them to a position from where they could be fired effectively. A fighter aircraft is nothing more than a gun platform."

"I see. So you think the Spitfire should be fitted out with a set of guns?"

"She's a Mark eighteen, isn't she? So that would be—"

163

"Two twenty-mills and two point-fives. Only the cannon actually project from the wings. I suppose we could fit a pair of dummy barrels to the leading edge. But no one has complained about their absence up to now."

Martin shook his head. "Real guns, Mike. Nothing else about the plane is fake, is it? So let's have the real thing."

Mike shrugged. "I can't see the point of it. People just want to see her fly, that's all. Guns would only add to the weight and affect performance. Do the other trustees feel like this?"

"Ah, that's my whole point. I'm thinking of something we could do together. Then, the next time there's a display, the Spitfire could add a new item to its program: low-level strafing—using blanks, of course."

A slight grin came over Mike's face. "It would scare the wits out of the crowd."

"And they'll love it. When the Spitfire makes its low-level passes, they're half-convinced it's going to crash on them and that's what adds to the excitement."

"And you wouldn't tell the trustees?"

"Not at this stage. Let them be as surprised as everyone else."

Mike remained unconvinced. "It's going to be very expensive, just for a bit of a stunt like that. How much would a pair of guns cost? And who's going to service them? I'm no armorer."

"You needn't worry about the cost. I'll pay for them. As for where we get them from—I just don't know at the moment. I thought you might have an idea."

"There's no market for twenty-millimeter cannons now —not in this country, as far as I know. Look, Mr. Martin, I don't think you should be thinking of putting so much money and effort into something like this, which has a very small benefit." A thought struck him. "Where would we stand legally, anyway? If the law won't allow you to own a handgun without a license, I can't see it turning a blind eye to a privately owned fighter aircraft with two twenty-millimeter cannon stooging round the countryside."

Martin said vaguely, "That's something we'll have to look into. Anyway it's just an idea at this stage, so we'll leave it there for now."

As he watched Martin walk back toward the house, the

164

engineer said thoughtfully to himself, "I'll believe it when I see it. We had all those promises about a new jet fighter to add to the collection. There's been no mention of that recently, I've noticed."

The following two days were hectic ones for Martin. After half a day spent telephoning various contacts, one finally gave him a name and address.

That afternoon he drove up the M1, came off at Northampton, then made his way to a village beyond Wellingborough. Just outside the village was a small sign, its paint peeling, pointing up a wide cart-track toward the registered office of Patcham Supplies.

As the car bumped along the track, Martin saw the fields on each side were littered with piles of rusting scrap metal. Each represented the remains of a motor-lorry, Bedfords and Dodges mostly. They had the look of bones left to bleach after the vultures had picked off all the meat. Further up the track the view on the left opened up onto a line of tanks. Several had their tracks missing and most had been emasculated by the removal of their guns. Martin's knowledge of army hardware was hazy, but he thought he recognized some wartime Shermans among them.

The track opened out into a concrete yard lined with a motley collection of motor vehicles, ranging from Champ scout cars to a Scammell tow truck. There was a Terrapin prefabricated hut with the sign "Patcham Supplies" along the top. Underneath was a red sign reading "This site is patrolled by guard dogs."

The door opened as Martin halted his car in the yard. The man who stepped out was in his fifties, wearing check trousers, a sheepskin coat, and a pork-pie hat. His features were brown and thin, and sharp gray eyes surveyed Martin from above a silver moustache.

"Afternoon," the man said. "I was on the point of packing in for the day, but I can give you ten minutes, Mr.—"

"Martin."

"I'm Harry Patcham. Patch 'em up and keep 'em going —that's the foundation of my business." An automatic smile went with the joke. He didn't seem surprised that it

165

provoked no answering smile from Martin. "Of course, if you want to browse I can leave you to it."

Martin came straight to the point. "I'm after a pair of twenty-millimeter cannon."

Patcham's eyebrows went up.

"I noticed you have tanks out there, and some aircraft. They must have had armament of some kind."

"True, but when they come to me they've always had their guns spiked, so to speak. Breech blocks or firing pins removed—things like that." Patcham studied him for a moment. "What line of business are you in? Exporting?"

"Not at all. I'm a trustee of an aircraft museum and I just want a set of guns to fit out a wartime plane."

Patcham smiled. "That's fair enough. Have to be careful these days. Let's go and see what we have."

He led Martin along a narrow path past the office and into the field behind, where a black Nissen hut stood. Patcham unlocked the door and switched on a light, and Martin saw that the hut was lined on both sides with storage racks containing dynamos, batteries, clutches, magnetos, nuts and bolts, and engine parts of all kinds. Most were well worn, some were rusty, but all were labelled.

As Martin followed Patcham to the far end of the hut, he said, "Is there much of a trade in ex-WD trucks?"

"Not really," the dealer said. "I cannibalize them. It's the spares that people want. Here—I think we might be in luck."

The last row of shelves carried machine guns of all kinds. Patcham made his way along, checking the labels. Finally he stopped.

"Give us a hand."

Martin helped him lift the heavy machine gun from the middle shelf. It was coated in black grease and there was no trace of rust on the mechanism.

"Is that what you're after?"

"If it's a twenty-mill, yes. I want a pair, in fact."

"They came in a set of four, from what I remember," the dealer said. "Yes—they're all here. Let's get them over to the office and we can talk business."

They wrapped two of the guns in newspapers before carrying them out. Once they lay on the floor of the office, Patcham sat at his battered desk and lit a cigarette.

"Good condition, aren't they?"

"As far as I can see. But you say the firing mechanism won't be working?"

"That's how I usually receive them. But that won't matter if you only want them for a museum piece. Will it?" Patcham examined the tip of his cigarette. "I'd say a hundred pounds"—he glanced at Martin—"each."

Martin took out his check book and asked, "Any idea where I can get some twenty-millimeter shells?"

The dealer watched him writing out the check. Then he said, "Funny sort of museum you must be running."

Martin signed the check and started to tear it off at the counterfoil. He stopped halfway and looked at the guns on the floor.

"I don't really know if I want them after all—unless I can get hold of some shells."

Patcham was staring at the check. Then he said slowly, "I'm not in the gun-running business, squire. I've got my professional reputation to think of. I'm not like some blokes—Teddy Askew, for instance, who operates from an office at Carter Street, Leyfield. He's welcome to that sort of business."

Martin nodded and handed him the check. "Is it all right if I take them with me?" He took out his banker's card and passed it over.

The dealer compared the two signatures. "Seems all right. You don't want a receipt, I suppose? Let's get you loaded up, then."

As they put the guns in the boot of the car, Martin said, "You can probably help me with something else I need. Petrol cans."

Patcham chuckled. "I've got about twelve thousand jerrycans—four-gallon ones."

"I want, say, forty of them. I'll collect them in a few days and we can settle up then."

"Sure. Anything else?"

"I don't think so."

Martin started the car. As he pulled away, Patcham walked alongside and called through the open window.

"Don't go making trouble with those guns, will you, squire? Could give the trade a bad name."

Martin drove through the works gate the next morning

167

at eight-thirty. Instead of going to the office he parked his car outside the engineering shop, went inside, and found Arthur.

"Whatever you're doing, I want you to drop it and take on a special job for me," he said, leading him out to the car.

The engineer said balefully, "Then why have we been breaking our necks this past week on the Algerian contract? That was supposed to be the priority job."

Martin opened the boot, lifted out one of the guns, and handed it to Arthur.

"I've got a pair of these. I want them stripped down, cleaned, and reassembled. And, if you're any sort of an engineer, you should be able to indentify what parts are missing."

Arthur cradled the gun in his arms and said, tight-lipped, "I presume you are being serious, Mr. Martin? This looks to me like a machine gun."

"It's a twenty-millimeter cannon and yes, I'm quite serious. It's for one of the aircraft over at Molyneux. Can you do it, Arthur?"

The engineer said, "A minute ago you were telling me, not asking me. Maybe I can do it. I won't know until I've tried. But to get back to my original point—what about the Algerian contract?"

"That takes second place for now." Martin picked up the other gun. "Where do you want them?"

They finally came to rest on a bench at the side of the workshop while Arthur arranged for a paraffin bath to receive the parts as the guns were dismantled. As he left the workshop Martin glanced back in time to see the engineer gesticulate in his direction for the benefit of the other men in the shop. Roughly translated, it said that the old man was crazy as a coot, but who were they to argue if he wanted to run an engineering works like a circus?

When he entered her office, Sheila looked at him coldly. "Enjoying your holiday?" she asked.

"I want you to find the number of a Teddy Askew of Carter Street, Leyfield," he told her. "Get him on the phone for me right away."

He went into his own office and a few minutes later the call came through. Mr. Askew would be in his office all day; yes, he would be interested in some business; and exactly what was Mr. Martin interested in? Very well, it would wait until they actually met.

As Martin put down the phone Gerald Harris strode into the room. The accountant's jaw was thrust forward and there was anger in his eyes.

"So you've surfaced at last! It's good to see one of our captains of industry is so dedicated to his task that he's prepared to put as much as half an hour a week into controlling the destinies of his company."

Martin said evenly, "I'm not in the mood for sarcasm, least of all from you. What do you want, Gerald?"

"What do I want? What does Martin Engineering want? A bit of leadership, a measure of sane management, and at least an iota of interest in whether the company survives or not."

"A rhetorical accountant—I never thought there was such a thing." Martin stood up. "I was just going, Gerald. If you've anything substantial you want to say—"

Gerald stood in front of him. "How serious are you about this company, Alec? That crazy Algerian contract is costing us a fortune, as well as throwing up all sorts of production snags that you should be here to sort out. Now I'm told you've kicked over the card table again. You've ordered Arthur to strip down and service some machine guns. Are we in business to make money or not?"

"Yes, we are," Martin snapped. "And all you're employed to do is tot up the figures. If they're red or black at the end of the day is my worry. Why don't you stick to your job and leave the management to me?"

"I'm chief financial officer of this company," Gerald blazed back. "That's more than adding up figures. It means keeping a constant check on the financial health of the company and taking action when necessary to ensure it remains viable. Like now. I've ordered Arthur to forget about those guns and get his men back onto their normal work. It's clear your judgment is so unbalanced—"

"You've what!" Martin grabbed a startled Gerald by the lapels of his jacket. "Go straight back to that workshop and tell those men to do exactly what I told them to do. Now!"

169

The accountant's face was pale as he disengaged his jacket and pulled away. "You just don't realize—"

"I damn well do realize! I want that job doing and doing quickly. This is my company still, and I'll use it to do what job as and when I like. And if you don't like the system here, Mr. Gerald Bloody Harris, then you can clear out and juggle with your figures elsewhere." He opened the door. "Now get out and tell those men to do the work I gave them."

The accountant left without another word. Sheila gave a sniff, then dropped her eyes as Martin glared at her.

"I'm leaving now," he told her. "You've no objection, have you?"

She made no reply as he walked out and shut the door behind him.

He drove up to London conscious of his deficiencies in the art of industrial relations. He would need to go out of his way to patch things up once this business was over, but right now he was gripped by an obsession. Anything which got in the way of the preparation of the Spitfire was a damned nuisance that just had to be brushed aside. His eyes fell on his watch as his hand gripped the steering wheel. The date figure was eleven. He had four days left.

Teddy Askew's office was a room above an estate agent's. He was large, florid of complexion, and completely bald. He spoke like a car salesman and showed no surprise at Martin's request.

"I can deliver one thousand shells tomorrow," he said, "at a cost of seven hundred and fifty pounds, payable in advance. What address is it?"

"Can't I take them with me?"

Askew removed the small cigar from his mouth. "I don't store anything here. These kinds of goods have to be handled with a great deal of discretion. They will be delivered tomorrow by an unmarked van."

Martin gave him the Molyneux address, emphasizing that the cases should be marked for his attention. Askew took his check without asking for any identification, and that was that. Somehow Askew seemed the sort of man who would have checked out Martin's background as soon as he knew he was coming. There was no doubt the figure

170

he had named was just a starting price, but Martin had neither the energy nor the inclination to haggle.

Martin stopped in London to buy the largest-scale ordinance survey maps available of northeast England and Scotland. That night, in his room at Molyneux, he spread out the maps on the floor. It was a part of the country that was comparatively unknown to him. Even in his service career he had not become thoroughly familiar with any area further north than Yorkshire, but seeing the word "Northumberland" on the map somehow caused a brief image to flash through his mind: an image of a windswept landscape, bleak and barren . . . yet with a concrete runway straddling it. He knew he had never flown up there, so where did that mental picture come from? Someone had painted it in his mind . . . Anita—no, Annette. He could not recall her surname.

An unconscious smile crossed his face as he remembered that period, two—no, three years ago, when Annette had worked as his secretary. Sheila, before going on holiday, had arranged with the agency for a temporary replacement. That wasn't always easy, most girls being unwilling to travel this far into the country. Annette had burst in like a breath of fresh air, apple-cheeked and nineteen years of age, breezy with a cheerful self-confidence that implied vast experience and unparalleled efficiency. That first morning the slow, irregular tap of the typewriter finally drove him to take a look outside his office, where he discovered Annette laboriously trying to find each letter in the keyboard with her two index fingers. No, she blithely admitted, she had no typing experience. As for shorthand, who needed it? Look, everyone knew a good secretary had to be much more than a shorthand-typist. She needed brains, intelligence, and sharp wits to be any good at all to her boss. Annette had all three, so he wasn't going to let such a bargain slip through his fingers for the sake of a bit of shorthand and typing, was he? He decided he wasn't, and she stayed the two weeks.

It turned out she was in her final year of an honors course at London University, and the vacation job she had lined up had fallen through. This was the only alternative the agency could offer.

It had been an exhilarating two weeks. Her easy infor-

171

mality and cheerful rudeness in answer to his more short-tempered remarks prevented the normal boss/employee barriers ever rising between them. She took a genuine interest in him and chatted at great length about her own background. He recalled her telling him of the family farm, in Northumberland, with a large area rendered useless by an abandoned wartime airstrip. "Nothing else within miles except our farmhouse," she told him. "Lord knows why they put it there—unless it was to annoy Dad, in which case it was a great success. It chops his farm clean in two."

He pored over the Northumberland map and finally found three different sites, each marked with broken lines and the legend "Airfield (disused)." Whether any of them was where Annette used to live didn't really matter. It was the location he was after, and one of these could be ideal. On second thoughts, that first one was too close to the A1, but the others seemed remote enough.

He marked their positions, folded up the maps, and went to bed. It would be a round trip of over five hundred miles and he had to do it tomorrow. If he took a van, he could pick up the jerrycans on the way. Pity he couldn't use the Rover for such a long journey, he thought as he went to sleep.

Had he done so, the whole operation would have been brought to a rapid and premature conclusion.

Hector Blair looked up from his desk. "How can he have gone to ground? He's an engineer, not Bugs Bunny."

"There's no sign of his having been home for over a week now," Jenkins said. "He doesn't appear at his office any more. His secretary claims not to know where he is, and I'm inclined to believe her."

Blair said bluntly, "Then you're going to have to find him."

"But you had him in here," Jenkins pointed out reasonably. "You can't have thought he was dangerous if you let him go."

"It's not a matter of holding him," Blair said irritably. "We've got to watch him, that's all. But now the fact that he's disappeared implies he might be up to something. Listen—use every means you can to track him down. Take as many men as you need. Get the police to cooperate, and keep me in touch with what you're doing."

As his assistant left, Blair looked glumly at the calendar. The truth was that Jenkins had touched a nerve in recalling how Martin had been allowed to leave his office. Blair had mentioned Martin's visit as an afterthought at the following day's joint security conference, and he had been surprised at the reaction of the other members. They took Martin far more seriously than he could. He tried to paint the complete picture for them, outlining all the evidence for the man's complete lack of credibility. But they insisted on regarding him as a real risk, to the extent of considering the virtues of taking him into custody on some pretext or other until the Conference was over.

Blair managed to convince them that close surveillance was all that was necessary. His people would be able to do that, with Special Branch aid where necessary. Now he began to wonder if it might not be better to admit he had boobed, and pass the whole thing on to the police. No, he could not do that, not at such a late stage. Never admit a mistake: that was the fundamental rule in his business if one intended to continue up the ladder. Just ensure that you'd considered and provided for every circumstance. Whatever went wrong, you then wheeled out the appropriate alibi and you were fireproof.

Once again his mind cast over the possible traps that lay in wait for him in this Edinburgh business. All were covered. No gaps at all. Except one, of course, but that was so ridiculous, so laughable that it was not even worth consideration. True, some strange things seemed to have been happening to Martin, if only half of what he alleged were to be believed. And there was no doubt the man himself genuinely believed in his obsession. So what did that prove? By definition, any neurotic's obsessions must be real to him. Still, if it was the only gap left, it might be worth covering, some way or other. He made a note to look into that closely.

But right now Martin himself was the real problem. I'll give Jenkins two days to come up with his whereabouts, he thought. It shouldn't be that difficult, for heaven's sake.

Martin steered the van along the cart-track and halted in the yard outside the Terrapin hut.

Patcham came out and said, "Everything's ready, squire. But that petrol order you phoned with caused a few problems. You're running a real risk, carrying nearly two hundred gallons of petrol like that. If the police stop you, you're for the high jump. So I know nothing about it, OK?"

"I'll not involve you. How much do I owe you, Mr. Patcham?"

They finally settled on three hundred and fifty pounds. Then they drove down to the filling station where the cans were waiting. In twenty minutes the van was loaded, the back doors locked, and Martin climbed into the cab.

"Thanks for your help."

The dealer waved an acknowledgment. "Always glad to do business. Good luck—with whatever it is you're doing."

It took him twenty minutes to reach the A1. Once there he headed north and settled down to a steady fifty miles per hour. The van was a 30cwt Commer. He had walked into the works at eight o'clock that morning, established that it was not required urgently that day, and had driven it out of the gate just as Gerald Harris's car was coming in. He didn't know if the accountant had recognized him and he really didn't care.

It was a cloudy day, but dry. Traffic was not too heavy and he was able to maintain his fifty miles per hour without difficulty. By midday he was near Darlington, and he pulled into a roadside pub for a meat pie and a pint of bitter. No whisky, he told himself. Half an hour later he was on the road again.

He passed through Newcastle at one o'clock and then started to consult the map that was opened on the seat alongside him. He had to come off the main road a couple of miles before Morpeth in order to reach the first of his objectives. He spotted the junction and turned off into an area of undulating moorland. In Colesford he stopped outside the village pub and studied the map once more. The airfield was a mile further on, over to the east.

Five minutes later he spotted the strip of concrete; leaving the van parked up against the ditch, he walked through the open gate and found a large wooden shed bearing the legend "Hillier Aviation Services." A twin-engined Cessna stood on the apron, apparently the only aircraft in residence. Seated in the cockpit, carefully edging the throttles back and forth, was a heavy-built man in his thirties with a short thick beard and wearing a sweatshirt and denim jacket.

As soon as he saw Martin he jumped to the ground and came across. "Hillier is the name. Can I help?"

"The map says this airfield is disused. I gather it's inaccurate."

Hillier gave a wry smile. "Only just. I'm the only one who operates from here. Are you looking for a charter?"

"Not at the moment. I use private aircraft on occasions and I'm looking for likely spots in this part of the world where we could put down."

Hillier was interested. "What line of business are you in, Mr.—"

"Alexander. I do a bit of this and that—various things." He felt the need to withdraw quickly. There was nothing doing here. "I was just passing and thought I'd take a look. I'll be on my way."

But Hillier had sniffed a likely prospect and he followed Martin out of the field. "Any charter work you want doing, Mr. Alexander, just remember the name Hillier. You'll find me more than competitive, and I'm on twenty-four-hour call."

"I'll do that," Martin said, climbing into the cab of the van and recalling with a pang poor old Fred Williams trying to sell him a similar line in hire cars.

The pilot was scrabbling through his pockets and finally came up with a business card, which he threw into the open window as the van pulled away.

"Give me a call any time."

The other airfield was about ten miles further on in Covington. Martin picked up the A1 again and then turned east toward Alnwick. He nearly missed his next turning, which was a glorified footpath on the right. He stopped and took in his surroundings. The only buildings in sight were a farmhouse and a barn.

He drove slowly along the track and finally, through a gap in the hedge, saw a strip of concrete on the left-hand side. He parked the van, climbed through the hedge, and found himself standing on a five-hundred-yard runway.

The concrete was chipped and cracked in places, but generally sound. Sheep were grazing on the other side and the cries of curlews drifted over the wind-bent grass. In the distance he could see the low curve of a dispersal shed. As far as disused airfields went, this was the real thing. Best of all, a mile to the north, a radio mast rose to about a hundred and fifty feet. From the air it would make an ideal reference point.

He returned to the van and drove another hundred yards along the track until he reached the farmyard. Chickens scuttled out of his way as he halted the van outside the stone house and climbed down. The side door was open and he was about to bang on the iron knocker when a man appeared from the barnlike building next door. He was in his sixties, his face lined and weather-beaten, with no trace of humor.

"Hello," Martin said. "I wonder if I can ask a favor."

"Must be a big one," the man said dourly, "if you've found your way up here to ask it."

Martin introduced himself. "I see you're busy and I shan't keep you long. Would it cause you any problems if I was to make use of that concrete runway? I presume it's on your land."

"It's my land, right enough. And that thing's been a damned nuisance to me these past thirty years, I can tell you. You'd be doing me a favor if you would pick it up and take it away with you."

Martin said with a smile, "I'm an amateur flyer and I'm planning a trip up here. What I'm looking for is a place where I can land and refuel my aircraft."

The farmer took a dog-end from behind his ear. "They've got a proper aerodrome at Newcastle, I believe. What's wrong with that?"

"Too much red tape. I can't be bothered using commercial airfields."

The man cupped his hands to light the cigarette. "They make you pay, I suppose."

Martin recognized the form. "I'm quite happy to pay you for the use of your land." There was a pause. "Say—ten pounds?"

The farmer shrugged. "At least it's not lambing time, when you might frighten the ewes. When did you plan to come?"

"This Saturday. Early morning. There's something else. That shed standing by the runway—could I store some tins of fuel in there?"

"It's not much of a shelter. I'll show you."

The farmer led him across the field to the shed. Inside was an ancient farm cart.

"See—it's open at both ends. I'd store feed in here but the rain blows in."

"It would serve my purpose," Martin told him. "I've got the stuff in my van. Could I use it for say, another five pounds?"

"It's not for me to discourage other people from throwing their money around," the farmer said.

As they walked back to the farmyard, Martin took three five-pound notes from his wallet and handed them over. There was the sudden sound of a diesel engine operating at high revs. In through the gate roared a tractor towing an empty cart. It spun round the yard and slammed to an abrupt stop behind the two men.

The driver was in her twenties, wearing a denim shirt and jeans. Her hand went automatically to straighten her short fair hair as she jumped down and saw Martin.

"Are you from Pollards?" she asked with a faint trace of a Northumberland accent. "Because I'm fed up complaining about this gear box." Her even white teeth highlighted her tanned features, which were set in a frown.

The farmer explained, "He's an airplane pilot. He wants to use the old runway."

She looked puzzled. "You want to fly from here? That runway hasn't been used since the war."

"It's just a matter of coming down to refuel," Martin said. "This area happens to be convenient."

"Make sure you don't hit any of the sheep," she said. Suddenly she smiled and her whole face came alive. "As long as you don't give the same trouble as the last lot of flyers who used it. Yanks. They left their mark behind them in more ways than one. Isn't that so, Dad?" The farmer glowered and she gave a laugh. "Dad's generation still thinks of those as the dark days—that's the men, of course. The women seemed to have enjoyed them."

"You're talking nonsense again, Annette," her father said shortly. "Aren't you supposed to go up to Matchett's this afternoon and sort out those accounts?"

"The VAT-man's really got you frightened, hasn't he, Dad? Let him wait for his money—that's always been your philosophy up to now. Anyway," she said, turning to Martin with a smile, "I'm going to offer our visitor a cup of tea. He looks as though he needs one."

"I'd welcome that, Annette. You used to make a fair cup of tea at the office."

She stared at him. Then she pulled a pair of spectacles from the pocket of her shirt and put them on before studying his features more closely.

"Why—it's you!" she exploded. "Martin—Alec Martin! How in heaven's name did you find your way up here?"

"It's almost a coincidence, but not quite," he admitted. "I remembered you telling me about this place, but it was just by luck that I found it."

"But you're *flying*—at your age? Ooops—" She put her hand over her mouth. "Well, you know what I mean, Alec. I know you're not really over the hill yet, but you must admit you're not exactly a dashing young adventurer, either. And why fly up to this God-forsaken place, anyway?"

Her father coughed pointedly and she turned to him. "This is Alec Martin, Dad. I worked for him once in the vac. We were great pals. Said I was the best secretary he ever had. Didn't you, Alec?"

"I don't know if I actually said that—"

"I was damned good by the end of the two weeks, and you know it. Anyway, you've just got to stay for tea. Come on in."

Martin said, "I have some stuff to unload. Can I be getting on with that while you brew the tea?"

"Surely. But don't be too long."

The farmer stood watching while Martin piled the jerry-cans in the shed; then he silently climbed onto the tractor and drove away out of the yard while Martin went inside. The girl had a small table set before a coal fire. As well as a pot of tea there were sausage rolls and scones.

"You're looking a bit underfed," she said, eyeing him shrewdly. "But I guess you haven't time for me to cook you a meal."

"That's true," Martin told her. "But I appreciate the

thought. If you'll allow me to content myself with what's here . . ."

He almost cleared the plates. The girl kept refilling his cup while she quizzed him on his real purpose for making the journey. When she realized he was being deliberately vague, she didn't press him further.

"Still cultivating ulcers by running that factory of yours?" she asked after a while, watching him closely.

"It's not as bad as that," he said. "You make it sound as though I'm a slave to the place."

"That was the way it seemed when I was there. I could never understand what you were getting out of it, except money."

There was a pause. "Satisfaction?" he hazarded, and she laughed.

"If that's what you're like when you're satisfied, I'd hate to see you frustrated. You know, Alec, I often thought there must have been a really nice guy inside you before you went into that business. Beats me why that wife of yours didn't make you give it up long ago."

There was a pause; then he said, "We're separated now."

"Proves my point, doesn't it?"

There was another pause. Finally he said, "I never really expected to find you still down on the farm."

She shrugged. "I'm surprised myself. It's just the way things worked out. Mind you, Dad looks on me as a spoiled woman—going off like that to spend three years in London. That's ruined me for being a placid country lass, content to feed chickens until one of the local lads took a fancy and set me up for life in a tied cottage."

"You got your degree, didn't you?"

"Sure. Not that it cuts much ice with Dad. With Mum dead, he needs a woman around the farm, and that naturally means me." She sighed. "So far I've managed to confine my activities to cooking, a bit of housework, and looking after his accounts. But mark my word, he'll have me shearing sheep and operating the dip before he's finished."

"It must be frustrating for you."

She laughed. "I'm only joking. Seriously, I don't mind giving old man Bailey a hand for the moment. But some

179

day I'm going to break free, and I'm trying to get him used to the idea."

Martin stood up. "I enjoyed that, Annette. I hope you'll understand if I have to rush off now."

"Oh, I understand all right," she said gloomily, following him out of the door. "All the fellers have to rush off once they see this place."

"I've arranged to fly back this Saturday," he told her. "It should be early in the morning."

"I'll be at my bedroom window, looking for that little speck in the sky," she said. "I might even shine a light for you. Take care."

She stood waving as he drove out of the gate.

On his way back to the A1 he studied the surrounding countryside. His navigational skill was so primitive he would need every visual aid possible in finding his way here on Saturday, including the light in Annette's window.

15

It was seven o'clock that evening when, consumed with weariness and his shoulder aching, he drove through the gate of the engineering works and put the van in the garage. He was surprised the place was still open, until he remembered that everyone was still working overtime on the Algerian contract.

He took a look in the machine shop and the first things he saw were the two cannon. They were still on the table where he had last seen them, but now they were spotless and gleaming, with a thin film of oil on the moving parts.

Arthur walked across with that look of smugness combined with condescension which craftsmen adopt when a layman examines their work.

"They haven't looked so good since the day they were made," he stated.

"You've done well," Martin said. "It's a matter now of getting them in working order—"

"That's in hand. We're machining the necessary parts now. These guns will be ready to fire by eleven tomorrow morning."

He watched Martin's reaction and was rewarded with a low whistle of surprise.

"I'd never have believed it, Arthur. I thought I was asking the impossible when I gave you this job. I never imagined you'd get it done so quickly."

In reality he had known that Arthur would never rest and would drive his men like slaves rather than admit defeat on a challenge like this.

"I'll collect them tomorrow. I'm grateful for your efforts, Arthur. And say thanks to the lads for me."

He left by the back gate and walked over to Molyneux in the gathering darkness. He was greeted by Mrs. Lowe as he let himself in. "There you are, Mr. Martin. I wondered if you would be coming back tonight. Come in and have some coffee."

Mike was in the lounge watching the news on television. He said, "Someone was here today looking for you."

"Oh yes?"

"He wouldn't give his name," Mrs. Lowe said, coming in with a plate of sandwiches. "He was in a white car. There were two of them, in fact. They looked like service types in mufti."

Martin took a sandwich and said carefully, "Did you tell them I was staying here?"

"Indeed I did not," Mrs. Lowe said. "Didn't you say you wanted some privacy? I told them where your home was, and your office, and I said the next time they would be able to find you here would be at the trustees' meeting."

"As it happens," Martin said, "I shan't be inconveniencing you much longer. I'll be leaving at the end of the week."

"It's no inconvenience to us; I thought I'd made that clear." She poured him some coffee. "He was very persistent. He kept asking questions as though he was trying to get me to contradict myself."

Mike chuckled. "Once Eileen realized that, she booted him out so quickly his feet didn't touch the ground."

"If there's one thing I object to," Mrs. Lowe said primly, "it's anyone implying I'm a liar."

A thought occurred to Martin. "Did they see my car by any chance?"

"I'd already moved that round to the back of the house," Mike said. "A delivery van came this morning with some packing cases addressed to you, and I didn't want to risk your car getting scratched." He glanced at Martin. "You used another vehicle today, then?"

"One of the firm's vans." As Mrs. Lowe went out, Martin said casually, "Remember what we were talking about the other day, Mike? Making the Spitfire as authentic as possible?"

"You mean by fitting the cannon?"

182

"I've managed to pick up a set. They're in pretty good condition."

"Twenty mills? Not the sort of thing that's easy to find these days."

"A friend of mine put me on to them."

"I see."

Martin said, "I think they'll look good when they're installed."

Mike shrugged. "I still can't see much point in it, myself. But bring them over tomorrow and we'll take a look."

As he lay in the camp bed that night, Martin pondered on the possible identity of the caller. It could only be Hector Blair's man, and he recalled Blair's threat to keep him in custody until after the conference. He could well have decided to implement that threat. Which meant Martin had to take every possible step to conceal his whereabouts over the next three days.

The next morning he entered the works by the rear gate and went straight to the machine shop. Arthur was waiting for him.

"They're all ready, Mr. Martin. Perfect working order."

"You're sure?"

"You can take my word for it."

Martin picked up one of the guns and examined it.

"I'll see there's a bonus for this," he said. "You've done a first-class job. Now help me load them into the van, will you?"

As they put the guns into the van he spotted Gerald standing silently watching from the back of the shop. But the accountant made no attempt to speak.

He drove the van over to Molyneux himself, bringing it to a halt outside the hangar. Mike came out and helped him carry the guns over to a bench, where the engineer studied them silently.

"Will you have any problems putting them in?" Martin asked, wiping the oil from his hands.

The engineer ran a finger over the gleaming metal. "Beautiful. I'm surprised you were able to pick them up in this condition." He paused and then made his decision. "We'll install them all right. I'm not an armorer but I've watched them do the job often enough."

"When do you reckon you'll get round to it?"

"Things shouldn't be too busy in the morning. We'll have a go then."

Martin nodded and walked away feeling relieved. As he saw Mike busying himself with the cannon, he switched direction and headed quietly for the office at the side of the hangar. Glancing back over his shoulder, he eased open the door and stepped inside without Mike's noticing him. The door eased shut behind him on a spring.

First he searched Mike's desk. Then he went through the filing cabinet beneath the window. Where was it? There was a small storeroom leading off the office and he made his way through. Another, older cabinet was against the wall, and it was in the third drawer down that he found what he was looking for: a slim blue Air Ministry publication entitled *Pilot's Notes for Spitfire 18*.

When he opened the office door, Mike was still busy with the guns. Silently Martin walked out of the hangar and back to the house, where he went straight to his room.

He glanced through the pages of the book. It was all there—pictures of the controls and instrumentation, all keyed in clear detail, the preflight checks, details of the performance limitations for both engine and airframe. He felt wry amusement at the thought of his learning how to fly an aircraft from a book, two days before he intended taking it into action.

The reality of what he was attempting had, over the past few days, assumed very clear proportions in his mind. He now had to consider the chances, not merely of success, but of survival. He was going to extend this flying museum piece well beyond its recognized limits, and there wasn't going to be anyone around to give a helping hand. At least, knowing Mike, the aircraft would be as airworthy as it possibly could be.

And that was the next problem. Mike. How could he keep the engineer out of the way on the fifteenth? It was something he should have considered earlier and now here he was with just forty-eight hours before he planned to abscond with the aircraft. What sort of convincing errand could Mike be sent on that would occupy him all day from early morning? . . . Then he recalled his conversation of a few days ago.

He went downstairs, closed the lounge door, and telephoned the Ministry of Defense in Whitehall.

Wing-Commander Beacham was surprised to hear from him. "We didn't have that drink we promised ourselves the other day."

"I'm sorry about that," Martin said. "Perhaps the next time you're up here we could get together—lunch maybe."

"That would be pleasant."

"I was thinking over what you were telling me, Wing-Commander, about the Hendon Museum. I haven't been able to get up there yet, but I know Mike Lowe would be fascinated to look round it—you know, our engineer. I was wondering if anything could be arranged."

"Well, of course. He's welcome any time. I'll give you the opening hours—"

"I do have them. In Mike's case, however, I'm sure he'd be more interested in what goes on behind the scenes —being in the same line of business. But he would be rather diffident about just going along there and asking questions. What I'm getting at, Wing-Commander, is this: would it be possible to send him a letter—a personal invitation to see round the place? He'd be really bucked to receive that."

Beacham pondered for a moment. "I could write him a note myself, then tip off the Hendon boys to look out for him and take him in hand. Did you have any date in mind for this?"

Martin tried to sound casual. "Let me see. I do happen to know this Saturday is a clear day for him. Perhaps Saturday morning quite early, so as not to inconvenience any of your chaps who may be going away for the weekend."

"As soon as that? Very well. I'll get off a note to him today, asking if he'd like to come along on Friday and stay over until Saturday. Will that do?"

"That's fine. I know he'll appreciate it, and I will too. Thanks for your cooperation."

He was perspiring as he put down the phone and he realized his hand was shaking. What on earth was the matter with him? All he had done was to tell a white lie that would cause nobody any harm at all, yet he was as keyed up as if he had perjured himself in court.

God, he needed a drink. If the Lowes kept whisky in the house, he would have stolen some without compunction. But their alcoholic indulgence extended no further than a bottle of sherry in the sideboard that seemed to have survived at least three Christmases.

He went back to his room and unfolded the ordnance survey maps once more. It looked straightforward on paper. But that pretty blue area, translated into the view from a low-flying aircraft, was a featureless waste of gray sea, waiting to swallow the unlucky or foolhardy pilot, particularly one flying a superannuated World War Two relic.

The Palestinian plane would approach Edinburgh up the Firth of Forth, the coastline providing the obvious navigational aid. To reach the airport it would have to fly inland and over the city itself, when the castle would come directly into view. He had to make his interception well before then, probably at the mouth of the firth. To do that, he would need height superiority to make up for the difference in air speed, which meant twenty thousand feet-plus. The maximum cruising time he would allow himself over the firth was forty minutes. If he did not make contact in that time, the Spitfire's fuel supply would be at a critical level. His only reassurance was that the terrorists intended making—literally—the greatest possible impact, and that would have to be during the opening ceremony, from ten to ten-thirty in the morning.

There was no more planning he could do. In an operation as bizarre as this, it was nonsensical to try to anticipate exactly what would happen. Countless things could go wrong, any of which could jeopardize or ruin his scheme.

Martin folded the maps. He had the aircraft, the armament, the refuelling facility, and the approximate interception time and position. The rest was up to Providence and his hazily remembered thirty-year-old ability to fly a Spitfire.

16

When Martin crawled out of bed the next morning at ten, his head was thick, as though a heavy cold were digging itself in. Declining Mrs. Lowe's offer of a full-scale breakfast, he had a cup of coffee and an aspirin before going across to the airfield.

The sky was overcast and there was a sharp wind as he made his way to the Spitfire, which was on the concrete apron in front of the hangar. Mike was prostrate on the starboard wing, his head and arms buried in the gun compartment. The gun barrels projected from the leading edges.

As he saw Martin, the engineer gave a thumbs-up sign. "They fit like a glove. I'll be finished in a few minutes."

When he finally dropped to the ground he said, "Haven't seen those fitted since—oh, the late forties. But it came back to me all right."

"Are they working?"

"I don't know of any gun that works without ammunition," Mike replied sarcastically. "But the pneumatic system works OK. All it needs is some shells and we've got a lethal weapon there."

Martin walked to the front of the aircraft and viewed the guns head-on.

"How about harmonization?" he asked after a while.

The engineer looked at him curiously. "I thought they were only for decoration, or for firing blanks. Why should they need harmonizing?"

"It was just a thought. Anyway, the aircraft looks a lot better for them. You did well to fit them so quickly, Mike."

The engineer pulled a letter from the pocket of his denim jacket. "I wanted to get it out of the way. This letter came this morning, inviting me to the RAF Museum at Hendon. It says if I want to travel up today I can stay overnight. Signed by Wing-Commander Beacham. He attends the trustee meetings, doesn't he?"

Martin nodded. "When he talked to me about it, I mentioned you would probably be interested in how they organized things. He must have taken me at my word."

"Thanks for suggesting it. As it happens, there's nothing urgent to be done here, so I can go this afternoon and leave Harold to look after things with more or less an easy mind."

Harold was hammering away at a strip of aluminum in the hangar.

Martin nodded. "By the way, just for my own satisfaction, show me how the shells are actually loaded into these guns." And Mike did so.

Mrs. Lowe laid on a bigger lunch than usual, presumably to sustain Mike on his journey. As they ate, Mike seemed almost excited at the prospect.

"It's a pity the invite isn't a double," he said to his wife. "It would be a break for you, too."

"No, thank you," she said firmly. "I see and hear enough of airplanes seven days a week. If you want to give me a break, take me as far away from an airfield as possible."

"How about you, Mr. Martin? They'd probably welcome you there without an invite. And things don't seem to be keeping you too busy at the works right now."

The portable radio in the kitchen was tuned to the one o'clock news. One item was a report that all the delegates had now arrived in Edinburgh for the opening of the conference the following day. The tightest security program ever seen in Scotland was in operation and would be tighter still when the PFF delegation arrived in the morning.

Martin shook his head. "I don't think so, Mike. I've got something else to keep me busy tomorrow."

Mike left at two-thirty. Half an hour later Martin made his way to the hangar.

Harold was brushing the floor, whistling as he maneuvered his broom round the undercarriages of the various aircraft.

"Hi, Mr. Martin," he said. "If you want Uncle Mike, he's gone for the day."

"I know that, Harold. Can you get the Land-Rover? I want to bring some stuff over here from the house."

When they had moved the ammunition boxes over to the hangar, Martin said, "Now I want you to tow the Spitfire out onto the apron."

Harold looked at him doubtfully. "What for? Uncle Mike finished working on that this morning."

"I've something to be fitted to it," Martin said briskly. "Come on, Harold, jump to it."

The tone of authority worked. The apprentice connected the tow-bar from the Land-Rover to the Spitfire's tail wheel and carefully maneuvered the aircraft onto the apron. When he had driven the vehicle clear, he came back and saw with surprise that Martin was on the port wing, removing the panel of the gun compartment.

"Open up those boxes, Harold," he said, "but don't go hitting them with a hammer."

Harold gave a whistle when he lifted the lid and saw the shells in the first box. "This is machine-gun ammunition, isn't it?"

"Start feeding it up to me," Martin ordered. "Don't be scared. There's no danger of it going off accidentally."

Martin kept the lad as busy as possible, in the hope this would prevent him thinking too deeply about what he could be doing and why. Finally all the ammunition was loaded.

As Martin screwed back the wing panels he said, "How much fuel is there in the tanks, Harold?"

"Fuel? I think the bottom main tank is about full. That's nearly fifty gallons."

According to the *Pilot's Notes*, that could give him anything up to an hour's flying, depending on height, boost, and supercharger setting.

"How many starter cartridges?"

Harold stared at him.

Martin repeated, "How many cartridges are there? The magazine takes five, doesn't it?"

"You want to start her up? But there's no one to fly her. Mr. Nielson only comes over for display days."

189

"I'm taking her up, Harold," Martin said casually. "I want to see how she handles with the extra load inside her. Just a couple of circuits."

"But I didn't know you were a pilot—"

"Listen, laddie, I was flying one of these against the Luftwaffe when your dad was in short trousers." Martin's voice was sharp. "Now why the devil don't you do as you're told and check those cartridges?"

The apprentice started checking the Coffman mechanism, looking back over his shoulder as he did so. "I thought only Uncle Mike could authorize flights with our aircraft. I mean—you have to have a pilot's license—"

"And what makes you think I don't have a pilot's license?" Martin asked wearily. "Now stop buggering about and tell me how many bloody cartridges there are. Are you as awkward as this with your uncle? If so, I wonder if it isn't about time we got a new apprentice."

Martin's tone of voice startled the lad. The people at Molyneux were not familiar with this shop-floor style that he used so frequently at the works.

"Four cartridges," Harold said sullenly, and stood back as Martin buttoned up his jacket and hauled himself into the cockpit.

Thirty years slipped away in a moment. The blue barathea of his trousers stuck into fleece-lined boots, Mae West over his uniform jacket, leather helmet in his hand. Into the narrow seat, landing on the parachute pack, as other aircraft all around barked into life, switch on the R/T, wait for instructions . . .

Except that there was no uniform, no helmet or boots. Just a gray suit, black leather shoes that needed repairing, blue shirt and navy-blue tie, occupied by a creaking fifty-year-old has-been. There was one solitary aircraft, stained and shabby with age, and the R/T switch connected him with nothing. The parachute pack was real, but God knew when its contents had last been checked. There was no elixir to be found in this grimy, oil-smelling box. Just a cold bud of fear in his stomach and a growing feeling of claustrophobia.

Harold was standing just clear of the wing, looking up at him. Martin automatically pulled the straps of the Sutton harness over his shoulders, then realized that, without

190

a flying suit, he had nothing to connect them to. No matter. For this trial flight he would not be indulging in aerobatics.

He turned on the electrical master switch and began to work through the cockpit drill. Booster pump off, generator warning light on, rpm override level at maximum, throttle open one and a half inches, fuel controls, ignition off . . . finally, brakes on.

He switched on the ignition, operated the priming pump plunger, then pressed the starter button. The Coffman cartridge kicked the engine into life. The cylinders fired one by one and the barking speeded up into a steady roar. He eased the throttle up until the rev counter showed twelve hundred, then held it while he watched the temperature gauges. Fifteen degrees for the oil, the *Pilot's Notes* said, and forty degrees for the coolant. The generator and fuel pressure warning lights had gone out.

There were no chocks and only the brakes held the aircraft from edging forward. At last the temperature readings were at the correct level. Martin took a deep breath and released the brakes. The Spitfire eased herself forward like the lady she was with scarcely a bump. One advantage of a concrete runway over grass.

He taxied in a zigzag course. This was essential with a Spitfire, as the engine blocked the pilot's forward view on the ground. He found his way to the start of the runway, where he braked for a moment and ensured the aircraft was properly lined up. Releasing the brakes again, he opened the throttle slowly to plus seven pounds. As the Spitfire gathered speed his hands and feet rested lightly on the controls and he relaxed into a growing familiarity with his surroundings.

The control surfaces were beginning to bite the air now and the aircraft was coming to life, eager and boisterous like a filly on its first outing. It was a feeling of uninhibited enthusiasm that Martin found himself beginning to share. Barely glancing at the instruments to confirm his instinct, he chose the exact moment to pull gently on the stick. At ninety knots the Spitfire sprang up from the ground with a dancing lightheartedness completely unlike a modern jet.

The ground fell away at a pace that took Martin's

stomach with it. He had the stick back and the nose was increasing its angle of climb with no apparent effort. He took the throttle up to plus twelve pounds, then raised the undercarriage and retracted the flaps. Within minutes the Spitfire was at seven thousand feet, flitting through fluffy cumulus formations. The ground, when he could see it through the clouds, had assumed a detached perspective with the patterned fields green and sparkling in the intermittent sun.

Martin looked round the cockpit. While it was as grimy and smelly as ever, now it was vibrant with life. He found his throat was tight with excitement, just as he recalled it being on his first solo. This time it stemmed from a combination of nostalgia and the realization of the immensity of what he was doing.

He pressed gently on the stick and rudder pedal and transcribed a graceful arc across the sky until the aircraft was heading east. Ahead he could see the fringes of the coastline and calculated he would be over the North Sea within two minutes. On the way he tentatively tested the aircraft's maneuverability against his barely remembered skill and was delighted when the two met in harmony. But for the lack of an oxygen mask and harness, he would have taken the trial to a more sophisticated level at a greater height. No matter. He knew he could handle the aircraft at a basic level and he could fill in some of the gaps during his journey north the following morning.

Once over the sea he switched on his guns and the sight came up as an orange-red light ring and two horizontal bars on the windscreen. He glanced down. No ships or vessels of any kind in sight. He took a deep breath and pressed down the button at the top of the control column.

Nothing.

It was locked in the "safe" position, of course, by a catch at the bottom. He pushed the catch up to "Fire," then tried to recall what the *Pilot's Notes* said. Pressing the top of the button fired the point-fives, pressing the bottom fired the twenty-mills, while a press at the center fired all the guns together. So it was the bottom for him.

He pushed the button. For a few seconds the aircraft seemed to stop in midflight as the shells spewed forth. The airframe shuddered violently as it absorbed the tremendous recoil. He watched the path left by the tracers ahead of him and made a rough calculation that the guns were harmonized to converge at around two hundred and fifty yards.

He released the button and the aircraft settled down. He realized he was still holding his breath and let it go with a deep sigh. The airframe had not experienced such a shakeup for thirty years, and he could only hope the shock had not been too much for it.

The sun was pleasantly warm on the side of his face as he banked into a turn and headed inland once more. The engine ran as smoothly as a sewing machine and Martin felt he could happily remain flying like this for hours. But his fuel was limited. Not only that, but there seemed to be an excessive amount of oil seepage on the engine cowling. That might be normal, but he would check with Harold when he landed. His eyes searched the gaps in the cloud until below appeared a town that seemed to be Kenley. From there he took his bearing to Molyneux.

Gently losing height as he approached the airfield, Martin felt a satisfaction that he had not known for a long time. The fear and depression had gone. Everything he had been planning was now coming into focus. He had the aircraft and his guns worked. He was sure now he could bring the necessary airmanship to bear. Depending on the weather, he had a chance of intercepting the Palestinian jet in the morning.

"All I need now is a decent night's sleep," he told himself. The tiredness he was feeling now should assure him of that.

The airfield came into view and he put the Spitfire into a broad circuit at fifteen hundred feet. Lower the undercarriage. Rpm override lever at twenty-six hundred. Flaps down. As the aircraft's speed decreased he made out the solitary figure of Harold standing in front of the hangar. He also saw two cars bumping their way across the grass from the house. As the aircraft banked to port he lost sight of them beyond the hangar. His height was now dropping below a thousand feet and he throttled back with flaps extended while preparing to line up with the runway.

The cars came into view once more. One was a dark

193

green sedan and the other a white Jaguar with a blue lamp on the roof. They were stopping in front of the hangar. His new-found confidence was shattered. Instinctively his hand went for the throttle. All he could think of was the need to get away from Molyneux as fast as possible. Then he saw the fuel gauge and knew he had no option but to make a landing.

He completed his circuit with the runway dead ahead and five hundred feet below. Ease the throttle some more. Dip the nose slightly forward. The concrete coming closer. Now it's flashing by beneath the wings. Speed down to eighty knots. Back on the stick, a gentle bump as the undercarriage connects. Roll at fifty miles per hour toward the hangar. All done instinctively while his mind raced ahead.

There were four figures standing with Harold watching him come in, two of them in police uniform. The engine coughed and spluttered as Martin throttled right back and poised his feet above the brakes and rudder pedals. As he neared the apron he swung the aircraft to the left and let it roll until it was a good fifty yards from the reception committee. He finally braked it to a halt, switched off the mags, and pushed back the canopy.

In the mirror above his head he could see Harold hurrying toward him while the police waited where they were. That was what he had prayed for.

"These men want to speak to you, Mr. Martin." Harold puffed as he came up. "Police, they are."

Remaining in his seat Martin spoke quietly and calmly. "Listen carefully, Harold, because I'm not going to repeat this. As soon as I take those men into the office, I want you to refuel this aircraft. Right away. I also want you to get an oxygen mask and flying suit and leave them in the cockpit here. Do you understand?"

The lad was gaping at him. "What's going on, Mr. Martin—?"

"Just do as you're bloody well told," Martin said with a pleasant smile for the benefit of the police as he climbed out of the cockpit and dropped to the ground.

He adopted a deliberately casual pace to walk across to the hangar where the group was waiting. It comprised a

194

police inspector, a constable, Hector Blair, and Jenkins. They watched him approach in silence.

"Why, it's Mr. Blair, isn't it?" Martin said in surprise. "Did you want to see me?"

Blair nodded stonily. "We'd like you to come with us, Martin."

"Where to?"

"Kenley police station for the moment. We've a number of questions that want answering."

Martin raised his eyebrows. "Are you arresting me?"

Blair glanced at the inspector before answering. "We want to talk. Informally. Now let's go, shall we?"

Martin shook his head. "We can talk here."

"It isn't suitable—"

"In the office."

He led the way into the hangar and through to Mike's office. On a nod from the inspector, the constable stayed at the main entrance to the hangar.

Martin sat in Mike's chair and pulled out his cigarettes. He offered them round and received three silent refusals. Blair took the most comfortable chair, Jenkins sat on an old collapsible wooden one, while the inspector, once he realized he'd missed out, stood in front of the door, hands behind his back.

"I'm flattered at such a high-powered delegation coming to see me," Martin observed pleasantly. From his seat he could see the clock above the door. Five thirty-five. Allow Harold twenty minutes to carry out his instructions. Say six o'clock to be generous.

Blair said ponderously, "You will recall the last conversation we had, Martin. When you told me of certain —ideas you had concerning the Edinburgh Conference."

"Just one idea," Martin corrected him. "Buzzing the castle."

The inspector blinked. If he had been put in the picture by Blair, he'd no doubt taken it with a large pinch of salt. Confirmation from the horse's mouth like this should make him revise his views on fancy security people who spent their time chasing nonexistent threats to security around the country.

Blair went on, "I think we agreed that you had been acting somewhat irrationally—due to stress of one kind or

195

another—and that the whole business was best forgotten."

"I don't recall you putting it exactly like that at the time," Martin said slowly. "And there was no sort of agreement. The whole thing fell through after my pilot was killed."

Blair shrugged. "Anyway, there was no further question of buzzing the castle. Now would you tell me, Mr. Martin, why you were flying that aircraft just now?"

"Certainly. This is the Molyneux Aircraft Museum, of which I am a trustee. That Spitfire is part of our collection, and I took it up for a trial flight."

"Is this one of your regular duties?"

"It's not a duty. I like flying. I flew a Spitfire in the war and I like to wallow in nostalgia as much as the next man."

"Do you have a current pilot's license?" Jenkins cut in quickly.

"You don't think I would break the law in that way, do you? Of course I have a license."

"Can we see it?"

"No." Martin smiled pleasantly. "One doesn't carry it around in one's wallet like a driving license. It's somewhere at my home."

"We can take you there now—" Jenkins began, but Blair silenced him and with an impatient wave of his hand.

"I'll put my cards on the table, Martin," Blair said. "Our people have been concerned because you disappeared from view for some time. After our last talk it was considered advisable to—well, to keep in touch. You see?"

Martin made no reply. He was looking at the clock, which showed five-forty.

Blair went on, "No one knew where you were, including your own staff. But late this afternoon we had a word with your accountant. He told us a strange tale about two machine guns being reconditioned at your factory. Yesterday you collected the guns in a van and drove off in this direction." He paused and looked steadily at Martin. "Those guns are for use in an aircraft, as I understand it. Have you installed them in an aircraft, Martin —the one you were just flying?"

196

"I have," Martin said. "And very realistic they look, too."

"Realistic?"

"Yes. They're only for show, of course. It impresses the audience on the display days."

Blair glanced at Jenkins, then went on. "My information is that those machine guns are in working order, and you went to a great deal of trouble to make them so. Why?"

Nearly five forty-five. Perhaps the refuelling was already finished. But there was still the problem of how the hell he was going to get out to the aircraft.

Martin sighed. "You don't know the mentality of the vintage-aircraft enthusiast. The equipment not only has to be there—it has to be in working order. Otherwise they feel cheated."

"Are the guns loaded?"

"Live ammunition? In a museum piece like that Spitfire?" Martin laughed. "If you fired a gun from that, the airframe would shake itself to pieces."

"We would like to take a look at the aircraft nonetheless."

"Look at it? What for?"

"To see if those guns are loaded," Blair said patiently.

Martin stared at him for a few moments. Then he said, "Why was it, Blair, that when I gave you some genuine information you chose to write it off as the vaporings of a crank? But now on the basis of some half-baked gossip from my factory, the whole weight of the security service descends on me?"

Blair stood up and said grimly, "We'll go and look now, shall we?"

At that moment the telephone rang. Martin grabbed the receiver like a lifebelt.

A man's voice said, "Is that you, Mike? Joe Roberts here. Look, I've just heard of a job lot of tires that might fit some of your kites. Would you be interested?"

Martin said, "I see."

There was a pause, and the caller said, "That's not Mike, is it? Is he there?"

"It's very difficult," Martin said. "I'm busy at the moment."

197

"I want to speak to Mike—Mike Lowe. Is he there or not?"

"I can't explain why. Look, can't it wait?" Martin looked at Blair and shrugged.

Joe became annoyed. "Mike asked me to look out for this sort of thing for him. If he's not interested—"

"It can't be that urgent," Martin said. "Anyway, I've got something even more urgent on my hands at the moment. I certainly haven't got time to look out a file for you."

"What the hell are you talking about?" Joe demanded. "I'm talking about tires. Look—is Mike there or not?"

"Oh, I see," Martin said with a sudden frown. "If it's that desperate I'll try. I'll take a quick look and see if it's in the back office. But listen," he cut in as the voice at the other end became more angry, "if it isn't there, you'll have to try something else. I just haven't the time to go delving at the moment. Now just hold on."

He put the receiver on the desk and said to Blair, "As usual with these people, it's a matter of life and death. I'll just take a quick look to keep him quiet, then we'll go and examine that plane."

He opened the door behind him and stepped through into the little storeroom. The door was on a spring that closed it behind him. He was relieved at that: to have closed it himself might have looked too suspicious.

There was a transom window about six feet up from the floor. Near it was the ancient green filing cabinet. Using the drawer handles to get a grip, he hauled himself on top of the cabinet, and by stretching to the left, he could just reach the bottom of the window frame. He pushed, and it opened with a faint creaking noise. Could it be heard outside? He waited a moment but nothing happened. Anyway, the fact that the hinges had not been oiled in years proved an advantage, for the window stayed up to where he pushed it.

Wedging his elbows within the frame itself, Martin hauled himself up so that his head poked through. He was at the side of the hangar facing the house. There was no one in sight. He wrestled his body through until only his legs remained within the storeroom. Now he faced the problem of reaching the ground without landing on his head. He twisted his body round until he was looking

198

at the roof of the hangar. Grasping hold of the bottom of the open window with both hands, he wriggled the rest of his body through. He dropped to the green, picked himself up, and started to run.

He stopped as he reached the end of the hangar. The constable had been left at the main door and it was impossible to reach the aircraft without passing him. Pausing to straighten his clothes and take a deep breath, Martin stepped round the corner and ambled in the direction of the Spitfire. The constable saw him coming, then did a quick double take. Martin could almost hear his brain ticking over as he tried to work out why the man who was being questioned by the brass should be wandering loose in this way.

Martin gave him a cheerful nod as he approached. "Looks like rain. Are they going to keep you hanging about here all evening?"

"I don't know, sir." He stared at Martin in an agony of indecision as he walked past. His orders had been clear enough: to stand where he was standing now. But no one had told him why. There had been no suggestion that Martin would try to make a break for it. And anyway, if he was making a break, he would be in rather more of a hurry, wouldn't he?

Martin slowed his pace deliberately and thrust his hands deep into his pockets as he strolled toward the Spitfire. He resisted the temptation to whistle nonchalantly: that really would be gilding the lily.

Christ. Harold hadn't finished refueling. The hose from the hand-drawn tanker was still in the wing tank. What the hell was keeping him so long?

In the office the three men watched the telephone receiver. Strange sounds were coming from it now.

Blair picked it up. "Hello—"

"What the blazes are you up to?" Joe demanded. "This call is costing me money and you're treating me like an idiot. Does Mike want those tires or not?"

"Tires?" Blair dropped the receiver and rushed across the office. He pushed open the storeroom door and saw the window.

"He's skipped," he snapped to the other two. "He can't be far—come on."

The three of them raced through the hangar, dodging round the vintage aircraft, and into the open. The constable turned round in surprise.

"Did you see him?" the inspector demanded.

"Why yes, sir. He went over to that airplane. I didn't realize he was trying to get away—"

The four of them raced across the grass toward the Spitfire. Martin was in the cockpit, while Harold was replacing the cover on the fuel tank. The constable was in the lead. Not only was he desperate to make up for the black he had made, but he had youth on his side.

The cartridge fired and the engine barked into life. Blair immediately swerved to the right.

"The car!" he called to Jenkins and the inspector.

They raced toward the Jaguar, which was standing a hundred yards away. The constable stayed on course for the aircraft itself. He reached it just as Harold started pulling the petrol bowser clear of the wing. The apprentice stepped backwards, collided with the constable, and the two of them rolled on the ground as Martin opened the throttle.

Within seconds the policeman disentangled himself and leaped at the cockpit, grasping for Martin's sleeve. The backwash of the propeller flattened him against the fuselage but he hung on.

Martin shouted, "Clear off, you bloody fool, or you'll get hurt!"

His voice was drowned by the sound of the engine, but in any case the constable would doubtless have ignored him. Persistence and dogged determination could certainly go down on his annual report. Martin deliberately put the engine up to maximum revs and released the brakes.

The aircraft moved off with a jerk that sent the constable spinning back along the length of the fuselage. Even then he made a grab for the tailplane. Martin grimly headed for the runway, and recalled wartime stories of riggers who accidentally became airborne. Reaching the runway, Martin abruptly used left brake and rudder to swing the aircraft into line with the concrete strip. The jerk sent the policeman sprawling to the ground. Increase throttle, flaps, release brakes, no time for an instrument check . . .

As the aircraft roared along the runway, the Jaguar halted directly in its path, straddling the concrete. The three men inside watched the Spitfire thundering toward them.

"Hasn't he seen us?" Jenkins asked. "He's not slowing down."

"You can't see directly ahead from a Spitfire in the tail-down position," Blair said. "Get ready to bail out of the car—look. He's swerving!"

As the tail started to lift and Martin saw the obstacle, he hauled savagely to port. The aircraft bumped and swayed as it hit the grass. For a moment it seemed as though it would tip over onto one wing.

"We've done it!" the inspector said. "He can't get up now!"

The Spitfire was bouncing on the grass surface but instead of slowing it was building up its speed.

Jenkins shook his head. "He's crazy."

"No, he isn't," Blair said tersely, slamming the car into gear. "They took off from grass all the time during the war. That plane was built to do just that."

Accelerator right down, he sent the car rocking and pitching across the grass after the Spitfire. For a few moments they were gaining on it. Then, with a gentle bounce, the Spitfire's wheels were clear off the ground. Blair brought the car screeching to a halt and leaned out of the window cursing as the plane gained height and the wheels retracted.

The constable raced up to the car, breathless, with his tie halfway round his neck.

"I did my best," he gasped. "He threw me off somehow."

Blair ignored him and snapped, "Inspector, you've got a radio in this car, haven't you? Call up your control. Tell them we're on our way back to your HQ and by the time we get there I want an open telephone line to the Ministry of Defense in London. The next decision is going to be a top-level one."

"What decision?"

"The decision to order the RAF to go and shoot down that Spitfire. Someone's got to make it."

17

Martin snatched a brief glance over his shoulder as the Spitfire climbed. Four white faces stared up at him, then dwindled rapidly away. Very soon the radio waves and telephone lines would be burning with urgent instructions for someone, somewhere, to do something.

Cloud level was low and drizzle splattered against the windscreen. At five thousand feet he levelled off. Solid cloud below hid the ground from his view. Martin looked around the cockpit. He was still unable to use his harness, but the flying suit lay in a bundle at his feet, together with the oxygen mask. Belatedly he checked the instruments. As far as fuel was concerned, the top and bottom main tanks were full, giving him eighty-five gallons, plus thirteen in the one wing tank that Harold had managed to fill before Martin had pushed him and his hose to one side.

He pulled the *Pilot's Notes* from his inside pocket and checked the table. At minus two pounds boost and eighteen hundred revs, his consumption would be forty-one gallons per hour. That should see him up to Northumberland and leave some leeway while he found his way to the airstrip. He set the supercharger switch to constant low gear, the rpm override lever to automatic, and throttled back until his speed was a hundred and eighty knots. Now the engine should be operating at maximum fuel economy.

Navigation was the next, and potentially greatest, problem. He had no radio and, at the moment, the cloud denied him any ground references. Heading north-northwest as he was, he should soon be over London. In a few minutes he would get below the cloud base and try and pick up a bearing from the city.

God, barely an hour ago he had been congratulating himself on the way everything was falling neatly into place. Now it had all blown apart. Sure, he had the aircraft all right, but that was all. No maps, all the security forces alerted, and the prospect of a night in the open in bleakest Northumberland, if he ever made it. How was he going to find his way up there in this visibility?

He pushed the stick forward and plunged into the cloud. Two minutes later the concrete spires of London appeared beneath him. He was at fifteen hundred feet as he flew over Whitehall trying to remember where he could pick up the M1.

Wing-Commander Beacham sat at his desk studying the card-index summary of reconnaissance photographic files from World War Two. The miles of film they represented were awesome in their number. How was he ever going to rationalize the reference system?

Frensham, the bright young civil servant who acted as his assistant, stood at the window watching the Whitehall traffic.

Then he looked upwards and said, "They're rehearsing the Battle of Britain fly-past early this year, aren't they?"

"Hmm?"

"There's a Spitfire going over. Quite low, as well."

These youngsters thought they knew it all, when they couldn't tell a Tiger Moth from a 747. Beacham didn't even bother going over to the window.

The only answer to this was to get the index onto the computer. After all, every other damn thing was on it. Why couldn't he admit to himself that he and his kind were anachronisms, living in a past that would never return?

Martin pulled up above the cloud base once more. He had seen enough to confirm he was heading generally in the right direction.

There was tension in his neck and the headache had returned from the morning. The bleakness of the sky around him was a reflection of his own emotion, a bleakness hovering on the brink of despair. Why? He had overcome every obstacle so far and his objective was as clearly defined as ever. Wasn't that objective still morally valid? By killing a group of fanatics, already committed to their own deaths, he could save many innocent lives. The equation was unarguable.

Height five thousand. Engine normal. Heading due north. Or was it? Two hours listening to the talk of a girl in Germany, a girl now dead, and he was cast in this fantastic role of crusader—or murderer. It wasn't enough. He could no longer justify his actions even to himself. Wasn't it possible he had reached the stage where he had lost any point of contact with reality?

It wasn't a shadow, as the sun was too low to create one. It was a darkness in the corner of his eye that made him glance to the left. A thousand feet above him, coming down in a shallow dive onto his tail, was a Buccaneer jet fighter with RAF markings.

Within five minutes of the Spitfire's departure, Blair was at Kenley police station and on the telephone to the Permanent Under-Secretary at the Ministry of Defense.

"The man's mad," he said. "Worse than that, he's clever. Quite frankly, sir, we have to believe that he's going ahead with this harebrained operation."

There was a pause before the Under-Secretary spoke. "What are his chances of success?"

"Of shooting down the Palestinian plane? I'd rather the technical people answered that, but it surely depends to a great extent on what action we take." He pondered for a moment. "Without any interference from our own people, I think it's conceivable that he could intercept the plane and shoot it down. He's already demonstrated the extent of his ability and resourcefulness. But I assume we're not just going to sit back and let him carry on with it."

"Indeed we are not. I'll get straight on to the RAF. They should be able to find him with all their damned electronic brain boxes."

The RAF were on the ball. Instead of alerting Strike Command, someone had the bright idea of checking with Training Command. Yes, they had a navigational training flight in progress within twenty miles of London. A Buccaneer, equipped with air-to-air radar.

The pilot was ordered to break off his scheduled program and give his navigator pupil a real live quarry to stalk. Pilot Officer Terry Barker, being a particularly able student, picked up the target within five minutes. Over the R/T the pilot, Flight Lieutenant James Hansen, called up ground control and reported a visual on the Spitfire, heading due north at approximately two hundred knots. What did they want him to do now, please?

No one seemed to be in a position to say. After a long pause, Hansen was ordered to keep the Spitfire in view, and further instructions would follow shortly.

In a room at the Ministry of Defense, the Under-Secretary faced the Group Captain who had brought the message from the underground control room.

"We have him in view. The simple question is, what do we do now?"

"Make him land, of course," the Under-Secretary said impatiently. "Your people can do that, can't they?"

"Not exactly. Can I use your telephone?" As he dialed he went on, "Our pilot can signal visually to him to land, and indicate pretty clearly that he must do so or he'll be in trouble. It appears his aircraft is not equipped with radio."

"Can't your pilot act more positively than that? What's the technique used by the Russians—buzzing, isn't it? Flying in close and forcing him down."

The officer raised his eyebrows. "That's rather a drastic measure. It only requires a slight miscalculation and you've got a midair collision—hello? Geoffrey? Alan here. I'm with the Under-Secretary now and he definitely wants the Spitfire to be persuaded to land. Can our pilot —what?" He listened for a moment. "I see. That makes it academic. Call me if there are any developments." He replaced the receiver and said to the Under-Secretary, "We've lost him."

"Lost him? But you've only just found him!"

Martin was surprised that they had pinpointed him so quickly. That Buccaneer pilot was probably feeling pretty smug right now, with a pat on the back to come from his squadron commander when he landed. Airborne radar was the answer, of course. If only these youngsters knew what it was like during the war, when all you had to guide you was a ground controller's voice and your own

God-given eyesight. It was a bus driver's job these days.

But radar did have a fundamental weakness.

Martin opened his throttle wide and pushed the stick forward. The Spitfire dropped like a stone. The Buccaneer immediately followed suit, but of course overdid things. It couldn't compete with the steepness of the angle the Spitfire had adopted, and its speed was its undoing. The jet shot ahead while the Spitfire, its engine screaming, dived straight down through the cloud.

Martin watched his altimeter closely. The cloud absorbed the plane like dirty cotton-wool and he could fly straight into the ground unless he was careful. As the pointer reached one thousand feet he pulled back on the stick. His speed was now nearly four hundred and fifty knots and the Spitfire was roaring and vibrating wildly. His left hand gently pulled back the throttle as the aircraft started to level off and the noise volume eased. He was now below the cloud at nine hundred feet. The Buccaneer was nowhere in sight, but he would need to get lower still to avoid those probing radar beams.

It was a flat suburban landscape below without any identifiable features. Rows of houses and straggling factories that could have been anywhere. He was down to three hundred feet and he seemed to be scraping the tops of some high-rise flats at a dizzy-making speed when he noticed a busy road to his left. He altered direction slightly and within a minute he was above a dual carriageway with three lanes of traffic in each direction and a bridge ahead. It was the M1 and that was what he had been seeking. All he had to do now was follow the motorway and it would lead him—where? He could not recall how far north the M1 now extended. He had an idea it faded out somewhere north of Yorkshire. Going to Northumberland by road he would probably have taken the A1.

After a while he thought to himself, "So why not do just that?"

The A1 ran parallel to the M1 and was, he guessed, about twenty miles to the east. Could he find it from the air? Banking the Spitfire to starboard he flew directly across country, his eyes scanning the ground below. A town directly ahead . . . river going in a loop . . . power station . . . it could be Bedford. Over open country again . . . and there, directly below, a dual carriageway. It had to be the A1, the Great North Road, heading arrowlike for Scotland.

Heavy traffic in both directions, many vehicles with their lights on because of the misty rain. He swung the Spitfire into line with the flow of traffic and came down to a hundred and fifty feet, his hands gripping the controls tightly. At this height disaster lurked only a split second away.

Flight Lieutenant Hansen reported that he was unable to regain any contact with the Spitfire. He gave the coordinates at which he had lost his visual, and control passed this on to the Defense Ministry.

"He's canny enough to get below the radar," said a wing-commander as the coordinates were translated onto a large moving display map in the underground conference room. "The information is that he's headed north. Well, look at this: the point where we lost him is as near as dammit to the M1. What's the betting that he's using the motorway as his navigational aid?"

Within five minutes all M1 police patrols had been alerted to keep a special watch for low-flying aircraft in the vicinity of the motorway.

Martin was feeling terrible. Holding the Spitfire to its rock-steady course was a physical strain that compounded his headache. He dared not increase his height, knowing that to do so would warm the hearts of radar observers over a wide radius. He had seen no trace of any other aircraft since joining the A1 and he wanted to keep it that way.

He also had to keep to this hedge-hopping level in order to stay with the traffic. Visibility was so bad now, with rain forming a fine mist, that even the headlights were difficult to see at times. He was flying just to the right of the road, following every bend and curve religiously. The cockpit was damp and steamy, as water penetrated the joints of the perspex canopy and trickled down onto his seat and the floor.

He found himself shivering. Suddenly dry clothing and a warm drink became the most desirable things in the world. Shouldn't he recognize the idiocy of what he was

207

doing and turn back now? Within an hour he could be crawling into a warm bed at Molyneux, equipped with hot-water bottles, whisky, and aspirins. True, he was in trouble enough already. They would have ascertained by now that he had no pilot's license, and sticky questions would be asked about his possession of two twenty-mill cannon complete with ammunition. But they were simple misdemeanors compared with the capital offense he was intending to commit.

A giant metal skeleton loomed out of the mist. The crossarms of the pylon were directly ahead, clutching heavy electric cables that dipped across the road. It was too late to climb.

He thrust the stick forward and banked sharply. The Spitfire screamed to no more than fifty feet above the traffic, left wing down at an angle of forty-five degrees. Martin held his breath as he watched the right wing tip. There might have been ample room to spare, but from his position it appeared the wing shaved the cable.

Thundering above the traffic as he levelled the aircraft out of its curving path, he could clearly see the startled faces of drivers below. Some even ducked their heads instinctively.

Ronald Hanbury was driving a Hillman with his wife Jenny alongside and the two children in the back.

"Look at that lunatic!" he fumed. "There's a law against low flying. In this visibility, too!"

"It wants reporting," Jenny said. "Let's stop and tell the next policeman we see."

"If he lasts that long," her husband said darkly. "The way he's going he'll kill himself before long—and some other poor beggars too."

Martin was perspiring heavily as he took the Spitfire back to one hundred fifty feet. Whether it was shock or the humidity of the cockpit he didn't know, but he felt as though he were running a fever. Every instinct urged him to turn back. With a conscious effort of will, he thrust his physical condition out of his mind and blew on the spark of his original motivation. In business one could never afford, in the stress and chaos of day-to-day management, to lose sight of the overall strategy. But now cold and damp reality threw the bizarre aspects of his plan into clear relief. What hope had he of intercepting a fast-moving jet at one precise point and, having found it, shooting it down?

He watched the fine spray of rain trailing from the wings. Should the weather be like this in the morning, he might as well not leave the ground at all. The British weather could prove the most ironclad safeguard of all for the Palestinians.

Look at that balance sheet again. There's a hell of a lot on the debit side, more than enough to convince the most committed patriot that he should give up. But the credit side must have something. His mind was confused now by the battle between pragmatism and idealism. Was it worth carrying on and failing, just so he could say he had tried? Over the weeks he had fought to suppress it, but now once more the picture of Greta began to force itself into his mind. She had given her life, while he was absorbed in self-pity just because his feet were wet . . .

This type of flying ate up the juice. According to the fuel gauge, he was now into the bottom main tank. Still enough to reach Northumberland and his stock of petrol, however. Oil pressure, electrics, everything as it should be. The engine running as smoothly as the day it came off the Rolls-Royce production line. Only the airframe itself showing the signs of age, with peeling paintwork and that brittle rubber seal seeming to attract the rain in through the canopy.

Or was the rain slackening off? The vehicles below were that much easier to distinguish. He must be into Yorkshire now, and that would be the lights of Doncaster ahead. Doncaster. What was it that had caught his eye during the road journey north?

The idle thought suddenly froze into an icy shock to his brain. He snatched the stick back and the Spitfire leaped upwards a hundred feet. It was barely enough to scrape clear of the coal mountain that reared up massively beside the road. Martin stared down grasping the trembling stick with both hands, sickness in his throat, at the bulldozers working like toys on top of the heap. Their drivers gazed up disbelievingly as the Spitfire's slipstream sent a cloud of wet coal dust slithering across the top of the mountain. The aircraft thundered past and picked up once more the line of the road, losing height as it did so.

God, for the second time he had literally scraped clear with his life. If that wasn't an omen . . .

The sky was definitely brighter ahead; the rain had eased. So he had had two narrow escapes? But that was it: he had escaped. Luck, fate, providence, whatever it was could be included on the credit side of that balance sheet. That decided him: he would stick with it for the moment at least. Besides, what would be the alternative? He could return to Molyneux and from there to the works. On his transistor radio in the office he would hear the minute-by-minute reports from the disaster area. What then? Gloat over Blair's disgrace, and then settle down to running a company that would soon no longer be his own? What the hell for?

Dimly, through the mists of his growing fever, he glimpsed again some of the boyish idealism that had started him on this adventure. Successful or not, it was going to fill a space in his life that Martin Engineering had never come near to doing.

The Group Captain pointed to the map.

"He could be anywhere in this area. We've got a dozen aircraft now covering the line of the A1 in the hope of spotting him."

"I thought it was the M1," Blair said.

"He must have changed his route. The police have had reports of a low-flying aircraft above the A1. Now that indicates to me that he's going straight up to Scotland."

"And what will he do there?"

"Land the aircraft, of course. But exactly where—that's the problem. Not a commercial airport, obviously."

Blair said, "Are there any derelict airfields he could use?"

"A number. We'll be checking them all. But that Spitfire can land on any reasonably level piece of grass."

Blair nodded thoughtfully. "Fuel is going to be his problem. The apprentice at Molyneux says the tanks were just over half full when he took off. In order to do what he proposes, he'll need a refill, won't he?"

"Certainly. But you know, Mr. Blair, from all I've been told about this man, he will have made provision for that somehow or other."

210

The two men looked at the map in silence for a few moments.

Blair said, "How long will it take to check all the derelict airstrips?"

"We're relying on the police for that. They'll be receiving from us the location of each one in the southeastern part of Scotland. Beacham of the Historical Branch is digging them out of his files. If there's nothing at the airstrips, then they'll have to start checking on every long, flat stretch of grass they can find. Let's hope it's not too wet—the poor devils could be at it all night."

Blair gave a sardonic laugh. "You're not serious, are you? How many level pieces of grass are there in Scotland? And how many can you examine in the dark?"

The Group Captain said stiffly, "If you can suggest anything else that would be more effective, then please tell us. At least we're trying to find him." He rolled up the map. "Anyway, there is one thing we're absolutely sure about, isn't there? In order to attack the Palestinian plane, he has to take off in the morning. From dawn onwards, the whole region will be saturated with RAF aircraft. He will be pinpointed as soon as he starts heading for the Palestinians' flight path. All it needs is for someone to give us the instruction." He said firmly, "This Martin is no superman, Mr. Blair. What he's proposing to do is—well, it's ludicrous. All right, he's done quite well so far, but it's been due to cunning rather than skill . . . the cunning of a madman outwitting his keeper. But give the RAF a free hand and he hasn't got a prayer."

"Thanks," said Blair as he stood up. "I'm off to a highpowered meeting with the Minister himself in the chair. I'll make a point," he added with heavy irony, "of conveying your optimism and self-confidence."

The airstrip had to be close. Martin wearily scanned the landscape ahead as he held the Spitfire down to a hundred and forty knots. Although the rain had stopped, in the gathering dusk visibility was as bad as ever.

The undulating fields of Northumberland all seemed exactly alike. He had left the A1 at Alnwick, following what he assumed was the road he had used with the van. But from the air, particularly in the half-light, he could not relate to the ground-level geography at all.

His sickness, combined with physical fatigue, seemed to slow his faculties to fifty percent of normal and his brain was hard-pressed even to match this. For the first time a feeling of panic began to take hold of him. He forced it down, telling himself that only his stupidity prevented his finding something as obvious as a concrete runway in a rural setting like this. The fuel gauge said very clearly that he had to find it within the next ten minutes.

Should he try a landing on level ground? Fields appearing flat from the air were notorious for developing the characteristics of a tank-testing area when seen at ground level. And his unannounced arrival amid a farmer's flock of sheep could very likely bring the police into the picture. He shrugged. Whatever the arguments against a forced landing, by definition that was something which offered no choice.

It was the radio mast that saved him. Invisible in the twilight, its red warning light glowed clearly as dusk descended. His heart leaped when he saw it about a mile away and immediately he altered course toward a point to the left of the light.

Two minutes later the runway was directly below. He put the Spitfire into a tight circuit that took him down to fifty feet and in line with the strip, which was now barely visible in the darkness. Throttling back to eighty knots he eased the aircraft down. The ground seemed to rush up toward him. Was his approach too fast? He had only seconds in which to decide whether to pull up and make another circuit. But even in the few minutes that would take, what little light there was would have gone completely. Taking risks was one thing, but a completely blind landing would be lunacy. He let the aircraft go.

The wheels hit the concrete with a force that bounced him out of his seat and jarred his spine up to the neck. His feet struggled to find their normal position and he jabbed repeatedly at the brakes as the Spitfire rushed through the darkness. He could not recall what lay at the end of the runway and he had no wish to find out the hard way.

Finally the aircraft eased to a halt. He moved the fuel cut-off to the fully aft position and the engine died. Then came wondering pleasure at the sheer, simple absence of noise. Martin sat in the cockpit for several minutes, devoid of energy even to push back the canopy. His clothes were saturated and his eyelids seemed to be gummed together.

He had flown with some degree of professional skill an aircraft which he had not handled for thirty years. In addition he had travelled over two hundred and fifty miles and reached his destination without any navigational aids save a compass. But there was no sense of achievement. All his mind could grasp was his desperate fatigue and his dehydrated body's ravenous need for fluids.

Finally he moved the canopy and eased himself out. The night air immediately chilled the exterior of his body, but it was a detached sort of cold: the fever still gripped his system. As he reached the ground, he staggered slightly on his aching legs and had to lean against the wing for support. The cold metal, with its peeling paint, had once more become lifeless and impersonal now that the aircraft was at rest.

"You're early. I didn't have a chance to put the light in the window."

The girl approached him out of the gloom, hands thrust deep in the pockets of her combat jacket. It was open and beneath it she wore a white sweater and jeans. Her blonde hair was as neatly groomed as ever, in contradiction to her casual dress. Her face was twisted into the little smile he recalled from their last meeting. Could it have been such a short time ago?

"I'm sorry if I've caused you any problems," he said. "The way things worked out, it was better for me to come tonight and leave in the morning."

"I'm glad you did," she said. "How do you plan to spend the hours of darkness? Tinkering with your magnetos, I suppose." She looked more closely into his face and her smile disappeared. "Hey, flying doesn't seem to agree with you, Alec. Is it air-sickness or something?"

"It's something, but I don't know what," he said. "Could be a touch of 'flu. It only came on in the last few hours. Whereabouts is the nearest pub? I want to get a bed for the night." A wave of dizziness overcame him.

"Don't be daft," she said abruptly, grasping his arm to steady him. "We've got a spare room. That's about as far as you seem fit to travel right now. Come on."

213

He hesitated as she started to lead him toward the farmhouse.

"Don't believe all those jokes about the farmer's daughter," she said, the smile back again. "You're not a commercial traveller, anyway."

"I appreciate the offer," he said, "but I was thinking of your father. I don't want it to appear I've come barging ing in uninvited."

"I've invited you. Anyway, the old man's down at the Swan for the evening. When he gets in he'll be too far gone to count how many people are in the house. Come on."

She led him in through the front door, into the living room, which was as cozy as he remembered it.

"Sit here," she commanded, pointing to the leatherette-covered armchair in front of a large coal fire. "I'll get you something to eat."

"And to drink," he croaked. He felt as though there were no drop of moisture left in his body.

She gave him hot soup and sandwiches, but he was unable to take the solid food. He drank what seemed like several pints of orange squash and then sat back with his eyes closed, allowing the warmth of the fire to relax his knotted muscles. Annette moved with quiet briskness in and out of the kitchen, and once it was clear he wanted nothing else, she slipped upstairs. When she came down ten minutes later he was almost asleep in the chair.

"Your bed is ready," she announced, firmly grasping his shoulder and persuading him to stand. "I'll show you where your room is."

Situated at the back of the house, it was no bigger than a box-room, almost filled by a huge old-fashioned bed.

"Put these on," she said, indicating a pair of worn pajamas on the counterpane. "You don't need any help, do you?" she added with an exaggerated eagerness that forced a grin from him. "I'll be back in a few minutes."

When he finally crawled between the cotton sheets he was conscious of the cold. Then Annette came in with two stone hot-water bottles.

"One for your feet and one to cuddle up to," she explained, lifting the sheet and thrusting them underneath. "Now just stay awake for about two more minutes."

She went downstairs again and returned this time with a handful of aspirins and a cup of hot milk. It was laced with whisky, he realized as he sipped it. When he had swallowed three of the tablets and finished the milk, she pulled the sheets up to his chin and smoothed the pillow.

"Now let's see what a night's sleep can do for you," she said. "You're neither use nor ornament to any woman in your present condition."

"Thanks, Annette. Now listen." He spoke as earnestly as he could. "Will you do me a favor? Please make sure I'm awake by seven in the morning. No later than that."

"Seven?" She raised her eyebrows. "You really do spoil yourselves down south. The livestock round here normally won't let you sleep on after five."

"I am serious. Please wake me by then."

"Don't worry, Alec," she assured him, tucking the sheets under the mattress. "I shall sleep curled up on the mat outside your door, ready to jump to your bidding. What else is a woman for?" She put her fingers to her lips and then planted them lightly on his forehead. "Now go to sleep and dream about me but wake me up if it gets really interesting."

As she went out of the room, the light from the landing before she closed the door glinted on her blonde hair. It became Greta's hair as he drifted into a half-sleep. Greta was there and he was rolling in the bed, his body on fire and his head drumming. She was placing something on his forehead that was cool and damp. He stared up at her anxious face.

"I'll do it, Greta," he croaked. "I promised you, didn't I? I'm going to stop them tomorrow."

18

The Secretary of State for Defense was in this most blistering mood.

"I've never come across such an almighty cock-up in my life," he snarled, slamming his briefing papers on the table around which were seated the senior staff of his department, both civil and military. "This thing has been building up for weeks, apparently, and I'm only brought into it now—when you've lost control and it's too late to do anything."

"It's not quite correct to say it's too late, Minister," Marquis, the Permanent Under-Secretary said quietly. "It's because there is something we can do that this joint meeting has been called—"

"I know why it's been called," the Minister snapped. "It's so you have a minister to take the can back for you. You've involved me so there's something on record to cover yourselves."

"I must protest, Minister," Marquis went on, more firmly. "We know exactly what can be done to prevent this man achieving his objective. But it requires ministerial approval right across the board—Defense, Home Office, Foreign Office. We feel that the initiative as far as the other ministers are concerned should come from yourself. The weight your views carry will ensure prompt and incisive action from them."

It was blatant flattery laid on with unblinking civil-service style and, as always, it worked.

The Minister remained silent as Marquis went on, "We're dealing with that most difficult and dangerous of problems—an unbalanced man with a lethal weapon. The sheer unpredictability of his actions has, up to now, been his most effective cover. But by this time everything has narrowed down to a situation whereby we know what he intends to do and when."

"You know everything except how to stop him," the Minister said sarcastically.

"Not true," Marquis said evenly. "There are three lines of defense, so to speak, in ascending order of urgency. First, we can find Martin before the morning, which is something the police are working on now. If they fail, then the next step is the obvious one: the Palestinians must be told to delay their arrival until we do find him."

The Minister snorted. "You don't *tell* these characters to do anything. What reason are you going to give? That the whole UK defense system is unable to protect them from one bloke in an antique aircraft? We'd be a laughingstock."

"Whatever reason we give, Minister," put in Harvey from the Foreign Office, "from this country's point of view postponement of their arrival will be the most straightforward solution."

Marquis went on, "Should they refuse, then it becomes a military problem pure and simple. The RAF will saturate the area and give complete cover to the Palestinian aircraft."

The Minister looked at the clock and shook his head in despair. "Nine o'clock at night and I have to go back to the House and present my colleagues with a basket of snakes like this." He rose. "We will reconvene this meeting at midnight, when I will report the PM's reaction."

The sheets were soaking wet and tangled into ropes around his legs. He held the Spitfire in a vertical climb, desperate to escape from the cotton-wool cloud that choked him. Greta was still there, anxiously sponging his forehead while he sought for any sign of the jet.

"They'll try to stop me," he told her. "Now they know what I'm doing they'll try everything they can. . . . They'll try to kill me. . . ."

The whirling mass of planes had British and German markings. Among them was a jet and he couldn't find it because of the smoke and flames. Blair was struggling to push the stick forward, but he wasn't going to let Blair ruin everything now.

"Look," he said to Blair, pointing to the left.

Blair looked out at nothing while Martin slipped away from him and into the mass of burning aircraft, pleased at the brilliant ingenuity of his ploy. But the jet wasn't there. . . .

The Minister was twenty minutes late for the midnight meeting. When he entered the room his face was drawn.

"All hell is loose now," he said grimly. "It's turned into a special Cabinet meeting. I have to report to them exactly what our course of action is to be."

Marquis said, "The police have found nothing yet, Minister. The feeling among ourselves is that the second course of action must be followed: delaying the visit."

The Minister said, "It was the first thing the Foreign Secretary attempted to do when he heard about this. The Palestinians were contacted and asked to make a later arrival." He shrugged. "They refused. Point blank. Let's face it, all they're coming for is to create embarrassment, and they regard our suggestion as being aimed at preventing that."

There was a pause. Then Marquis said, "We have no option but to proceed to Phase Three. The RAF will give them an escort—"

"No," the Minister said. "They emphasized that there is to be nothing of that kind. It would give the impression that they are afraid of their enemies and that the whole world is not necessarily on their side. And an official escort from a nation like Britain would be anathema to them. They will fly in alone."

There was a buzz of conversation around the table.

Marquis thought for a moment, and said, "Very well. But the RAF will still take care of the situation. As soon as Martin's aircraft takes off, it will be located. They will force him down—or, at least, out of the path of the Palestinian aircraft, creating a safe corridor. That will be feasible, Air Marshal?"

"Indeed," said the blue-uniformed figure to his right. "Martin was able to avoid detection during his flight north by flying at nought feet. He can't meet the Palestinian jet without climbing much higher than that, and then we've got him."

"I can report that to the Cabinet?" the Minister said, rising to his feet.

"Yes, sir."

As the meeting started to break up, a thin figure at the far end of the table spoke diffidently. "This lack of co-operation by the Palestinians—surely it couldn't mean there's some substance in Martin's story?"

But the Minister had already left the room.

The fever had gone. Martin sat up in bed as the feeble dawn light seeped through the window. Annette stood by the bed and felt his forehead.

"You're not the hot stuff you were during the night. In fact you seem almost normal."

"What time is it?"

She looked at her watch. "Six-fifty. You can go back to sleep for ten minutes."

"What's the weather like?"

"Dry and overcast. Moderate westerly wind. Pretty cold."

He pondered on that for a few moments. Then he noticed she was wearing a dressing gown. "Did you get up specially to wake me?"

"You're joking, aren't you?" He looked puzzled and she went on, "I've been here most of the night. Didn't you notice? So much for the impact of my vibrant charm."

The distorted half-dreams of Greta came back to him. "I did see you. I just had the feeling you were someone else—"

"Who is this Greta? She certainly seems to fill a big part in your life. I gathered she isn't your wife?" She looked at him questioningly.

"She was close to me. But she's dead now." He pushed the sheet aside and put his feet on the floor.

"Just a minute," she said. "You aren't really serious about getting up at this time, are you? You're really not fit—"

"I feel a lot better this morning than I have done for several days," he told her. "Now I've a lot to do, and I want you to help me. To start, could you pass me my

219

clothes and then possibly make me some breakfast? I'm glad to say I'm quite hungry."

There was a shakiness in his limbs as he dressed, but he felt he could overcome that.

Over a meal of cereal, bacon, and eggs that Annette served to him by the fire downstairs, Martin spoke to her with quiet urgency.

"As soon as I've finished this, I have to go out and fuel-up the aircraft. It would be easier if there were two of us. Could you give a hand?"

"You're daft. It's cold out there, and anyway you're not fit to fly that airplane."

"I've flown feeling a damn-sight worse than this. Will you help?"

She sighed. "I suppose so. I feel now as though I'm thoroughly involved in whatever you're up to. You're not going to tell me what it is, I suppose?"

"I can't at the moment. Do you know the village of Colesford? It's about ten miles from here."

"I know Colesford. I don't know anyone who lives there."

"That's good." He searched through his pockets until he came up with a business card. "What time is it now?"

"Seven-thirty."

"It's probably a little too early to call him."

"Call who?"

He showed her the card. "A man named Hillier who flies an aircraft out of Colesford. Annette, are you willing to do something out of the ordinary?"

"Try me," she said mischievously.

"Listen. I'm going to ring Hillier and tell him I'm a newspaperman who wants to arrange a charter flight for a photographer. You're going to be the photographer."

She stood behind the chair and felt his forehead. "Still cool enough. So you must know what you're doing. What *are* you doing, Alec?"

He was silent for a few moments. Then he said, "I want you to take my word for it, Annette, that this is all of vital importance to a lot of people—good, decent people. I can't tell you any more right now, because it's far too complex. But by the end of the day you'll realize what you've been involved in. And you'll have no reason to feel ashamed, I promise you."

"Oh." She sat on the rug between him and the fire, her legs tucked beneath her. She stared at the flames as she spoke. "Whatever you're planning to do yourself, Alec, I gathered from the things you said in your sleep that it involves a strong element of risk to your life."

He shrugged. "Crossing the road is risky. Not to mention driving that tractor the way you do."

"What I mean is, if I do cooperate, is it going to lessen the personal risk for you?"

"Yes. I suppose it could.'"

"Very well. Now how do I set about looking like a photographer? I've got an Instamatic upstairs."

He smiled. "I don't think you'll need to display an actual camera. Have you got a bulky leather bag? That can look as though it's packed with equipment."

She was puzzled. "But this Hillier character is going to expect me to take some pictures, isn't he?"

"It won't get that far. Don't worry, you won't need to take any. Now will you come and help me fuel-up the Spitfire?"

As they stood up a thought struck him. "Your father—where is he?"

"He's been up for a couple of hours. He's down at the bottom meadow now, wiring some fences. We have pretty savage sheep around here, you know. Wait." She went into the kitchen and came back with an ancient, oil-stained army greatcoat. "Not quite Dad's Sunday best. He only uses it when it's cold."

As she helped him into it, he said, "So today isn't cold by his standards?"

"Lord, no. If the frostbite doesn't attack more than your nose and fingertips, it's a mild spring day. Come on."

A chill wind swept across the fields as they walked over to the Spitfire. The sky was gray but the sun was fighting to break through. Thank God at least it was dry.

Annette helped Martin carry the jerrycans to the plane, and then she brought a large funnel from the building where the tractor was housed. The fumes as he emptied the cans into the Spitfire's tanks gave him a sick feeling, but he hid his problem from Annette. Finally the last can was empty. He gratefully climbed off the wing and drew a deep breath of fresh air.

"You're looking a bit green," she told him.

221

"I'll be all right. Let's get back to the house and arrange your little jaunt."

Hillier himself answered the phone.

"I don't know if you recall, Mr. Hillier, but we had a chat a few days ago. Alexander is the name—I'm in newspapers among other things."

"I remember our chat, although I didn't realize you were a newspaperman. How are you, old chap?"

"In a bit of a spot. Our usual charter company has let us down, and one of my photographers needs an aircraft. Would you be available, by any chance?"

"Could be. Let me check the diary—"

"You won't need a diary. I want this right away. Take-off at nine-fifteen, in fact."

Hillier gave a whistle. "You newspaper chaps expect a lot for your money."

"Sorry about that, but news doesn't happen to a time-table. What will the charge be?"

"Depends where you're going and the distance involved."

"This is a flight out over the North Sea—say a two hundred-mile round trip."

"Oil-rigs, I suppose. Well, let me see." After a few moments he took a deep breath and said, "I can do it for one-fifty."

"Right. The photographer is on her way over. She'll give you the exact destination."

"A woman? They're into everything now. Where do I send the bill?"

"I'll pay cash, if that's more convenient."

"It certainly is." That meant the transaction would not go through the books. "I'll start warming up the engines. We'll be ready to go as soon as she arrives."

As he put the phone down, Martin suddenly thought of something. "How will you get over to Colesford? You can't very well do it by tractor."

She laughed. "It's all right. I've got the Marina back from the garage."

"Good. Now, have you got an atlas? Preferably one showing the British Isles on a large scale."

Annette brought the red atlas from the trunk in her room. Opening it at the page covering northeast England,

222

he began to work out a course over the North Sea. Finally he wrote it down on a piece of paper and handed it to her.

"That's the course you want the pilot to take."

"Right," she said. "Now that only leaves one thing—the money. Haven't I got to give him some cash?"

"That's the agreement, but I don't have that much cash. You'll have to cash this check and give it to him in a day or two."

"Now just a minute," she said sharply. "What's to stop you paying him yourself? Just how risky is this business for you, Alec?"

"It's not the risk," he said. "It's just that, once it's over, I'll have to go south again. It would be more convenient if you could give him the cash. Now when you arrive at his airstrip and he finds you haven't got the cash with you, he'll grumble a bit. But he'll still take you. Mr. Hillier needs the business."

The outer door opened and Mr. Bailey walked in. He grunted toward Martin as he opened the sideboard and took out a large ball of twine.

"I'm going out for a couple of hours, Dad," Annette said. "I'll be back for lunch."

"Not going up in that airplane of his, are you?" Bailey asked suspiciously.

"No, Mr. Bailey," Martin said. "Mine is only a single-seater. I'll be leaving shortly myself, by the way. Thanks for your hospitality, and for the use of your runway."

Bailey said, "At the Swan last night, Sidney Parsons was asking about an airplane like yours."

Annette glanced at Martin and said quickly, "He's the local bobby."

"Said they'd been asked to watch out for any airplanes landing in the area last night. You're not in trouble with the police, are you?" he asked, looking Martin directly in the eye.

Martin shook his head. "Nothing like that. I won't get you into trouble, Mr. Bailey." There was a pause. "What did you tell him?"

"Nothing. At that time I thought you weren't due until the morning." He opened the door and spat on the ground before stepping out. "None of their business, anyway. Bloody VAT."

223

As the door closed behind the farmer, Martin said in puzzlement, "What did he mean by VAT?"

"That's his obsession. He reckons the whole country is geared to trying to squeeze as much money out of him as possible. That's the only reason the police are interested in airplanes landing here, in his view: they want to know how much he's getting paid."

She went upstairs and came down with an old Gladstone bag.

"This is the nearest I can get to a briefcase. Believe it or not, Granddad Bailey used to store his money in it and keep it under his bed."

"It'll do."

Martin watched as she took a duffle coat from a hook behind the door and struggled into it.

He said, "Luckiest thing I ever did, coming here. I'd search for years and not find a girl like you."

"What?" She frowned as she pushed the toggles of the coat through their loops. "Does that mean you've actually noticed me at last? And, what's more, noticed that I'm a girl? Wow. We might uncover a streak of romance in you yet, Alec."

"I'm serious," he told her. "You're really some girl, helping me out in this way on the basis of a very brief acquaintance. I could be up to any amount of no good for all you know."

She sighed as she picked up the bag. "I'm the girl who spent the night in your bedroom, remember. I can vouch for the fact that, given the chance to get up to no good, you remained a shining pillar of virtue."

She walked up to him and studied his face. "You look in reasonable condition now. Try and get back in one piece, Alec. It would mean a lot to me."

She kissed him lightly on the mouth and then went to the door. She turned and smiled at him. "See you later, maybe?"

"I hope so."

She went outside and reversed a red estate car out of the shed across the yard. With a brief wave she sent the car bouncing out of the yard and along the track.

As she disappeared, so did the smile on Martin's face. He stood in the doorway staring at the sky. The sun was still trying to find a way through the broken cloud to the east. There was a moderate wind from the west, which might mean a clear sky before long.

A slight shiver passed through his body. He told himself it wasn't the fever coming back, simply the cold wind. That and the fact that he was proposing to set out now to kill two men. He pulled the coat tight and trudged over to the runway. The Spitfire stood silent against the background of wind-worn grass, its wings coated with dew. He used his sleeve to wipe the moisture from the windscreen. The canopy had been open all night and the cockpit itself looked cold and damp. Then came the realization that the Spitfire was headed in the wrong direction.

He made a conscious effort to shake off the sluggishness he felt. Pull yourself together, you damn fool. You've got a vital job to do that you've been setting up for weeks. Don't cock it up now, just because of a bit of hangover from a cold.

Where was Bailey? Annette had said something about the bottom meadow. A glance at his watch suddenly made him hurry. Eight forty-five. God, he had to be airborne in fifteen minutes. What was the matter with him? He shook his head violently from side to side as though to clear the grit that was clogging his mind. He was acting like a bloody zombie, losing track of time as well as overlooking all the obvious things.

He found Bailey two fields away. The farmer was standing by a gate that led onto the road, talking to a police constable whose white panda car was parked outside the gate. Both men looked round as Martin hurried up. The farmer stared at him and Martin realized he was studying the army greatcoat.

"Annette lent it to me—hope you don't mind," he said quickly. "Mr. Bailey, there's something needs doing. Could you come along and help me sort it out?"

Bailey looked uncertainly at the constable and then back at Martin. "What sort of thing?"

"The machine I brought along—I need help in starting it up."

"Oh. I see." After a moment's rumination he turned and nodded to the constable. "See you, Sidney. Regards to Alice."

He followed Martin back along the path, but doggedly refused to increase his pace above the usual deliberate plodding. Martin had to hold back and wait for him.

"Sidney was asking me about airplanes again," the farmer said after a while. "The way he described it, they're looking for one like yours."

He was alongside Martin now and, looking straight ahead, he went on, "From what he told me, the character flying this airplane is planning to do something daft with it. He's not a criminal, you understand, but they want to stop him making a fool of himself."

They walked in silence for a while. Finally Martin asked, "Did you tell him about my aircraft?"

"Course not. What the hell is it to do with them, who I allow on my land? There's too much nosing into other people's affairs these days."

They reached the Spitfire. Bailey looked at it uneasily and said, "You don't want me to turn that propeller around?"

"Nothing like that. I have to get the aircraft pointing the other way. Could we use your tractor to turn it?"

Bailey brought the machine over from the farmyard. Martin attached the tow-rope to the tail wheel and directed the farmer as he maneuvered the aircraft around. As Bryant disconnected the rope, Martin climbed into the cockpit. It was as cold and damp as it looked. He switched on the main fuel cock, set the wing transfer selector cock to normal and the rear fuselage tank cock to off. Throttle open one and a half inches, rpm override to maximum, fuel cut-off fully aft.

Next he switched on the main tank booster pump for thirty seconds to prime the system, then set the fuel cut-off control fully forward. All this he did while checking the *Pilot's Notes* and thanking his stars that he had managed to steal them from Molyneux. While flying the aircraft was still an instinctive procedure for him, the book was vital for the essential preparations.

After setting the cartridge starter breech, he operated the priming pump until the sudden increase in resistance showed the fuel had reached the priming nozzles. He switched on the ignition, then gave two more strokes to the priming pump. Leaving the plunger out, he pressed the starter button.

With black and white smoke puffing from the exhausts, the engine clattered into life and sent squadrons of crows flapping up from the surrounding fields. He screwed down the priming pump and turned off the priming selector cock. After opening the engine to twelve hundred rpm he left it to warm up as he lowered himself to the ground.

Bailey had stood watching the procedure with interest. Martin stripped off the greatcoat and handed it to him.

"Thanks for your help," he shouted above the noise of the engine and started to pull on the flying suit. Harold had done a thorough job when he threw it into the cockpit, for he had included the life jacket as well.

Martin glanced at the sky. The cloud was breaking up fast and there were broad patches of blue to be seen. As he was about to climb back into the cockpit, Bailey tapped him on the shoulder.

"Wherever you're going, the best of luck to you," the farmer shouted. "Annette is convinced you're a good 'un, and you're doing something worthwhile."

"When did she say that?" Martin asked in surprise.

"We had a long chat this morning, before you woke up. She's a bit on the wild side, is Annette, and I can't always work out what she's talking about. But she's good at two things—judging horses and people. You're OK, Mr. Martin."

He stepped back to the edge of the runway and gave a brief wave as Martin climbed into the cockpit. Martin nodded to him as he fastened the Sutton harness and his eye went over the instruments.

The oil and coolant temperatures were well up. Now the controls. Elevator neutral, rudder full left, flaps up . . . everything was now as it should be. The plane was fuelled, armed, and ready to fly. While the pilot wasn't a hundred per cent, he felt better than he had twelve hours previously. He looked at his watch. One minute off nine o'clock. Annette's aircraft should take off fifteen minutes from now. To the east the sky was now a bright blue.

Martin felt the tension building up inside him. Against all the odds, the weather was opening up to his advantage. If it stayed like this, the Palestinian plane would be approaching the Firth of Forth in perfect visibility. That would be in less than one hour from now. And he was going to be there to meet it.

Opening the throttle wide, he used brakes and rudder to steady the aircraft and line it up with the runway.

On the road alongside the farm, Police Constable Sidney Parsons was about to start the engine of his panda car. He paused as a wave of sound roared over the hedges toward him. Whatever machine it was that Jack Bailey was talking to that chap about, it made a heck of a racket.

The sound grew louder.

Above the hedge a blue-gray shape moved at increasing speed into the air. The sun glinted on the canopy as the Spitfire banked away to the right and its wheels disappeared into the slots beneath the wings.

Constable Parsons reached for the hand-set of his radio.

19

A few miles south of Aberdeen, in an underground control room, a group of men watched a bank of radar screens. Hector Blair felt out of place among the gold braid and blue uniforms. Not only was he in civilian clothing, but he felt decidedly scruffy after his night flight up from London. The Air Commodore who had shared the Andover transport aircraft with him had contrived to remain as starched and fresh as if he were on the parade ground.

"How many aircraft have you in the air now?" Blair asked the Air Commodore when he next turned away from the screens.

"Twenty actually in the air, covering the route the Palestinians will follow. Another dozen on standby that will take off as soon as we get a trace on him."

"Armament?"

The Air Commodore said, "We took note of your request. As theirs is a deterrent rather than an attack role, our aircraft are armed with guns as opposed to missiles." He smiled. "A quick burst of those gatlings across his bows should give him pause for thought if he proves uncooperative."

"You're certain you can pick him up on radar?" Blair asked. "You didn't have much success yesterday."

The officer pointed to a separate screen that had been set up on a temporary rig at the side of the room.

Blair studied it and said, "What's so special about this one?"

"Our normal radar network is aimed out to sea—quite naturally, of course, because that is where a hostile force could normally be expected to come from." He grimaced. "In this case, of course, it's an internal threat. So Coastal Command have stationed a Nimrod aircraft on a patrol course inland. That's acting as a satellite for us—scanning and bouncing the picture down to this temporary rig."

Blair nodded. The Nimrod, a long-range submarine hunter, was packed to the brim with detection devices of all kinds.

He said, "But even the Nimrod won't be able to pick him up if he follows his usual pattern of hedge-hopping?"

The Air Commodore said patiently, "True. But he can't make his attack unless he gains some height, can he? No, Martin won't be doing any low-level flying today. And as soon as he pops up on our screen, we'll have him."

Blair looked at the twenty-four-hour clock on the wall. Twelve minutes past nine. The Palestinians should be starting to cross the North Sea any moment now. In less than an hour they would be touching down at Edinburgh's airport, Turnhouse. So where was Martin?

Blair felt a knot of unease in his stomach. He was surrounded by a dazzling display of scientific expertise, all geared to pinpointing that ancient Spitfire and surrounding it with a blocking screen of aircraft as soon as it appeared. Martin didn't stand a chance. But why didn't Martin himself realize that?

Martin's trouble, of course, was that he was living thirty years in the past and had no grasp of the enormous technical odds he was facing. In his obstinacy, he would believe that sheer cunning and flying skill were enough to defeat the most sophisticated defensive system of the 1970s.

And the root of Blair's unease was that he suspected Martin could be right.

At that moment the operator at the temporary screen called out, "We've got something here."

Blair joined the others as they gathered round the screen. The operator in radio contact with the Nimrod passed a piece of paper to the Air Commodore.

He studied it, then gave a nod. "This is Martin, all right," he told Blair, satisfaction in his voice. "He's taken off from somewhere in Northumberland and he's on a direct interception course for the Palestinian aircraft." He picked up the telephone that was linked to the RAF gound controller for the fighters. "Get all your aircraft to converge on this bearing," he instructed.

As the orders went out, Blair watched the screen. It made sense. Who else but Martin would be taking off from that point and heading on that course at this particular moment? But the feeling of unease was still there.

"Can I make a suggestion?" he said to the Air Commodore, who had just put down the phone. "Keep your aircraft on station covering the Palestinians' route, and use your reserves for intercepting this unidentified one."

"Unidentified?" the officer said with impatence. "But it's your people who told us roughly where and when to expect Martin. That's him on the screen, doing just what you expected."

"Nevertheless," said Blair doggedly, "I feel we should not jump to conclusions. Please do as I say."

"This is now an operational situation," the Air Commodore said stiffly. "The RAF is in control and we do not take our instructions from civil servants."

Without replying, Blair went over to one of the telephones. He had arranged an open line to the Ministry of Defense, and within seconds he was through to the Secretary of State.

He rapidly explained the situation and concluded, "It's my considered view, sir, that we must not leave any possibility uncovered."

The Minister sounded fretful. "Surely those radar boys know what they're about, and the RAF is capable of making an intelligent assessment. The brass-hats don't like us civvies interfering in actual operations. I think you're making too much of this, Blair."

"Perhaps so, sir. But you'll recall the Cabinet's decision: they instructed you to take any action which you considered necessary to protect the Palestinian aircraft, including the ultimate sanction against the Spitfire itself. I am here now as your representative. The RAF have to be told that they must accept my decisions as coming from you and implement them accordingly." He paused. "I consider the course of action I have just outlined to be essential. If you decline to accept that, then I will put down your decision in writing here and now and have it witnessed. I have to cover myself."

There was a snort at the other end of the phone that indicated a suppressed explosion. Then there was a pause. Finally the Minister said, "Let me speak to the officer in charge."

Blair passed the phone to the Air Commodore with a feeling of grim satisfaction. The civil service methods were unbeatable. An experienced politician knew his career could be wrecked by a piece of A5 paper, which would carry far more weight at an inquiry than any amount of verbal self-justification.

The officer's expression was tight-lipped when he put down the phone. Ignoring Blair, he went over to the other phone linking him with the ground controller. Tersely he ordered that those aircraft in the air should resume their original stations, while the reserve force was to be used for the interception.

Then he turned and studied the radar screen in silence. In another corner of the room the teleprinter started its chatter. When the message was completed, the operator tore it out and handed it to the Air Commodore.

There was triumph in his voice as he turned to Blair. "The police report that one of their patrols saw a Spitfire taking off from a disused airfield in Northumberland twenty minutes ago. What do you make of that, Mr. Blair?"

"Twenty minutes?" Blair snapped. "They were told to notify us immediately of anything they saw."

"The message adds, 'Regret delay due to fault in officer's radio.' "

Blair took the message from him and studied it. "Covington. Where is that?"

He went over to the large-scale map spread out on the table. After a while he found the village and studied the position of the disused airstrip in relation to the coast.

Finally he said to the Air Commodore, "Can you indicate on this map the point where your radar made its first contact?"

With the help of one of the radar operators they eventually pin-pointed a spot ten miles south of Covington.

Blair nodded. "You will see that there is also an airfield in that area. Can you think of any reason why Martin should take off from Covington and then fly south to another airfield, when his target is to the northeast?"

The officer shrugged. "Surely all the evidence up to now has been that this character is irrational?"

Blair said, "Unpredictable, yes. Irrational, no. Our problem in dealing with Martin is a straightforward one: he knows exactly what he's doing, whereas we have to guess. And up to now we've been very poor guessers."

"Well, it won't take long to clear this one up," the Air Commodore said, studying the radar screen and then glancing at the clock. "Our aircraft should be intercepting him four minutes from now."

The coastline came into view. Through the side window of the Cessna, Annette watched the fields giving way to a strip of beach and then they were over the sea.

"Good weather for photography," Hillier said from the pilot's seat alongside her. He was wearing sunglasses and a long-peaked cap, in emulation of the barn-storming pilots he saw in American movies. Annette thought the only prop missing was a well-chewed cigar between his teeth.

He was right about the weather. The cockpit was splashed in brilliant sunlight and the sea was reflecting a blue sky.

"Shouldn't you be getting your cameras ready?" Hillier asked, glancing at the Gladstone bag on her lap. "We'll be reaching your destination in about fifteen minutes."

"There's plenty of time," she said casually.

Where was Martin now? Over the sea somewhere, she assumed. It was clear that her role was to be a decoy of some kind, and all she could hope was that she was fulfilling it efficiently. The possibility that whatever Martin was up to might bear the stamp of illegality did not trouble her. She was a law-abiding girl as far as it went, but she did not believe in blind obedience to any law, constitutional or moral. Her basic creed being the ultimate freedom of the individual, she regarded it as logical to apply her individual judgment to every philosophy or cause that sought to involve her. Clear thinking was one of her principal intellectual assets. This, combined with the pragmatism she inherited from her father, enabled her to avoid the more specious and ephemeral causes. She was an idealist, but she leavened her idealism with a commonsense view of life as a finite period of time in which only so much could be achieved—and enjoyed.

Her empathy toward Alec Martin was for a man who, when he believed in something strongly enough, would take very positive action—as he was doing now. A criminal he was not, at least by her standards, regardless of what the law might say. She had heard enough from him in his delirium to be convinced of his sincerity.

"Strange. Looks as though we've got company."

Hillier pointed toward the right, from where three jet aircraft were converging on the Cessna. Annette looked in the other direction and saw another three on that side.

"They're above us as well," Hillier said in bewilderment. "What the hell is going on?"

The RAF roundels were visible as the jets swept in and took up position on each side of the Cessna. Annette could clearly see the pilot of the nearest aircraft. He was looking across at them and waving his hand as though to push the Cessna back.

"He's telling us to turn round!" Hillier exploded. "Who the hell do they think they are? We don't take orders from the RAF!"

Annette said nothing. The jets began to pull ahead and took up a close formation pattern around and in front of the Cessna. After rocking their wings, they began a gradual bank to port. To avoid a collision, Hillier had to turn with them. The Cessna was being forced inexorably back to the coast.

"Take no notice," Annette said suddenly. She had the feeling that, the longer they could delay things, the better Martin's chances would be. "They can't force us back."

"Lady, they're doing it," Hillier pointed out. "I don't like it any more than you, but I can't fight the RAF. We'll just have to go back and sort it out on the ground."

"I hope it was a help, Alec," Annette murmured to herself as the plane headed inland.

In the underground room, the message from the RAF flight leader brought an expression of disbelief to the air Commodore's face.

"A Cessna! Surely Martin hasn't switched planes—"

"Of course he hasn't," Blair snapped. "It's just as I anticipated. He's made monkeys out of us. That Spitfire is now on an interception course with the Palestinian plane.

234

Where's the phone? Get me put through to the Edinburgh air-traffic control!"

"There's no cause for panic," the officer said. "We've still got complete coverage of the Palestinian route."

"No thanks to you," Blair said harshly. "And there's no point in taking any more chances. We've got to divert that plane." He picked up the phone connecting him to the head of air-traffic control. "What contact have you got with the Palestinians?" he demanded.

"A radar fix only," the controller said. "They're dead on course, but we can't make any radio contact at all."

"Why not?"

"I've no idea. We've been trying to raise them for ten minutes. They just don't answer."

"If it's a radio fault, they might still be able to hear you," Blair rapped. "In case they can, tell them they must divert. They can go anywhere they damn well like as long as they keep clear of Edinburgh!"

He put down the phone, then dabbed his forehead with his handkerchief. The standard of air-conditioning in the room seemed to be deteriorating.

"A radio failure," he said, shaking his head. "Why does modern science contrive to let us down at the worst possible times?"

The Air Commodore watched him with something like amusement. "There's no need to get into such a flap, you know. All we're dealing with is one middle-aged man who hasn't flown for years, in a slow, antiquated aircraft. If we can't cope with him, the RAF may as well go home."

Blair muttered something beneath his breath. The Air Commodore was about to ask him to repeat it. Then he saw the expression on Blair's face and guessed it would not be anything to his or the RAF's advantage.

In an Edinburgh suburb, faces in the street stared upward as the Spitfire roared past, just two hundred feet above them. They looked startled, and were no doubt wondering what number they should ring to complain about low-flying aircraft.

Martin looked at his watch. Nine thirty-five. Ahead was the Firth of Forth and in three minutes he would turn east following the line of the firth. This was the dangerous time. He had to gain height rapidly now, and so make his first appearance on the radar screens. If the decoy had worked properly, the RAF would only just be discovering how they had been fooled. By the time they regrouped and headed for his radar fix it would, with luck on Martin's side, be too late.

His eyes scanned the instruments once more. The oil pressure was slightly down. It had flickered on occasions during the past ten minutes and there were fresh oil streaks on the engine cowling ahead of him. But the sound of the engine was healthy enough . . . and as long as it survived the next twenty minutes, that would be sufficient.

As the water of the firth appeared below, Martin pulled the Spitfire into a turning climb. The sun was bright, picking out in sharp detail the outline of the two bridges to his left. He built up the revs to twenty-six hundred with nine pounds of boost. The rev counter swung over and the airframe vibrated as the Spitfire struggled for height.

Five thousand feet . . . seven . . . ten . . . At thirteen thousand the supercharger engaged high gear. At twenty thousand he levelled off at maximum speed of four hundred ten knots. The firth had now diminished to a blue patch that widened abruptly into the expanse of the North Sea. His eyes roved around the sky ahead. It was difficult to focus and the pulse in his head was banging. God, the fever couldn't be . . . no, it was something he knew . . . that time over Holland . . . his hands slipping off the controls and Colin bellowing over the R/T . . . "Oxygen, you blasted fool!"

Martin took a deep gasping breath and pulled the oxygen mask to his mouth. The first breaths were ice-cold. He turned the regulator back slightly to adjust the flow. It was like a neat double whisky. Everything was suddenly clear, his brain razor-sharp, his hands holding the controls with delicate precision. It was 1944 and he was young and alive with energy. . . .

Six planes alongside him—no, seven including the one that was taking up position ahead of him. What impressed him most was the absolute steadiness with which the Phantoms held their course. It was as though they were all locked in on invisible wires connecting them to the Spitfire. The one in front was rocking its wings.

The realization that his bluff had failed hit him like a hammer blow.

20

He pushed the stick forward sharply. The Spitfire's nose dropped and he was hurtling toward the sea. A fraction of a second later the jets were on the same course and tightening up their stations around him once more.

Immediately he reversed his move. Wrenching back on the control column he sent the Spitfire clawing skyward at a sixty-degree angle. As the blood drained from his head he felt close to blacking out. It took longer for the jets to duplicate the maneuver as they had all overshot him in the dive. He flipped the Spitfire into a banking movement to port and skidded across the sky.

The Phantoms were too fast and too heavy to match the move. By the time they pulled round in a graceful sweep that ate up most of the sky, the Spitfire was on a climbing course to the northeast. Their turbines chalking the sky with vapor, the Phantoms took up the chase and within seconds they were once more jockeying into position around him.

Martin took a deep breath and threw the Spitfire into a controlled spin. The jets made no attempt to follow his corkscrew course downwards. Instead they spread out into a moving circle that followed a slowly descending spiral, covering him like a blanket. A thousand feet above the sea, Martin pulled the Spitfire level and searched desperately for a way to break clear. The jets enclosed him like venomous insects, waiting to spring in for the kill.

For five minutes he wriggled and turned, dredging up from his memory long-forgotten maneuvers in an effort to shake the Phantoms clear. Finally he grasped the folly of what he was doing. It was nine forty-five and he was playing the game that they wanted: the RAF pilots' aim was to kill time. All right—if he couldn't shake them off, he would take them with him. At ten thousand feet he put the Spitfire on a course due east and opened the throttle.

The jets took up their original stations around him. This time however they moved in much closer. Martin found himself gripping the controls tightly as he watched their wing-tips come within inches of his own. It was clear they were trying to break his nerve. To hell with them. If the wings did touch, they would be as likely as he to lose control. He held the Spitfire steadily to its course.

It took a couple of precious minutes and a look at his compass before he realized the subtle game they were playing. So gradually that it was barely noticeable, they were edging to the north. Surounded as he was by the jets, they inevitably became his external points of reference. Acting with clockwork unison, they were able to nurse him off his course.

In fury and desperation he once more threw the Spitfire into a dive. Like leeches they came down with him. He could see the individual pilots barricaded behind crash helmets and oxygen masks, casting impersonal glances toward him as though he simply represented one more technical problem that required solving.

Damn it, he was going east whether they liked it or not. He levelled out at twelve thousand feet, the jets holding their positions beside him. Then one of the Phantoms pulled clear, its pilot juggling his position with careful deliberation until he was directly in front of the Spitfire and about half a mile ahead. The gap between the two aircraft shortened. Suddenly the Spitfire began bucking wildly and the controls almost tore themselves from Martin's grasp. The exhaust blast from the jet was tossing him like a leaf in the wind. Another Phantom took up position beside the first, and the combined backwash practically sent the Spitfire rearing onto its tail.

Martin had never felt so ill in his life as, his stomach heaving, he struggled to hold the reeling Spitfire level. Almost without regret, he saw streaks of black suddenly appear on the windscreen. At the same time the oil-pressure gauge began to drop. He pulled back on the throttle, put the aircraft into a gentle left turn, and headed back toward Edinburgh.

In the underground radar room people stood silently beneath the wall-mounted amplifier. Blair sat astride a chair, his chin sunk in his arms which were resting on the back of it.

The voice of the RAF controller came through clearly. "A message from Foxhound Leader. I'll put him on to you live."

A crackling led into the next voice.

"Foxhound Leader here. We've got him nicely sewn up. He's coming quietly." Blair looked up sharply. The pilot went on, "We're nursing him back to Turnhouse Airport. Better have the emergency crews standing by— he's producing a bit of smoke from the engine."

The Air Commodore smiled at Blair with satisfaction. "What did I tell you? I said you could leave it to the boys in blue."

Blair picked up the telephone linked to the airport controller. "Where's the Palestinian plane now?" he demanded.

"We make him thirty miles off the coast, heading for the firth."

"How about radio contact?"

"We still can't raise a squeak from him. But he's on his proper course."

Blair thought for a moment, then said, "The RAF is bringing the intruder to you. Make sure he's landed and out of the way before you accept the Palestinian plane on circuit."

"What do you think we are?" said the controller in a pained voice. "We're not in the habit of allowing our aircraft to run into each other."

Blair went to the other phone linked to the Ministry.

"Everything is under control, sir," he told the Secretary of State. "The RAF have nabbed Martin and are bringing him in now."

"Good work," the Minister said. There was relief in his voice. "No unpleasantness, I trust?"

"There was no need to apply the ultimate sanction, sir."

"Good. Give my congratulations to all concerned. I'll

239

back it up with an official communication later. Right now I'm going home for some sleep."

No suggestion that I might need a rest too, Blair thought glumly as he replaced the phone. But somebody had to clear up all the loose ends and that was going to be a job and a half. First he had to try to scrounge a car to take him to Turnhouse Airport. He wanted to meet Martin face to face.

The sun glittered on the wavelets in the firth and the heat was building up inside the cockpit. How long would the engine last? He had throttled back and lost height to a thousand feet, but oil was now covering most of the port side of the engine cowling. All he could hope was that he might be able to nurse the Spitfire to the ground somewhere.

The jets held a steady course all round him, despite problems in keeping down to the Spitfire's speed. They weren't taking any chances until he was on the ground, safely locked up. Martin glanced at his watch. Nine fifty-three. How could so much hope, exhilaration, and frustration have been packed into only twenty minutes?

His fury had been replaced by a bitter fatalism. There was absolutely nothing more that any human being could be expected to do. God knew he had tried his damnedest. His failure was an honorable one, at least. Surely no one could deny that?

Two miles ahead was the first of the Forth bridges, the famous railway crossing. In a couple of minutes the Palestinians would be using these same landmarks to guide them to the castle.

You damn fools, he mouthed savagely to the jet pilots surrounding him. Why don't you look behind you? That's where the real threat is, not in this clapped-out flying anachronism.

Oil was filming the windscreen, distorting the forward view. But the engine note remained steady.

The delegates would now be assembled, the children poised to begin their display. Ten minutes from now would come the explosion, then the heaps of smoking, tangled wreckage. . . .

Everything had been in vain: the weeks of planning,

the deceptions, those sleepless nights, the battles with Koster—and the deaths of Greta and Philip. Failure. But not his fault. Then whose? If only the decoy had worked . . . but Annette could not be blamed for that. She would have done exactly as he asked her. Whatever went wrong would distress her as much as him.

What would he tell Annette? Tell her that what he had sought to involve her in had turned into a bungled failure?

"Try and get back in one piece, Martin. That means a lot to me."

Maybe she actually meant it, believing that he was actually going out to achieve something, the knight on the white charger. But in the stories the knight always won, which was why they were only stories.

The first of the bridges was less than a mile ahead. He glanced to the side. The jets had eased away from their close-quarters position, their pilots relaxing in the knowledge that the Spitfire was a spent force. The pressure guage was still crazy, but that incredible Rolls-Royce engine refused to waver.

Nine fifty-five. He gave a gentle touch to the stick, and almost imperceptibly, the Spitfire began to lose height.

Suddenly all the other emotions drained from him. It was as though some inhibiting link between two parts of his brain had broken, leaving only a cold, implacable determination. His mind was clear and everything had a startling immediacy. He could almost feel the roughness of the bridge steelwork ahead of him, the icy lash of the waves as he slammed the throttle forward. The engine pitch ascended to a scream and the Spitfire shot forward in a shallow dive.

The jet pilots reacted with split-second reflexes and immediately gave chase. As Martin calculated, they overcompensated and the Phantoms, with their excessive weight and power, shot ahead of him. At fifty feet above the firth he levelled off. The bridge was approaching at a dizzy speed. He aimed at the center of the arch linking the left-hand span. Common sense told him there was adequate clearance at this height, but nonetheless instinct made him force the aircraft down lower still.

The slipstream sent creamy spray whipping from the wave tops as, at twenty feet and three hundred and fifty knots, he hurled the Spitfire beneath the bridge. He was in shadow for a fleeting second but it felt as though the whole weight of the bridge were crushing down on him.

Then it was sunlight and he had the stick back as far as it would go. The Spitfire rocketed upwards in a curving loop. He could feel the G-force pulling back the skin from around his eyes. Frantically he centered the stick and the aircraft, inverted, hurtled back over the top of the bridge. As he hung from his harness, his eyes were held by the sheer scale of the network of iron girders below and around him. Then they gave way to the waters of the firth once more. He rolled the Spitfire over onto an even keel and started a steady climb toward the east.

There was no sign of the Phantoms. They would be well up the firth by now, scattered over miles of sky while they desperately tried to regroup. How much of a lead had he gained on them? Maybe no more than a minute, but it could be sufficient. Meanwhile the oil-pressure gauge was sinking lower and hot oil was spraying all over the windscreen. But the engine was still turning.

While Squadron Leader Jim Baylis felt professional satisfaction when the Spitfire conceded defeat, there was nevertheless a faint sense of disappointment at the back of his mind.

It was pure sentiment, of course. He would not have felt it had the aircraft been anything but a Spitfire. It was because this was the aircraft that, in story books, pictures, and films, had been his boyhood source of inspiration. The Battle of Britain, with the Spitfire and Hurricane in the role of twin Davids against the Nazi Goliath, first sowed in his mind the idea of a flying career. He considered himself one of the most fortunate of men to have been able to follow that career exactly as he had planned it. All that was needed to complete his dream was to be taken back thirty-five years so that he could have been an active participant in the fight for civilization.

The stab of nostalgia when he first aligned his Phantom with the Spitfire over the sea had been profound. Simply to watch that graceful creation in flight was an emotional experience. The pilot, whoever he was, handled it well, and competing against his skill had been thoroughly stimulating. The Spitfire had to lose, of course, and it was his

242

job to ensure that it did. But defeat did not belong with his image of the Spitfire and he wished, quite irrationally, that it had been some other type of aircraft.

What gave added poignancy to the occasion, as he reminded his navigator, Len Cooper, was the fact that the first time the Spitfire fighter ever went into action against an enemy was on October the 16th, 1939 . . . over the Firth of Forth.

But sentiment was not allowed to cloud Baylis's professional approach to the task he had been given. His reason for being here was to ensure, at all costs, that the Palestinian aircraft reached Edinburgh safely. Having ordered the rest of the flight to escort the Spitfire to the airport, he took up station at the entrance to the firth and awaited the visiting jet.

It finally came into view at nine fifty-six, a Gulfstream executive jet, gleaming white, flying at twelve thousand feet and on course for Edinburgh. At that moment came the call over the R/T.

"The prisoner's escaped from custody, Foxhound Leader. He's doubled back toward you."

Even before the Spitfire came into view, Baylis called his controller.

"He's on a collision course with the Palestinian aircraft. Request instructions."

"Wait, Foxhound Leader."

In the underground control room Blair had just been told that a car was ready for him, when the conversation came over the Tannoy. He rushed back and grabbed the phone.

"Ultimate sanction," he snapped to the controller. "At all costs the Palestinian aircraft must be protected. I repeat —at all costs!"

The controller was unhappy. "What authority—"

"There are witnesses here to my instruction," Blair rapped. "I'm speaking with the direct authority of the Cabinet itself. You and your pilot are completely indemnified. Destroy the Spitfire!"

He put down the receiver, his lips tensed into a tight line. A moment later the other phone rang. He picked it up.

Martin felt no elation, no sense of achievement, as he saw the Gulfstream gleaming white in the sun a thousand

243

feet above him and two miles ahead. There was an inevitability about it. After all, wasn't this the moment that all the work, the lies, the scheming—and the dying—had been leading to?

He put the Spitfire into a climb and checked through his list. Gun-sight on. Guns on. Check oil-pressure—nonexistent, if the gauge was to be believed, but somehow the engine still struggled on.

A shadow above him. A Phantom cutting across his path. The pilot looking toward him, waving him back with what looked like desperation. Martin ignored him and concentrated on the white jet. He had twelve seconds left to make his interception.

Baylis swung his Phantom round into a beam attack from above. The Spitfire came into his sights and his hand closed on the button. At the same moment Martin pushed the throttle to maximum with eighteen pounds of boost. The book said the engine could take no more than five minutes of this and it was to be used only in a situation of "operational necessity"—an Air Council euphemism for sheer desperation. The noise was unbelievable, a screeching roar of protesting metal as the oil-starved engine was flogged right past its limits of tolerance. But it responded, like a racehorse tackling one last impossible fence that it knows will mean its death. The Spitfire leaped upwards, closing the gap and heading directly at its target.

The Phantom's shells spewed forth, cutting through the air literally inches behind the Spitfire's tailplane. Baylis desperately swung round to take aim once more, in the certain knowledge that it was too late.

Martin's mind was ice-clear as he jockeyed the Spitfire into a head-on attitude to the white jet. The two aircraft had a combined approach speed of almost a thousand miles per hour. This, and the vision distortion due to the oil on the windscreen, meant that aiming as such was out of the question. It was simply a matter of pressing the button and hoping.

He flicked off the safety catch and his thumb hit the top of the button. Oh God, nothing. The bloody stupid rotten stinking guns aren't firing at the precise moment you need them because . . . because the book tells you. It tells you. Top of the button for the point fives, bottom for the cannon, center for all guns. With a groan he slid his thumb down and the twenty-millimeter sheels ripped through the sky.

But already it was too late. The jet soared above him, its shadow darkening the cockpit, and he knew he had failed. Solely and simply because of his own stupidity. The Spitfire had not failed him. It had done everything that he had demanded from it, and more. It was Alec Martin who had not been up to it. In a final gesture, he threw the Spitfire into a tight banking turn and began a futile attempt at pursuit. The engine was still at full boost and black smoke was pouring from the exhausts. The Griffon could explode at any moment but what the hell did that matter.

His eye caught the rearview mirror. It was filled with the head-on shape of the Phantom, coming down on him like an avenging hawk. Martin's muscles tensed as he waited for the shells to stitch his aircraft from end to end. Flames spat from the gatling unit beneath the Phantom's nose. The cockpit darkened once more and the jet fighter's shadow was passing over him. Martin stared upward in disbelief, his muscles still tensed, as the Phantom took up a position on the tail of the Gulfstream jet.

Another burst from the gatlings and the Palestinian aircraft seemed to halt in midflight. To Martin it was like watching a film frame by frame. A lick of flame from above the flight deck, spreading along the length on the fuselage. Then the aircraft blasted itself apart, at first like a yellow flower opening to the sun, and then into a flaming ball of twisted, melting metal.

Martin had seen many aircraft destroyed in the air. On escort duty he had been close to a Lancaster when a German anti-aircraft shell found its bomb bay. It was that moment all over again. Blazing fuel shrouded the Spitfire as he clenched the control column with both hands and desperately tried to hold the plane level.

Surrounded by flying chunks of white-hot metal, the Spitfire tumbled onto its back. Then, with a terrifying suddenness, silence engulfed him. Its engines seized up solid, the Spitfire spiralled downwards toward the water of the firth below.

He pulled back the canopy with both hands, released the Sutton harness, and tried to struggle against the centrifugal force that glued him to his seat. Finally the Spitfire rolled lazily onto its back and he dropped clear.

As the air cut through his clothing, he found the ring and pulled the ripcord. The parachute tore itself free from the pack then, with a jerk that jarred his shoulders, the white canopy blossomed above him.

Drifting down toward the choppy waters, he watched the Spitfire nearing the end of its spiral descent, quite close to the part of the tail-unit of the Palestinian jet that was all that remained on the surface. At the last moment the fighter seemed to level out, as though guided by a ghostly hand on the control column. Quite gently it touched down on the water, creating hardly a splash. For a few seconds it floated, rocking slightly with the movement of the waves and then, as though drawn by something beneath the surface, the Spitfire slid quietly out of sight.

A helicopter was clattering its way over from the shore as the Phantom flew low above the water and dipped its wings before turning for its base.

MEMORANDUM TO: THE SECRETARY OF STATE FOR
DEFENSE

FROM: DIRECTOR, INTERNAL SECURITY
COORDINATION OFFICE

The confidential report on the incident
over the Firth of Forth on May 15 has
already been submitted to you. This is a
form of addendum which you may feel should
be considered separately from the main
report. I submit it as a personal note to
clarify my particular role in this
incident, and I would respectfully ask you
to regard it not as an excuse but as an
explanation.

The official reason for the loss of the
Palestinian aircraft, as released to the
media, was that a collision with a flock
of birds had resulted in a spontaneous
explosion. In fact, as the confidential
report makes clear, this was not so. It
was destroyed by an RAF fighter aircraft,
and the report emphasizes that the RAF
pilot concerned was acting under direct
instructions from me. This I confirm.

My reason was, quite simply, that I
received information which convinced me
that Mr. Alec Martin's warning about the
real purpose of the Palestinian flight was

based on fact. Although Martin's warnings
had been discounted from the very
beginning, I took the precaution of
arranging for a special watch to be kept
on the airfield in Germany where the
Palestinian plane was to refuel. Despite
great difficulties, our agent did manage
to see certain movements around the
aircraft which suggested one of the
occupants was being covertly removed and
was smuggled away by car. That this was in
fact Zaidi, who had been photographed by
the press boarding the aircraft, made
sense in the light of Martin's story. This
agent's report reached me at the moment
after I had ordered the Spitfire to be
destroyed. Clearly a decision had to be
taken immediately.

I thereupon countermanded my original
instruction and ordered that the
Palestinian aircraft be destroyed instead.

The violence of the explosion that
resulted, indicating that the aircraft
was carrying explosives, does, I submit,
vindicate my decision; as also does the
fact that Zaidi appeared in Germany
shortly after this, claiming that his
aircraft had been hijacked by Israeli
terrorists. It should be remembered that,
at that stage, the only official statement
that had been issued by this country was to
the effect that a foreign aircraft had
crashed in the vicinity of Edinburgh and

that, on security grounds, full details
were being withheld for the moment.

It is fair to assume that this message was
read by Zaidi as confirmation that his
operation had succeeded and he therefore
moved on to the next stage of his plan. In
the event, as will be recalled, his
allegation had remarkably little impact,
being followed, as it was, by the MoD
statement that the aircraft had crashed
into the Firth of Forth. General opinion
seemed to be that, if the Israelis had in
fact adopted hijacking as a diplomatic
tool, it had proved singularly ineffective,
as indeed had Zaidi himself, for allowing
his aircraft to be taken from him. His
influence seems to have waned considerably
as a result.

I therefore submit that, reckless though
it may appear to some people, my decision
was the correct one. However, I accept
that, in the absence of direct proof to
substantiate the above theory, I grossly
exceeded my authority in transmitting that
order to the RAF in your name.

As it has been decided to take no action
against Martin himself in this matter, and
the confidence of ministers in their civil
servants has to be maintained, it has been
made clear to me that I am to be the
sacrificial lamb, so to speak.

I do not complain at what my people would

regard as the injustice of this. History has shown that it is often the case that one man acting according to his conscience can serve his country and his fellow men far more significantly than many governments operating within a parliamentary consensus. But such a man must also be prepared to accept the role of martyr.

In keeping with the high standards of this department, therefore, I hereby respectfully inform you that my resignation is at your disposal.

                              H. BLAIR
                              Director